Ladies' Night *at*

FINBAR'S HOTEL

The authors are listed in alphabetical order. As for which author wrote each chapter, we leave it to the reader to decide.

MAEVE BINCHY was born in Co. Dublin and taught in various girls' schools until she joined the *Irish Times* in 1969, which she still writes for. Her last six books, including *Evening Class, The Copper Beech, The Glass Lake* and *Tara Road*, have all been number one bestsellers in many countries around the world, and have frequently been adapted for television and cinema, most notably *Circle of Friends*. She is married to the writer Gordon Snell.

DERMOT BOLGER was born in Dublin in 1959. The author of six novels (including *The Journey Home* and *Father's Music*), seven plays (including *The Lament for Arthur Cleary* and *In High Germany*) and several volumes of poetry, he devised, edited and co-wrote the bestselling collaborative novel *Finbar's Hotel*, and is also the editor of *The Picador Book of Contemporary Irish Fiction*.

Born in Dublin, **CLARE BOYLAN** is the author of six novels (*Home Rule, Holy Pictures, Black Baby, That Bad Woman, Room for a Single Lady* and *Beloved Stranger*) and of two collections of short stories. Her non-fiction works include *The Agony and the Ego*, essays on the art and strategy of fiction writing, and *The Literary Companion to Cats*.

Born in Dublin, 1969, **EMMA DONOGHUE** is now based in Canada. Her novels include *Stirfry*, soon to be filmed, *Hood*, and *Kissing the Witch*. Her plays are *I Know My Own Heart*,

Ladies and Gentlemen and *Trespasses*. She also writes lesbian history and biography, and most recently has edited *The Mammoth Book of Lesbian Short Stories*.

ANNE HAVERTY's first book was *An Independent Life*, a biography of Constance Markievicz. Her novel *One Day As A Tiger* won the Rooney Prize, was shortlisted for the Whitbread and was Ireland's entry in 1998 for the Aristeion Prize. A collection of poems, *The Beauty of the Moon*, is a PBS recommendation. She lives in Dublin.

EILIS NI DHUIBHNE was born in Dublin in 1954. Her collections of short stories include *Blood and Water, Eating Women is not Recommended* and *The Inland Ice*, and she has published two novels, *The Bray House* and *The Dancers Dancing*. She is also known as a poet, a playwright in Irish and English and a children's author.

KATE O'RIORDAN was born in London and brought up in the West of Ireland. She now lives in London. She is the author of two novels, *Involved* and *The Boy in the Moon*. She has written for stage and screen and is currently adapting her last novel for BBC Films. Her third novel is published in May 2000.

Following a career as one of Ireland's leading journalists, **DEIRDRE PURCELL** has written six critically acclaimed bestsellers: *A Place of Stones, The Childhood Country, Falling for a Dancer, Francey, Sky* and *Love Like Hate Adore*. She recently adapted *Falling for a Dancer* as a four-part serial for BBC television. She lives in Dublin.

A novel by

Maeve Binchy

Clare Boylan

Emma Donoghue

Anne Haverty

Eilis Ni Dhuibhne

Kate O'Riordan

Dierdre Purcell

Each chapter in the book has
been written by a different author,
listed alphabetically and not in the order
they appear. We leave it to discerning
readers to identify them.

Ladies' Night *at*

FINBAR'S HOTEL

Devised and edited by Dermot Bolger

PICADOR

First published 1999 by Picador
an imprint of Macmillan Publishers Ltd
25 Eccleston Place, London SW1W 9NF
Basingstoke and Oxford
Associated companies throughout the world
www.macmillan.co.uk

and simultaneously in Ireland by
New Island Books
2 Brookside, Dundrum Road, Dublin 14

ISBN 0 330 37304 8 (Picador)
ISBN 1 874597 82 0 (New Island Books)

New Island Books receive financial support from
The Arts Council of Ireland (An Chomhairle Ealaíon), Dublin, Ireland

This selection and the concept of *Finbar's Hotel* are copyright © Dermot Bolger and all stories are copyright © their respective authors: Maeve Binchy, Clare Boylan, Emma Donoghue, Anne Haverty, Eilis Ni Dhuibhne, Kate O'Riordan, Dierdre Purcell. It is the desire of the writers not to disclose authorship of individual stories within the book.

The right of Dermot Bolger to be identified as the
editor of this work has been asserted by him in accordance
with the Copyright, Designs and Patents Act 1988.

1 3 5 7 9 8 6 4 2

A CIP catalogue record for this book is available from
the British Library.

Typeset by SetSystems Ltd, Saffron Walden, Essex
Printed and bound in Great Britain by
Mackays of Chatham plc, Chatham, Kent

CONTENTS

ROOM 101 – TOUCHY SUBJECTS

1

ROOM 102 – DA DA DA – DAA

33

ROOM 103 – THE DEBT COLLECTOR

69

ROOM 104 – GOD'S GIFT

101

ROOM 105 – THE MASTER KEY

137

ROOM 106 – THE WEDDING OF THE PUGHS

191

THE PENTHOUSE – TARZAN'S IRISH ROSE

223

From "Town Talk" – the *Irish Times*

Saturday, 23rd May

The literati, glitterati and – as **Fiona McNally** was fond of remarking in her inimitable fashion, when queen of Dublin's Leeson Street night-club scene – the "cliterati" were out in low-cut force last night for the reopening of that unique Dublin institution, Finbar's Hotel.

Now extensively refurbished, if not rebuilt from scratch, **Mrs Van Eyck** (as Fiona McNally now insists upon being called) was denying claims that she was trying to out-Clarence Dublin's Clarence Hotel in terms of chrome chic and splendour, while also dropping hints that "those four harmless Northside boys from U2 really should leave hotel management to those of us who remembered to grow up".

Certainly **Bono** and **The Edge** were among the few luminaries of Dublin society who appeared not to have made the trip down the quays to help launch the good ship Finbar. Everyone else seemed present except for Fiona's husband and business partner, **Ricky Van Eyck**, the Dutch rock star who made his fortune and reputation with his band **Echo, Echo** in the late 1970s with a string of what this paper's rock columnist described as *"impossibly long, indigestible and drug-induced instrumental dirges"* that became hits in Turkey, Finland, Spain and eleven other European countries. Proof, if proof were needed, as **Paul McGuinness** remarked to **Michael Colgan**, that the 1970s were not just about enjoying yourself.

B. P. Fallon and **Ferdia Mac Anna** were just two of the rockheads present who claimed to remember his famous opening (and only) words at his sole Irish concert in 1982 in the National Stadium: "Hey, you dudes out there, it's cool to be here in Iceland."

Digitally remastered (with a picture of Fiona on the cover) Echo, Echo's *Greatest Hits* is now apparently insatiably popular in the emerging republics of Eastern Europe, where Mr Van Eyck is presently on tour, leaving Fiona as a grass widow to bravely bask alone in the limelight last night. As **Alan Stanford** whispered in his best Lady Bracknell voice, "her hair has turned quite gold from grief".

Survivors present from the punk era were fondly recalling Fiona's initial attachment to Finbar's Hotel, when, fresh out from Sion Hill School in 1977, she made her first public appearances in the dingy basement night-club there as a singer fronting *Fiona & The Frogmarchers*.

B. P. Fallon was insisting that Fiona & The Frogmarchers lasted for three gigs in Finbar's (others present claimed it was only two – still one more than most Dublin punk bands) before her garage-chain-owning father realized that the money he'd been paying to subsidize his daughter's fledgeling University College Dublin education was actually being used to pay for the hire of Finbar's basement (where **Bob Geldof** once cracked his skull head-butting the low ceiling during the Boomtown Rats' debut gig) from the legendary original owners, the **Fitz-Simons** family.

But since then, until her disap-pearance to Holland some years ago, Fiona McNally made social columnists like myself feel that we were missing out on the whirlpool of Dublin life if we didn't print her name at least once a week. From being expelled from univer-sity to opening Ireland's first lin-gerie shop, managing several almost successful bands and cor-nering the market in early U2 bootleg tapes (of which "Live in Tullamore" was the undoubted classic), few stories of parties in the 1980s seem complete without some appearance by Fiona Mc-Nally.

We must, of course, quickly state that not all stories were true – lest we walk the same plank as the *Evening Herald*'s late **John Feeney** who mistakenly described her in 1983 as the main supplier of confidence-inducing cocaine to Dublin's bright young things. Still the out-of-court settlement did at least fund **Fiona's Restaurant,** as famous for being "the in-place" to be seen as for its notorious staff pay and conditions.

Since its closure by Environ-mental Health Inspectors in 1993, Fiona has spent much of her time abroad, although her press release style faxes concerning her on-off engagement to the American rap star **Ice Cop Killer Daddy Do** did liven up many a dull night in newsrooms around Dublin before the advent of Mr Van Eyck.

However, last night was a glamour occasion for letting bygones be bygones and one can only marvel at the wonders that careful replastering has done to this once crumbling Dublin institution. It is young professionals in on the quayside from now on and woe betide an appearance by any of the "Biffos" (Big Ignorant F**kers from Offaly) who were the mainstay of Finbar's Hotel for so many years.

Bertie Ahern and **Celia Larkin** were spotted talking to **Conor Lenihan**, no doubt recalling his late father's nights here with half the Fianna Fáil front bench in waiting – when the back room of Finbar's was the favoured haunt of priests, politicians and prostitutes, and gardai raiding after hours were offered "a pint or a transfer to the Aran Islands" by the late Douogh O'Malley.

Joseph O'Connor and **Anne Marie Casey** were hogging one corner with **Colm Tóibín**, **Anne Haverty**, **Clare Boylan**, **Hugo Hamilton**, **Mary Rose Doorly** and **Emma Donoghue**, engaged in conspiratorial literary whisperings, while Mrs Van Eyck informed people that **Roddy Doyle** had promised he would try to get along, provided the televised Chelsea match didn't go into extra time, and that **Maeve Binchy** and **Gordon Snell** would arrive at any moment.

Sadly no representatives of the former staff seemed present, though many guests recalled Finbar's famous night porter, **Simon O'Connor**, who is currently ill with cancer in St Luke's Hospital.

Back in the days when hotel fire safety in Finbar's Hotel meant keeping the hands of the owners away from matches, whiskey and insurance claim forms at the same time, staff like Simon, **the Count** and **Johnny Farrell** were known to work occasional discreet miracles.

But perhaps not even they could have attempted the geographical miracle that Fiona Van Eyck conjured in her opening speech in single-handedly deciding that Dublin's Temple Bar Latin quarter now stretches as far as her shining new establishment opposite Heuston Station. But then, as the late **Kenny Everett** might have said, at least she has done so "in the best possible taste".

TOUCHY SUBJECTS

Sarah's eyes were as dry as paper. Jet lag always made her feel ten years older. She stared past the blonde chignon of the receptionist in Finbar's Hotel. Twenty to one, according to the clock on the right. One take away eight was minus seven. No, try again. Thirteen take away eight was five. Twenty to five, so, Seattle time. Morning or evening? Wednesday or Thursday?

She shut her eyes and told herself not to panic. A day either way would make no difference. *Please let it not make any difference.*

'Ms Lord?' The Dutch or Danish receptionist was holding out the key for Room 101.

Sarah took it and tried to smile. There were four different clocks behind the desk, she realized now. The one she'd been reading was New York, not Dublin. So here the time was a quarter to six, but according to her body clock it was . . .

Forget it.

Bag in hand, she stumbled across the marble floor towards the lifts.

A young assistant porter in Edwardian stripes brought up her double espresso ten minutes later. Sarah felt better as soon as she smelt it. She even flirted with the boy a little. Simply a matter of 'That was quick,' and a tilt of the eyebrows, just to shake herself awake. He answered very perkily. *Every little hormone helps.* Even if, to a boy like that, thirty-eight probably seemed like ninety.

Her heart thudded as the caffeine hit home. She dragged the chair over to the window; sunlight was the best cure for jet lag. Not that there was ever much sunlight to catch in Ireland, but at least it was a clear evening. Her eyes rested on the long glitter of the river as she drained her espresso. Time was you couldn't even have got a filter coffee in Dublin; this town had certainly come on. You could probably get anything you needed now if you paid enough. She winced at the thought; too close to home.

Knotted into the starchy robe, she flexed her feet on the pale red and black carpet and considered the dress spread out on the bed. She knew it was comical, but she couldn't decide what to wear. This was a big night, most definitely, but not the kind of occasion covered in the book on manners her mother gave her for her eighteenth birthday. (Sarah still kept it on her cookery-book shelf in Seattle; guests found it hilarious.) Whatever she wore tonight had to be comfortable, but with a bit of glamour to keep her spirits up. Back home, this sleeveless dress in cream linen had seemed perfect, but now it was creased in twenty places. Like her face.

Sarah was tempted to keep on the dressing gown, but it might frighten Padraic. She wished she knew him better. Why hadn't she paid him a bit more attention at all those Christmas dos? She was sure there was a chapter on that in her etiquette manual: *Take the trouble to talk to everyone in the room.* Last year her entire corporation had undergone a weekend's training in Power Networking, which boiled down to the same thing, with motives bared. *Work the party. You never know when someone might turn out to be useful.*

Was she using Padraic? Was that what it all amounted to?

No more bloody ethical qualms, Sarah reminded herself. This was the only way to get what she wanted. What she needed. What she deserved, as well as the next woman, anyway.

The dress was impossible, it would make her look like cracked china. She pulled back on the purple suit she'd travelled in; now she was herself again. Cross-legged on the bed, she waited for her heartbeat to slow down. Six twenty. That was OK; Padraic was only five minutes late. All she wanted was to lie down, but a nap would be fatal.

There was that report on internal communications she was meant to be reading, but in this condition she wouldn't make any sense of it. She stretched for the remote and flicked through the channels. How artistic the ads were, compared with back home. Sarah paused at some sort of mad chat show hosted by a computer. Was that Irish the children were talking? How very odd.

Please let him not be very late.

The Irish were always bloody late.

*

Padraic was relieved that Finbar's Hotel was way down on the quays opposite Heuston Station, where he was unlikely to bump into anyone he knew. He stood outside for a minute and gawked up at the glistening balconies. He remembered it when there was only a peeling façade, before that Dutch rock star and his Irish wife had bought it up. What would it cost, a night in one of those tastefully refurbished rooms? It was a shame all the yuppies had to look down on was the Liffey.

The first things he noticed when the doors slid open were the white sofas, lined up like a set of teeth. Ludicrous; they'd

5

be black in a month. Padraic grinned to himself now, to relax his jaw. Greg in Marketing had this theory about all pain originating in the back teeth.

Padraic was the kind of man who always wore his wedding ring, and it hadn't occurred to him to take it off. But as he stood at the desk and asked the receptionist whether Ms Lord had checked in yet, he thought he saw her eyes flicker to his hand. He almost gave in to an silly impulse to put it behind his back. Instead, he tugged at the neck of the striped Breton fisherman's jersey he had changed into after work.

The receptionist had the phone pressed to her ear, now. She sounded foreign, but he couldn't tell from where. What was keeping Sarah? What possible hitch could there be?

Poor woman, he thought, for the twentieth time. *To have to stoop to this.*

'Padraic?'

He leapt. He felt his whole spine lock into a straight line. Then he turned. 'Máire, how *are* you! You look stunning! I don't think I've seen you since Granny's funeral. Didn't I hear you were in England?' The words were exploding from his mouth like crumbs.

His cousin gave him a Continental-style peck on the cheek. 'I'm only back a month.'

Her badge said Máire Dermott, Reception Manager. He jabbed a finger at it. 'You're doing well for yourself.' If he kept talking, she couldn't ask him what he was doing here.

'Oh, early days,' she said. Then, in a discreet murmur, 'To be honest, they head-hunted me when the first manager walked out. I didn't quite know what I was letting myself in for.'

His eyebrows shot up. 'It all looks fabulous, anyway,' he

said, wheeling round and waving at the snowy couches, the bright paintings, the rows of tiny lamps hanging like daggers overhead. He edged away from the desk, where the receptionist had got Sarah on the phone at last.

'So how's Carmel?' asked Máire. 'And the boys?'

Padraic was about to give a full report on his respectable family life when the receptionist leaned over the desk. 'Excuse me, Mr Dermott. If you would be so good as to go up now, the room is 101. And please tell Ms Lord that the champagne is arriving.'

He offered Máire a ghastly smile. 'Friend of Carmel's.'

Her face had suddenly shut down. She looked as snotty as when they were children doing Christmas pantomimes and she always made him play the ox.

Padraic gave a merry little wave of the fingers. 'Catch you later,' he said, backing away.

On the way to the lifts he glanced into the Irish Bar, which looked just like the one he and Carmel had stumbled across in Athens. And there huddled on a stool was that scumbag Neil Nolan, the debt collector who'd tried to come the heavy with Carmel's brother. Two years had diminished him. Was this whole hotel full of people Padraic didn't want to meet?

He pressed repeatedly on the lift button as he saw Neil Nolan leaving the bar, then put his hand against his hot face. It was God's own truth, what he'd told his cousin about Sarah being a friend of Carmel's. But it was also, under the circumstances, the worst possible thing to say. His father's side of the family were notorious gossips. Once again, Padraic Dermott had dug himself a pit with his own big mouth.

Sarah was standing in the door of Room 101, her heart ticking like a clock. When she saw him coming down the long corridor she felt a rush of something like love. 'Hi!' she called, too loudly.

'Hey there!'

They kissed, as if at a cocktail party. Padraic's cheek was a little bristly.

'Come in, come on in with you!' She knew she sounded stage-Irish; she was overcompensating. She didn't want him to think she was some transatlantic ice queen who'd forgotten how to travel by bus.

Thank God there were armchairs, so they didn't have to sit on the bed. Padraic hunched over a little, hands on his knees, as if ready for action. She tried to remember if they'd ever been alone in a room together before.

'How was your flight?'

'Oh, you know.' Sarah yawned and shrugged, then realized that he probably didn't know. 'How's business these days?' she asked.

'Not bad,' he said, 'not bad at all.' She could see his shoulders relax a little into the satin-finish chair. 'We're diversifying. Loads of opportunities.'

'I'll bet,' she assured him.

'And yourself?'

'Well, I got that promotion.' She added a little rueful smile. Not that he would have any idea which promotion she meant.

'Of course you did!'

Did she detect a touch of irony? Surely not. 'And the lads?' she asked.

'Doing great,' he told her. 'Eoin's in the senior school this year.'

Sarah nodded enthusiastically. 'I brought them some

stuff . . .' Her voice trailed off as she nodded at the heap of presents on the sideboard. The last role she wanted to play was the rich Yank, buying herself a welcome.

'Ah, you're very good.' Padraic was craning over his chair to see the parcels.

Then a silence flickered in the air between them.

'D'you ever see anything of Eamonn these days?' His tone was ostentatiously light.

'Not really,' said Sarah. 'He's in Boston.'

'Mmm. I just thought—'

'That's nearly as far from Seattle as from Dublin.'

'So they say.'

Padraic was looking as if he wished he hadn't mentioned Eamonn's name. She hadn't sounded touchy, had she? She hadn't meant to, if she had. It was only the general twitchiness of the occasion. Padraic just sat there, looking around at the furnishings. And then, thank Christ and all his saints, a knock on the door.

The boy in stripes brought in the champagne on a tray. Was that a hint of a smirk on his face? It occurred to Sarah for the first time how this might look to someone who didn't know the circumstances. She squirmed, but just a little. In her twenty years away from Ireland she had taught herself not to give a shit what anybody thought.

Five minutes later, Padraic's hands were still straining at the wire around the cork. Sarah thought for an awful moment that they'd have to ring down and ask for the boy to be sent back up.

'Excellent!' she said, when the pop came, very loud in the quiet room. The foam dripped onto the table. 'Ooh, doesn't it make a mess!'

And then she realized she sounded just like that nurse in the *Carry On* films, and the laughter started in her throat, deep and uncouth.

Padraic looked at her, owl-eyed, then started laughing too. His face was red. He filled both glasses to the brim.

'I swear, I didn't mean—' she began.

'I know you didn't.'

'It was just—'

'It was,' he said, knocking back half the glass and wiping one eye.

Sarah felt a bit better after that little icebreaker. She offered to refill his glass.

'Better not,' said Padraic, all business now. 'You know what Shakespeare said.'

She tried to think of all the things Shakespeare ever said.

'Drink,' he explained. '"It makes a man and then mars him . . . provokes the desire, but takes away the performance."'

'Really?'

Padraic added, 'It's the only quote I ever remember.'

Sarah nodded. Privately she was sure Shakespeare had never said any such thing; it sounded more like Morecambe and Wise. It was time she took charge of this conversation. 'Listen,' she began in the voice she used at meetings. Was she imagining it, or did Padraic sit up straighter? 'Listen,' she tried again, more gently, 'are you sure you're OK about this?'

'Absolutely,' said Padraic.

'No but really, you've only to say.' She let the pause stretch. 'It's a lot to ask.'

'No bother.'

Typical bloody Irishmen, can't handle any conversation more intimate than buying a paper. Sarah pressed her fingertips together hard and tried again. Her voice was beginning to shake. 'I hope you know I wouldn't be here if there was any other way.'

'I know that, sure.'

'I can't tell you how grateful I'll be – I mean, I am, already,' she stumbled on. 'The only thing is, I get the feeling Carmel kind of talked you into this?'

'Nonsense,' he said, too heartily. 'I'm more than happy. Glad to be of use.'

She winced at the word.

'Well, now.' Padraic got up and straightened the sleeves of the shirt he wore beneath that ridiculous striped jersey. 'I suppose I should get down to business.' From his jacket pocket he produced a small empty jar that said *Heinz Carrot and Pea for Baby*.

Sarah stared at it. 'How suitable.' Her throat was dry.

He peered at the ripped label. 'Would you look at that! I grabbed the first clean jar I could find that wasn't too big,' he added a little sheepishly.

Compassion swept over her like water. 'It's perfect.'

They stood around as if waiting for divine intervention. Then Sarah took a few light steps towards the bathroom. 'Why don't I wait—'

'Not at all,' he said, walking past her. 'You stay in here and have a bit of a nap.'

She heard the key turn in the bathroom door.

A nap? Did he seriously think she could sleep through what might turn out to be the hinge of her whole life?

*

Padraic knew he was being paranoid, but just in case. Sarah might think of some further instructions and burst in on him in that scary suit with the pointed lapels. Anyway, he'd never been able to relax in a bathroom without locking the door.

The jar looked harmless, standing beside the miniature elderflower soap. He tried perching on the edge of the bath, but it was too low; he feared he might fall backwards and damage his back. *Dublin Businessman Found Committing Lewd Act in Luxury Hotel.* All right for the likes of George Michael, maybe, but not recommended for a career in middle management. And his cousin Máire would never forgive him for the publicity.

He tried sitting on the toilet – with the lid down, so it would feel less squalid, more like a chair. He leaned back, and a knob poked him between the shoulder blades, and the flush started up like Niagara. He stood up till the sound died down. Sarah would think he was wasting time. Sarah would think him a complete moron, but then he'd always suspected she thought that anyway.

Now these weren't the sort of thoughts to be having, were they? Relaxing thoughts were what were needed; warm thoughts, sexy thoughts. Beaches and open fires and hammocks and . . . no, not babies. Would it look like him, he wondered for the first time, this hypothetical child?

He hadn't been letting himself think that far ahead. All week he'd been determined to do this thing, as a favour to Carmel, really, though Carmel thought he was doing it for her best friend. He'd been rather flattered to be asked, especially by someone as high powered as Sarah Lord. He couldn't think of any reason to refuse. It wasn't your everyday procedure, and he wasn't planning to mention it to his mother, but really, where was the harm? As Carmel put it the other night, 'It's not like you're short of the stuff, sweetie.'

Still, he preferred not to dwell on the long-term consequences. The thought of his brief pleasure being the direct cause of a baby was still somehow appalling to Padraic, even though he had three sons and loved them so much it made his chest feel tight. He still remembered that day in Third Year when the priest drew a diagram on the blackboard. The Lone Ranger sperm; the engulfing egg. He didn't quite believe it. It sounded like one of those stories adults made up when they couldn't be bothered to explain the complicated truth.

Padraic sat up straighter on the glossy toilet seat. He did ten Complete Body Breaths. It was all he remembered from that Stress Training his company had shelled out for last year. Two hundred quid a head, and the office was still full of squabbles and cold coffee.

He unzipped his trousers to start getting in the mood. Nothing stirring yet. All very quiet on the Western Front. Well, Sarah couldn't expect some sort of McDonald's style service, could she? *Ready in Five Minutes or Your Money Back.* She wasn't paying for this, Padraic reminded himself. He was doing her a great big favour. At least, he was trying to.

He zipped up his trousers again; he didn't like feeling watched. If he could only relax there would be no problem. There never was any problem. Well, never usually. Hardly ever. No more than the next man. And Carmel had such a knack . . .

He wouldn't think about Carmel. It was too weird. She was his wife, and here he was sitting on a very expensive toilet preparing to hand her best friend a jar of his semen.

At the sheer perversity of the thought, he felt a little spark of life. *Good, good, keep it up, man. You're about to have a wank*, he told himself salaciously, *in the all-new design-award-winning Finbar's Hotel. This is very postmodern altogether. That woman out there has flown halfway round the world for the Holy Grail of your little jarful. Think what the Pope would say to that!*

This last taboo was almost too much for Padraic; he felt his confidence begin to drain away at the thought of John Paul II peering in the bathroom window.

Dirty, think honest-to-God dirty thoughts. Suddenly he couldn't remember any. What did he used to think about when he was seventeen? It seemed an aeon ago.

He knew he should have come armed. An hour ago he was standing with *Penthouse* under his arm at the Easons magazine counter, where the cashier had looked about twelve, and he'd lost his nerve and handed her an *Irish Independent* instead. Much good the *Irish Independent* would be to him in this hour of need. He'd flicked through it already and the most titillating thing in it was a picture of Mary Robinson signing a petition.

This was ridiculous. *You're not some Neanderthal; you were born in 1961.* Surely he didn't need some airbrushed airhead to slaver over? Surely he could rely on the power of imagination?

*

The door opened abruptly. Sarah, who had turned her armchair to face the window so as not to seem to be hovering in a predatory way, grinned over her shoulder. 'That was quick!'

Then she cursed herself for speaking too soon, because

Padraic was shaking his head as if he had something stuck in his ear. 'Actually,' he muttered, 'I'm just going to stretch my legs. Won't be a minute.'

'Sure, sure, take your time.'

His legs? Sarah sat there in the empty room and wondered what his legs had to do with anything. Blood flow to the pelvis? Or was it a euphemism for a panic attack? She peered into the bathroom; the jar was still on the sink, bone dry.

Five minutes later, it occurred to her that he had run home to Carmel.

The phone rang eight times before her friend picked it up. 'Sarah, my love! What country are you in?'

'This one.'

'Is my worser half with you?'

'Well, he was. But he's gone out.'

'Out where?'

Curled up on the duvet, Sarah shrugged off her heels. 'I don't know. Listen, if he turns up at home—'

'Padraic wouldn't do that to you.'

There was a little silence. In the background, she could hear a soap opera theme on the television, and one of the boys chanting something, over and over. 'Listen, Carmel, how did he seem this morning?'

Her friend let out a short laugh. 'How he always seems.'

'No, but was he nervous? I mean, I'm nervous, and it's worse for him.'

'Maybe he was a bit,' said Carmel consideringly. 'But I mean, how hard can it be?'

Who started giggling first? 'Today is just one long *double entendre*,' said Sarah eventually.

'How long?'

'Long enough!'

And then they were serious again. 'Did you bully him into it, though, Carmel, really?'

'Am I the kind of woman who bullies anyone?'

This wasn't the time for that discussion. 'All I mean is, I know you want to help.'

'We both do. Me and Padraic both.'

'But you most of all, you've been through the whole thing with me, you know what it's been like, with the clinic . . . And I swear I wouldn't have asked if I had anyone else.' Sarah was all at once on the brink of tears. She stopped and tried to open her throat.

'Of course.' After a minute, Carmel went on more professionally, 'How's your mucus?'

'Sticky as maple syrup.'

'Good stuff. It's going to happen, you know.'

'Is it?' Sarah knew she sounded like a child.

'It is.'

All at once she couldn't believe what she was planning. To wake up pregnant one day and somehow find the nerve to go on with it, that was one thing, but to do it deliberately . . . *For cold-blooded and selfish reasons*, as the tabloids always put it. In fantastical hope, as Sarah thought of it. In fear and trembling.

'Are you sure you can't come over for a little visit?' asked Carmel.

'I really can't. I've a meeting in Brussels tomorrow morning, before I head back to the States.'

'Ah well. Next time.'

*

Padraic was leaning on the senior porter's desk, which was more like a lectern. He spoke in a murmur, as if at confession.

'Our library on the third floor has all the papers as well as a range of contemporary Irish literature, sir,' muttered the slightly stooped porter, as if reading from a script.

'No, but magazines,' said Padraic meaningfully.

'We stock *Private Eye*, *Magill*, *Time* . . .'

'Not that kind.' Padraic's words sounded sticky. 'Men's magazines.'

The old man screwed up his eyes. 'I think they might have one on cars . . .'

'Oh, for Christ's sake,' he said under his breath.

Then, at his elbow, just the woman he could do without. 'Are you all right there, Padraic?'

'Máire.' He gave her a wild look. She was just trying to catch him out, at this stage. Was she following him all over the hotel to examine the state of his trousers? Just as well he didn't have the bloody erection he'd spent the last fifteen minutes trying to achieve. She'd probably photograph it for her files.

'This gentleman—' began the porter in his wavering voice.

'I'm grand, actually.' And Padraic walked off without another word.

What did it matter if they thought he was rude? Máire had clearly made up her mind that he was cheating on Carmel with her best friend. When the fact was, he would never, never, never. He wasn't that type of guy. He had his faults, Padraic admitted to himself as he punched at the lift button, but not that one. He was a very ordinary man who loved his family. There was nothing experimental about him; he didn't even wear coloured shirts.

Then what the fuck am I doing here?

He didn't have a key to Room 101; he had to knock. Sarah let him in, talking all the while on a cordless phone. Her smile didn't quite cover her irritation. 'Cream,' she said into the phone. 'Cream linen. But it didn't travel well.' He gave her a thumbs-up and headed into the bathroom.

Now he was well and truly fucked. Tired out, without so much as a picture of Sharon Stone to rely on. Funny how it seemed so easy to produce the goods when they weren't wanted. He considered the gallons of the stuff he'd wasted as an adolescent, when he locked himself into his mother's bathroom on a daily basis. He thought of all the condoms he'd bought since he and Carmel got married. And tonight, when all that was required was a couple of spoonfuls . . .

He sat on the toilet and rested his head on his fists. What on earth had induced him to agree to this mad scheme? It just wasn't him. He knew Irish society was meant to be modernizing at a rate of knots, but this was ridiculous. It was like something off one of those American soaps with their convoluted plots, where no one knows who their father is until they do a blood test.

Sarah was still on the phone; he could hear her muted voice. Who was she talking to? She was probably complaining about him, his lack of jizz, so to speak. Padraic stared round him for inspiration. A less sexy room had never been devised. Sanitary, soothing. The only hint of colour was Sarah's leopardskin toilet bag.

Reckless, now, he unzipped it and rifled through. *Pervert*, he told himself encouragingly. Looking through his wife's friend's private things . . . her spot concealer, her Super-Plus tampons, her pills (*aha, Prozac, how very Seattle*). He felt something stirring in his trousers. He sat down again and reached in. He clung to this unlikely image of himself as a lecherous burglar, an invader of female privacies. A man who could carry a crowbar, who might disturb a woman who was having her bath, some independent single business-woman with sultry lips, a woman like Sarah . . .

Oh my God. If she only knew what he was thinking, barely ten feet away—

Never mind that. *Hold onto the fantasy. The crowbar.* No, chuck the crowbar, he couldn't stoop to that. He would simply surprise . . . some beautiful, fearful woman, and seize her in his bare hands and—

If Carmel knew he had rape fantasies she'd give him hell.

Never mind. Do what you have to do. Keep at it. Nearly there now. Evil, smutty, wicked thoughts. The gorgeous luscious open-mouthed businesswoman . . . bent over the sink . . . her eyes in the mirror . . .

By now he had forgotten all about the jar. His eye fell on it at the last possible minute.

Now wouldn't that have been ironic, Padraic told himself as he screwed the lid back on with shaking hands.

It didn't look like very much, it occurred to him. He should have brought a smaller jar. A test tube, even.

He gave himself a devilish grin in the mirror. Endorphins rushed through his veins. Now what he'd love was a little snooze, but no, he had a delivery to make.

Sarah was reading some spiral-bound document, but she leapt up when he opened the door, and the pages slid onto the floor. 'Wonderful!' she said, all fluttery, as he handed over the warm jar. Her cheeks were pink. She really was quite a good-looking woman.

'Hope it's enough,' he joked.

'It's grand, loads!'

19

It occurred to him for the first time that she might need some help with getting it in. *Oh God, please let her not upend herself and expect me to . . .* But he was too much of a gentleman to run away. He hovered. Sarah, acting like she did this every day, produced a gigantic turkey baster.

'Wow!' said Padraic. 'I hope they didn't search your bag at customs.'

'No, but it did show up on the X-ray screen.' She gave a breathless little laugh.

'Wow,' he said again. Then, 'It might have been easier to do it the old-fashioned way!'

It was a very cold look she gave him. Surely she couldn't think he meant it? A touchy subject, clearly. (Weren't they all, these days?) Padraic knew he should never make jokes when he was nervous. He felt heat rise up his throat.

'I'll get out of your way, then, will I? Treat myself to a whiskey. Maybe you'll come down and join me after?'

He couldn't stop talking. Sarah smiled and nodded and opened the door for him.

*

She tried lying on the bed with her bare legs in the air, but it was hard to keep them up there. *Hurry, hurry,* she told herself; the jar was cooling fast. How long was it they lived? Was it true that boy sperm moved faster but girl sperm lived longer? Or was it vice versa? Not that she gave a damn. She'd take whatever God sent her, if he was willing to use this form of Special Delivery. *Please just let this work.*

Finally she ended up lying on the carpet with her feet up on the bed. She felt almost comfortable. It was crucial to feel happy at the moment of conception, someone at work had told her. Awkwardly, leaning up on one elbow, she unscrewed the lid of the jar and began to fill the turkey baster. It was certainly easier at the clinic, where all she had to do was shut her eyes, but it felt a lot better to be doing this herself, without anyone peering or poking. Just her and a little warm jar full of magic from a nice Dublinman with a name. Nothing frozen, nothing anonymous.

There, now, she had got a good grip on the plunger. She would just lay her head back and take a few relaxing breaths . . .

The knock came so loud that her hand clenched.

'No, thank you,' she called in the direction of the door.

No answer. She took one huge breath and pressed the plunger.

Afterwards, she could never remember hearing the door opening. All she knew was that the assistant porter was standing there staring, in his ludicrous striped jacket, like something out of Feydeau. And she was on her feet, with her skirt caught up around her hips. 'Get out,' she bawled. She tugged at the cloth and heard a seam rip. There was wetness all down her legs.

The boy started to say something about turning down the sheets.

'Get out of my room!'

The door crashed shut behind him.

Afterwards, when she had mopped herself up, Sarah scrubbed at the carpet with a damp facecloth. The mark was milky, unmistakable against the square of red wool. They'd think she and Padraic had done it right here on the floor.

She wanted to go down the corridor and find that young porter. She longed to spit at another human being for the first time in her life. 'Look, boyo,' she would scream in his ear, 'if I can make myself pregnant I'm sure I can turn down my own sheets.'

But she hadn't, had she? All she'd done was stained the carpet.

*

The funny thing was, now he'd started, the dirty thoughts wouldn't stop coming. They raced merrily through his head. All the way down in the lift Padraic watched the other passenger in the mirrored wall. She was fifteen years too old for the red dress and black leather waspie, but still, not bad at all. A hooker, or just somebody's bit on the side? This hotel was a stranger place than it looked from the outside; behind all that fresh paint you'd never know what was going on. He shook his head to clear it as the lift glided to a stop. He let the woman get out first.

The Irish Bar was stuffed with people, singing rebel songs Padraic hadn't heard in years; it seemed to be some sort of wake. No sign of Neil Nolan, thank God. After two whiskeys Padraic felt superb. Relief and alcohol danced through his body together, while his hormones played 'It Had to Be You'.

Tonight had demanded his all, and his all was what he had given. With a bit of luck, one lonely frustrated woman's life would be transformed, and a little bit of his DNA would grow up next door to the Pacific Ocean. With a light tan, and rollerblades . . .

There was his cousin, consulting a clipboard and talking to the barman. He shouldn't have got so het up earlier; she was only taking an interest. He'd been in a bit of a state, he could admit that now. When he'd finished his third whiskey

Padraic gave a little wave but Máire didn't seem to see. He squeezed his way over and waited for a break in the conversation, then put his hand on her arm.

'Hello again,' she said.

'It's not what you think,' he announced satirically.

'Right.' She seemed to be speaking to her clipboard.

'No, really. I mean, yes I'm here to meet a woman, obviously, but it's about a hundred and eighty degrees opposite to what you're obviously thinking.'

Máire looked up, and her eyes were hard. 'Listen, Padraic, it's none of my business.'

'Yeah, but—'

'I've a lot on my plate tonight,' she muttered rapidly. 'Moans and groans about double bookings, and a scrawny old bitch upstairs bathing in milk and raw meat, as if anything but divine intervention would improve her face at this stage.'

'But the thing is, Carmel knows I'm here,' he assured her, tugging at her sleeve. 'Old school friend. Carmel set the whole thing up, in fact.'

His cousin looked slightly revolted, and he was just about to explain, when he remembered that he had promised both Carmel and Sarah never to tell a soul about their little arrangement. So he had to let go of Máire's sleeve. She was out the door like a shot.

Knees against the bar, he idled over his next drink, planning how to describe the evening to his wife. *Oh, we got the business over with in the first ten minutes – nothing to it.* But he mustn't make it sound like too much fun either. Carmel was being remarkably kind to her friend, when you came to think about it – lending out her husband like a sort of pedigree stud. He savoured the image.

Funny, he thought. That old porter's paging another Mr Dermott. Then two things occurred to Padraic: that it was him who was being paged, and that he was very nearly pissed. He'd only had a few, but then he'd forgotten to have dinner.

'The lady upstairs would like to know when you're coming back, sir,' said the porter. A little too loudly and pointedly, Padraic thought.

He was up in Room 101 in three minutes.

'I'm so sorry,' Sarah stuttered. 'I can't believe—'

He acted like a gentleman. He assured her it could happen to anyone. (Anyone, he mentally added, who made a habit of inseminating herself in hotel bedrooms.) He swore the stain would hoover out: 'These people are professionals.' (He could just imagine the chambermaid telling Máire that her cousin had spurted all over the carpet.) He grabbed the empty jar and headed back into the bathroom.

*

This time, Sarah said to herself, she'd stay calm.This time she'd lock the door. This time she'd get it right. And then tomorrow she'd be on her way back to Seattle, and . . . *Maybe. You never know. Carmel said it would happen.* This was still the right day. Her chances were pretty good.

Padraic popped his head out of the bathroom. Only now did she notice how dark red his face had gone. 'I might be a little while.'

'How many have you had?' She didn't mean it to sound quite so cutting, but she thought she had a right to know.

He leant on the door jamb. All the softness went out of his voice. 'What's that supposed to mean?'

She shrugged.

'I thought my shift was over, you know,' he went on acidly. 'As far as I knew you'd got what you wanted, you were finished with me, and I had the right to a drink.'

'You've had more than one,' she pointed out neutrally.

'And if you'll give me a minute,' he shouted, 'I can still fucking well get it up.'

They avoided each other's eyes.

'Jesus,' he added, 'no wonder—'

He turned to go back into the bathroom, but Sarah was on her feet. There was nothing she hated more than unfinished sentences. 'No wonder what?'

'No wonder you have to resort to this sort of carry-on.'

Her eyes stood out in her face. 'You mean because no man would have me? Is that what you think?'

'I never said that.' Padraic was leaning his head against the door jamb now. 'It's just, you must admit, you come on a bit strong.'

'That's because this is my last chance,' she bawled at him.

He shifted on the spot. 'Don't say that. Sure, a fine-looking woman—'

'Getting a man is easy,' she spat.

He was taken aback. The pity in his eyes faded.

'It's having children with one that's turned out to be impossible,' she said between her teeth.

'Why didn't you and Eamonn—'

'Because we were divorced by the time we were thirty. Then the guy I was with for six years after that didn't happen to like children. And the next one did, but he had a single-figure sperm count. Is this what you want to hear, Padraic? You're welcome to all the details.' Sarah's voice was shaking like a rope. 'I'm thirty-eight years old. I've been paying a clinic seven hundred dollars a month for fertility drugs that make me sick, and frozen sperm that doesn't work. What else do you suggest I do?'

He considered the carpet. 'I was just . . . I suppose I was wondering why you left it so late.'

'Oh, don't give me that. Just don't you dare.' She felt breathless with rage. 'How was I meant to know what I wanted at twenty-five? Men have no fucking idea. You'll still be able to make a woman pregnant when you're seventy!'

Padraic flinched at the thought.

After a minute, very quietly, he asked, 'But sure . . . why me? Couldn't you just have gone out one night and picked up a stranger?'

Sarah sat on the edge of the bed and wept. Her elbows dug into her thighs.

'I didn't want the child of some pick-up,' she said at last, very slowly, the words emerging like pebbles. 'Quite apart from what else I might pick up from him.' She waited till her voice had steadied enough for her to go on. 'I wanted the child of a nice man, and all the nice men were taken.'

After a long minute, she felt the bed bounce as Padraic sat down beside her. 'Not all, surely,' he said after a minute. He sounded like a child who'd just been told the truth about Santa Claus.

Her smile came out a bit twisted. She turned her head. 'Don't worry about it, Padraic,' she drawled. 'I get by just fine without the husband and the jeep and the house in the suburbs.'

He didn't know how to take that. She watched him staring at his shoes.

'All I want is a child.' Sarah said it softly. She was never so sure of anything in her life.

'Fair enough,' he said after a minute. 'You haven't seen me at my best tonight,' he added hoarsely.

She gave a little sniff of amusement and wiped her eyes. 'I suppose not.'

'You try getting an erection in a toilet without so much as a copy of *Playboy*. I'm not seventeen any more, you know.'

Sarah giggled and blew her nose. 'Sorry. I should have brought you some hardcore from Seattle.'

'*Pan-Pacific Perv-Girls*.'

She laughed painfully. *Go on*, she told herself. *Make the offer*. 'Shall we just call the whole thing off, then?'

She could tell he was tempted. Just for a minute. Until he thought of what Carmel would say.

'Not at all,' said Padraic. He stood up. 'A man's godda do.'

'Are you sure?'

'I'm going back in there,' he declared, 'and I'm not coming back out empty-handed. You just lie down and think of Ireland.'

'No,' she said, jumping up, 'I'll go in the bathroom. You could do with a change of scenery.'

She handed him out his jar, then locked the door. She looked herself in the eye, turned on the cold tap and washed the salt off her face.

*

Padraic stood before the wardrobe mirror and stared down into his trousers. Not an enticing sight. Visibly tired, old before its time. He eyed his face and counted his wrinkles. Salmon couldn't eat after they mated, he remembered; they just shrivelled away. What was there left for him in this life, now he had served his time, genetically speaking?

But tonight's job wasn't quite over yet.

He felt utterly exhausted. Nerves, alcohol, and a fight to round it all off. But he had to rise to the occasion now. *Noblesse oblige*. He thought of Carmel's last birthday. He'd been knackered from work, and half a bottle of champagne hadn't helped, but he knew she wanted to be ravished, he could almost smell it off her. So he had claimed to be full of beans, and though it took an enormous effort it was all right in the end. He'd known it would work. It always worked in the end, him and Carmel.

Padraic lay down on the bed. He wanted to be home in her arms.

This room had no more resources than the bathroom, really. He flicked through the TV channels (with the sound down, so Sarah wouldn't think he was time-wasting). Not a drop of titillation. After five minutes of *Dirty Dancing*, he realized he was finding Patrick Swayze far more appealing than the girl, and that raised such disturbance in the back of his head that he switched off the telly.

He lay down again and scanned the room. The prints were garish abstracts; nothing doing there. There was the phone, of course. If only he had memorized a number for one of those chatlines. He'd rung one once, in a hotel room much nastier than this one, somewhere in the north of England. All he remembered was that the woman on the recording had a terribly Royal Family accent, and spoke very, very slowly to bump up his bill.

If he rang downstairs and asked for the number of a chatline he was sure to get Máire. She'd tell her mother. She'd probably tell *his* mother.

Padraic shut his eyes and tried out a couple of trusty old fantasies. Only they weren't working any more. He wondered whether one traumatic evening had rendered him permanently impotent. Could you get that Viagra pill in Ireland yet? He felt exhausted at the thought. Somehow the idea of having a voluntary sexual impulse seemed like a remnant of his youth. Maybe that was it, his lot.

All at once he knew what number to ring.

'Hello there,' said Carmel, and her voice was so warm he thought he could slip right into it and sleep. 'Are you coming home soon?'

'Any minute now. I just need a bit of help,' he admitted.

'Are you still at it?'

'She spilt the first lot.'

Carmel let out a roar of laughter. 'I should have warned you,' she said. 'When we shared a flat, Sarah was always knocking over cups of tea.'

'Are you comparing my precious seed to a beverage, woman?'

'The comparison is entirely in your favour.' Her voice changed for a minute; her mouth moved away from the phone and he heard her say 'You go and brush your teeth, love. I'll be up as soon as I've finished talking to Daddy.'

He wanted to tell her to say goodnight from him, but he wasn't meant to be thinking like a daddy now.

Carmel's voice was all his again now, going low. For a respectable wife and mother she could sound like a shocking wee slut. 'Are you ready for round two, big boy?' she asked.

'I don't think I can.'

'Can't means won't,' she said in her best schoolmistress voice.

He laughed into the phone, very softly.

'All right now,' she crooned. 'Enough of this nonsense. Shut your eyes.'

'I just want to come home.'

'You are home.'

'I am?'

'You're home in your bed with me. Nothing fancy.'

'Not a seedy motel?'

'Not Finbar's Hotel either. We could never afford it. You're home in bed with me and the kids are fast asleep and you're flat on your back, with your hands above your head.'

'Surrendering, like?'

'Exactly.'

Carmel, he thought a few minutes later with the part of his mind that was overseeing the rest, should consider a career move. She could make a mint on one of those chatlines. And to think of all this lewdness being saved up for a big eejit like him. He kept his eyes squeezed shut and pretended his hands were hers. She always knew what to do. She was working him into a lather. She was going to make it all right.

*

Sarah was leaning against the sink, praying. It had been so long, she hardly remembered what to say. She got the words of the Hail Mary all arseways, she knew that much. *Blessed is the fruit?* Mostly what she said was, *please.*

The bathroom door opening made the loudest noise. Padraic's grin split his face like a pumpkin. She seized the jar. Half as much as last time, but still, there must be a hundred thousand ambitious little wrigglers in there. She rushed over and lay down on the carpet.

'Will you be all right now?' he asked.

'Yeah, yeah,' she said, 'you go on home.'

He gathered up the pile of presents for his boys. When he

was at the door he turned to give a little finger wave. She had already filled the turkey baster.

'See you at Christmas, I suppose,' he said. And then, 'Fingers crossed.'

They both crossed their fingers and held them in the air.

Sarah started laughing before the door shut behind him. She was still laughing when she pressed the plunger.

DA DA DA – DAA

It was a childhood of smells. Sourish, unpasteurized milk, straight from the churn in the Creamery; liquorice leather and fusty, raddled horsehair in the Saddler's; miniature golf ball chewing gums which smelled of plastic in the sweet-shop. A grainy, whiskey-breath kitchen, each morning. Pungent wafts of cheese and onion crisps from rain-sodden uniforms – girls huddled together, passing sos in the school-yard shed. Bicycle grease. Old rain. New rain. Cigar smoke . . . It was a childhood of predictabilities. Sunday matinees. Closed shops, Wednesday afternoons. Mazola fish on Fridays. Kids playing Dracula on the street most evenings, dishcloths wrapped around their necks for capes, tomato ketchup drools from their mouths. Around the next corner – another gang taking over the street with a skipping rope, or a burst football, or someone's father crumpled drunkenly in the gutter. Usually your own. A reeking, predictable childhood. But that was then.

This was now. Poppy gazed around the lobby of Finbar's Hotel. The white leather sofas so soft you could nearly hear the baby calves crying. Marble floors and columns – not quite white, a low-fat milk colour. She searched for some-thing else, the pale, reflective crispness of the lobby – yes, she had it – she had walked into an apple. Four brass-rimmed clocks on the wall behind the reception desk – for important people who not only dealt with their own time. She was one

35

of them. The time in New York – it still passed, without her. An elderly porter in livery stood behind an ornately scrolled lectern, for desk seemed too paltry a word for a man who delivered directions to hotel guests with all the evangelical zeal of a preacher. His waving arms encompassed Dublin. He was the heart, the very soul of this rejuvenated city. All arms, all smiles – servile to the point of recompense, even if she sensed a tiredness there. Poppy waited for her room.

She was called that because she had once liked poppies. Not the flowers, the potatoes. Her real name was Maura. She hadn't been Maura for the longest time, and she rarely ate potatoes these days. Even designers in the rag trade had to look vaguely anorexic. She lived on grilled fish, plain pastas with a drizzle of olive oil, side salads. Small mountains of chocolate, Toblerones, if she felt depressed. Which was rarely, now that she was successful.

Voices rose and fell in the Irish Bar to her right. It looked as if there was some sort of pre-party group, gathering together. Off-duty staff, still in their uniforms, were raising and clinking their glasses with the people there. She couldn't tell whether they were sad or happy. So she assumed that someone had died. The porter looked across with a vinegar expression every time someone's laughter pealed through the whiteness.

Her gaze carried over to the open door of Fiona's Bar, where an ancient American couple drank at the counter. They were a sight. A grizzled turkey of a man, reeking of new money – no class, and his equally grizzled wife, decked out in taffeta. A throwback to the 1930s in emerald green no less. Dear oh dear. Poppy shook her head. She watched with growing amusement as their petulant, fake-breasted granddaughter wheedled and preened – prising a wad of

money from the turkey's wallet. Then a coochycoo blown
kiss and a toss of her serious hair before she flounced out
toward the lobby. Tanned, lithe and lethal. Poppy could hear
her whispery high-pitched voice call back to her grandparents. She would see them at eight. I'd have my doubts
about that, Poppy smiled to herself. This looked like one
dysfunctional family. Poppy knew *that* smell.

Her attention was distracted by the advancing figure of
Richard, her secretary. He carried two flutes of champagne,
cream cricket sweater draped around his shoulders, Ray-Bans
set back on his bleached, cropped hair – he returned her smile
confidently, but he was mincing like a camp poodle, so she
knew he was nervous. First time to Ireland for this second-
generation Bronxer. Secretly, he'd expected to be lynched. So
he swaggered, flaunting the homosexuality that had so
repelled his Roscommon father. So nervous, he couldn't yet
see that the fabled Ireland of his youth, the endless, monoto-
nous, force-fed sentimentality of his parents, had no bearing
on this new country. For all the world as though he couldn't
see the blatant y.e.s. tattooed on the buttocks of the porter's
young assistant. She felt sorry for Richard. Then she felt a
pang of pity for the poor assistant, standing rigidly to attention
in a heavy Edwardian uniform. He was sweating.

Seeming immune from everything, Karl Brown, the company accountant who had flown in with them, sat on one of
the white sofas smiling as he stared around. He had already
got his room while they were fussing over details of the
showing. Poppy wondered if anything ever fazed him. Even
his divorces had seemed amicable, as though nobody could
fall out with him. Now his only thoughts were of golf on
some of Ireland's most exclusive courses and a leisurely
search for his Cork roots – the company reward for some

creative accounting in the last quarter. He would take no part in the presentation but she knew that, in time, every detail would be recounted back to New York in his rich moderated tones.

Just as Richard placed the drinks on the glass table, an elegant woman, in a black leather catsuit, with blonde, serious hair, approached Poppy. Her smile was businesslike, efficient to the point of contempt.

'Mizz Fitzpatrick,' she said, checking a clipboard. 'Please accept my apologies for the delay. Your room is nearly ready. There was a bit of a mix-up – it's been a crazy week. Two rock groups and all that comes with them – not that we ever discuss who's staying here, you understand. I was just about to offer you a drink – but I see you're being looked after.'

The woman extended a hand with glittery nails. Poppy put out her good hand. The other was stubbed to the quick.

'Fiona Van Eyck,' the woman said in that unmistakable south-side Dublin accent. 'I'm the owner.' She did a little self-deprecating moue. 'For my troubles.'

Before Poppy could say anything, another harassed look-ing woman, wearing a RECEPTION MANAGER badge, came running from behind the lobby desk.

'Everything's fine, Mrs Van Eyck.' She sounded more north-side. 'I've explained the delay to Miss Fitzpatrick.'

The blonde rolled her eyes with irritation.

'Thank you, Máire. I'm not doubting you, pet. You know I just like to keep my hand in.' She smiled beatifically. 'When you'll let me, of course.'

North-side flushed to her roots. Richard wriggled on leather. Been there, done that. Ate the T-Shirt. Poppy sipped with a wry expression. She'd designed the T-shirt.

'Actually, I was just coming over to give you this message.' The woman called Máire thrust a folded-over card at Poppy.

'Thank you.' She ran it through the crevices of her good-nailed hand.

'The woman said it was urgent. Very urgent,' Máire said, before retreating from her employer's glower.

'Nothing so urgent you can't enjoy your stay with us, I hope,' Mrs Van Eyck purred. 'Business or pleasure, may I ask?'

Poppy toyed with the card. She wanted to read it. But she also wanted to teach Richard a lesson in coolness. She smiled, just enough frost to keep them all at an appropriate distance. No matter, that her meeting later tonight, was the most significant – no, *nuclear* event of her life. So far.

'Business,' she responded. 'As a matter of fact, I'm selling snow to Eskimos.'

The blonde threw her head back and laughed with honesty. Poppy liked her from that moment. She felt instinctively that they could get on. But in another life. If she weren't in New York. Richard had vacuumed the contents of his glass – still jittery – so she felt compelled to put him at ease.

'I've got the top Dublin store guy coming round this evening – we'll mention no names –' Van Eyck rolled her eyes appreciatively. Poppy continued – 'to look at our collection.' Why she felt compelled to explain further, she had no idea, perhaps there was a reciprocity in the blonde woman's feigned indifference. She wondered about the Dutch surname. It seemed vaguely familiar. 'We've booked the U-Turn suite, for the showing,' Poppy continued. 'Plaids, tweeds, wellingtons with suede rolldown tops, harpy

39

nightgowns, emerald lingerie, capes with Book of Kells embroidered insignias, you know, Oirish stuff.'

'There's money in that.'

'Indeed there is.'

'Sell what you are, that's what I say,' Fiona said.

'Oh, and sometimes what you're not,' Poppy said.

Richard lit a cigarette. The porter's assistant brought him an ashtray. Their eyes met. Poppy thought: That's you all fixed up.

'God, Dublin is different,' she said.

'To what you remember?'

'Yeah.'

'It only looks different, believe me.'

'My stuff is all over the world now. And it's taken me the best part of ten goddam years to crack Dublin,' Poppy said. 'Don't ask me why it should be so important to me.' She shrugged. 'But it is.'

'So now it's snow to Eskimos.' Fiona smiled. 'Good luck. Success is all the sweeter after a decent wait.'

'I hope so.'

Fiona excused herself and wandered off. Poppy noticed that another guest, a dumpy, middle-aged woman, didn't get so much as a look from the selective owner. Probably because she looked like somebody's secretary. The woman had a laptop open on the sofa beside her and was typing at a furious rate. Occasionally she glanced up like a startled rabbit. Then clickety-clack again. It was a horrible thought, but for a split second Poppy considered hiring her to sit like that in the corner of the U-Turn suite – a prime example of the way everything was wrong and dated about how certain Irishwomen still dressed. The woman stopped working. Gathered her things and headed for the Echo Rooms restaurant. Doubtless a fair old appetite stoked up from all that frenzied typing.

She watched Karl Brown serenely watch customers cross the lobby. He was unlike most American males with their fixation for younger women. She wondered who he might find tonight. She had observed his almost imperceptible courtship techniques before and his way of always finding somebody different, someone interesting, someone in whom only he could spot magic. She sipped her wine and casually opened the card. It told her that her father was on his way and to call her mother urgently. The last word was underscored several times.

'Everything OK?' Richard looked concerned. 'You look green.'

'No,' Poppy said through gritted teeth. 'Everything is most definitely not all right.'

She headed for the reception desk, about to demand her room, no matter what state it was in. Máire Dermott handed her the electronic key.

'I was just coming to get you,' she said, 'number 102, on the first floor – the lifts are over . . .'

But Poppy was already running upstairs. She wrenched the door handle before getting a green light, and had to insert the key again. Inside, she ran to the phone.

'Mam? Mammy? What the hell does this note mean? What's he coming here for? Who told him where I am? You did? Well, thanks a whole bunch. This was meant to be a quick in and out trip. You know I'll be home for a week next month – couldn't you have stopped him, for Chrissakes? Yes, I was going to ask you how you are. How are you? How's *he*?, more to the point . . . What's that – mad? Oh, shite . . . on a scale of one to . . . oh no – a definite ten or a maybe ten? Ten. Yes, I know you've had to put up with him for the last fecking thirty-odd years and yes, I should be more generous about one lousy night – just not this particular night . . . Oh, feck off you too.'

She slammed the receiver down and the phone instantly rang. A Dutch receptionist, to say that her father had arrived, could they send him up. The girl sounded so calm, she had no idea that she was facing a walking, ticking, ringing time bomb.

'Send him up,' Poppy snarled.

Richard called from 107 to say that his room was neat and he was going to make a start in the U-Turn suite, if that was OK with her. The buyer had confirmed his arrival time of seven thirty. Richard wanted to know if he should reserve dinner for all of them after the showing. And how was her room?

'Yes, yes and grand.' She cut him off.

Two hours to get rid of him. Poppy paced over the red and black chequered carpet. Surely it could be done in two hours. History told her otherwise.

Peremptory knock on room door. Oh little man, she thought, you've had a busy day.

'Dad!'

He barged past her, carrying an old typewriter case and a grey suit on a hanger. A lock of hair danced on his forehead.

'Frocks in New York and cocks in Australia,' he said. He set up shop by the window. Checking over his life. 'Glasses, train ticket, wallet – where's my handkerchief – where is it? Oh here it is. Right. Glasses, train ticket, wallet, handkerchief. That's it, isn't it?' He was breathless. She saw that she was supposed to agree that he had all the essentials.

'That's it, I'd say.'

He sat, cross-legged on the chequered carpet. A solitary chess pawn.

'Thank Christ for that. Yesterday, I had thirty-six things on the list. Thirty-six things! There're only twenty-four hours in a day, for feck sake. Anyway. I made it. Here I am. Jesus Christ – cigars!' He jumped up again, checked his trouser pockets and pulled out a box of Coronas. They were added to the growing pile on the table. 'Snotty little bastard – the porter – gave me a look as if to say, "This fellow is carrying a perfectly good suit, but he's too casual to wear it." He thought I was dismissing him, so he dismissed me first. I sent your sister in Australia a fiver. She's destitute again. I sent her a note too, back of a cigar box job – I said, "Here's my last fiver, if you insist on backpacking or whatever it is you're doing out there – it might come in handy. If an Aborigine doesn't rape you first. Keep it in your shoe."'

'She'll be delighted.'

He sniffed, sat cross-legged again, studying his splayed fingers. A legacy from his drinking days. He gave it up, nine years back. Now, he was just mad. He looked smaller, thinner if that was possible. Deep furrows on his brow, grooves along his sunken cheeks. Slicked-back shiny hair, except for the loose lock. The punctured face looked closer to seventy than sixty. Dressed in rags, as usual. He still hadn't looked at her.

'How's New York?'

'Grand.'

'I don't know how you stick the place.'

She thought, I'm thirty-five, reasonably attractive, success-ful, trading up to a Mercedes next month, granted I'm single, but that's all right in New York. Lots of women are. She thought, bury me now and make sure the casket is locked. He'd only follow.

'Did you put your pills on the table?' she asked, to make him dance.

'No,' he said sourly.

'How *is* the angina?' Ah, you'll dance yet.

'Wonderful. Your mother has asthma again. Ass–ma, my ass.'

'She sounded a bit wheezy, on the phone.'

'You should hear her off the phone.'

'Would you like a sandwich or something?'

'What do you think?'

'You tell me.'

'I'd have a sandwich if I'd the time. But I don't. I've been retracing steps. I went to that hotel in Thurles on the way. You know, the one I nearly set fire to. They didn't remember me. I suppose it was twenty years ago. I said sorry anyway. Then I said sorry again to the nurses in the mental, in Cork. They were never as bad as I made out. Then I got the suit – what do you think?' He lifted the hanger.

'Very nice. Look, I'm going to order a sandwich for myself in any case.'

'Do that.' He looked around with a pained expression. 'Christ – what a godawful room. Small fortune a night, I suppose? It's like stepping into a washing machine. I'm booked into Mrs Deasy's off the South Circular. Ten pounds a night and an enormous devil of a slip-slop breakfast in the morning. Lets you sleep until ten, if you want. How's New York?'

'Fine. I said.'

No, she thought. Don't bury me. Cremate me. Scatter the

ashes over the coasts of Africa. Still he'd find her. She ordered sandwiches and a pot of tea from room service.

Retracing steps. The last bloody thing on earth she'd ever want to do.

'I'm going to see my counsellor at St Pat's,' he said.

'This evening?' she asked, hopefully.

'In the morning.' He stroked the suit. 'I have things to say.'

If he had things to say, he'd say them. Of that much she could be certain. Poppy slumped onto the bed. He cast her a watery smile.

'If you've anything to say yourself, you'd better get a word in edgewise.' He checked the watch on the table. 'Round-about now – that's – if you have – 'cause I'm barking most of the time these days. Precious few moments of lucidity. I'm having one just this minute.'

'I've nothing to say.'

'God knows that's the truth. Now so, I want you to know that your life is a sham. You've no business wasting your talent on frocks and suchlike. You're a pure disgrace. I gave you that talent.'

'Since when are you the artist?'

'If I set my mind to drawing, I'd be good at it. No. I'd be fecking fantastic. But I'm a poet. I'm thinking of starting a novel. But I don't think there'll be time. Anyway, the world is too undeserving. Actually, I'm a businessman. I've a card here somewhere.' He was growing increasingly agitated. She would have to calm him down. He jumped up and began to pace. 'I'm not God,' he said, 'but I can see eighty years behind, eighty years ahead. You're wasting your life. All of you. The whole wretched shower of you. D'you hear me?'

Not retracing steps? She was back in the small kitchen of

her childhood, watching Daddy do the books for his butcher's shop out front, sipping whiskey, wreathed in cigar smoke. Stabbing the lined pages with his pen. Her mother wheezing in bed upstairs. Drinking cold milk, while he ranted about the ignorance of the world, an ignorance concentrated almost exclusively amongst his customers. '*Bastards!*'

'Calm down, Dad.'

He stopped in mid-pace. Hands riffling the sleek hair – the only thing left of him intact.

'Calm down! How can I calm down? When all the people . . . the places . . . the things I've done . . . they're all jumbled up in my mind. It's an omelette in here. Where can I take them? I'm not sure where I'm going myself . . .' He whirled about, wild-eyed. 'D'you know what the punk asked me on the phone last week?' The punk was her younger brother. 'He thought he was being clever, the gobshite – he asks, he asks, "Seeing as I'm so virtuous, would I consider myself a modest man?" The fecking bollocks.'

'And what did you say?'

'I said – I said – "If you consider my intellect and my not so inconsiderable talents – then yes, I would say that I'm a modest man."'

'That softened his cough.'

'Damn right.'

They smiled. He sat on the floor again. A demented elf. She had to steel herself to staunch the old flow of pity. If it crept in, it would set her back years. She had cried for a fortnight after their visit to New York. Parents looked pathetic and vulnerable outside their own territory. And so much smaller. Forever walking in the wrong direction. Hesitating on pavements – walk – don't walk, they crossed every junction like the devil himself was after them. Her mother was petrified, the pace, the noise, the cabs. He walked around with a hand in his trouser pocket, the other holding a cigar aloft, trying to look at ease. Every time he looked up the solid flanks of Manhattan multi-storeys, he said, 'Ye haven't much sky here.' That was all he ever said about New York. At last something had frightened him into silence.

A knock on the door practically sent him under the bed, scurrying for cover.

'What's that? What's that?'

'The sandwiches, most probably.'

'Oh.'

The assistant porter held the tray high. He liked his job. A bit defensive in his glance. Not a bit wrong with being a porter, it said, unless you wanted to be something else. He hovered by the table. SHANE, his badge told them.

'D'yis mind if I move some of that stuff there?'

'What?' He was on his spindly legs again. 'Oh Christ no! I'll do it. Let me do it. They're my things.'

'Right y'are. Which of yis will sign here for me?'

'Will you sign or will I do it?' her father asked.

'You do it.'

'What name will I put?'

'Put your own.'

He had to find his glasses. Then he had to find his own pen. He had to light a cigar to give him ballast. He peered at the chit over the spectacle lens.

'Here is it? Right. Ja-a-mes F. Fitz-pat-rick. That all right?'

'Sound out. Enjoy the sandwiches now let yis.'

'Do I give him a tip or what?' her father hissed.

'Yeah. Go on.'

'What? What'll I give?'

'What change have you?'

Young Shane edged slowly to the door, mindful to keep his eyes averted.

'None!' Her father shrieked. 'I've no change at all. Oh, Jesus, Mary and St Joseph. We're fucked!'

Poppy shook her head. She rose from the bed and slipped a pound coin into Shane's waiting cup of hand. It was more than a week's wages the last time anyone seriously wore a uniform like that.

When she turned, James Fitzpatrick was wolfing sandwiches, two at a time. She saw him waltzing around the kitchen floor at home with a leg of chicken in one hand, his conductor's knitting needle in the other. 'Listen to this bit – just listen to this.' Mozart or Beethoven or Schubert taking over the room. The lock of hair gyrating on his forehead as he conducted. 'Come out now, Kate Bush. What've you to say to that?' He had a thing about Kate Bush ever since Poppy said she liked her. It was customary for him to have a thing about anyone or anything the family praised. He was so easy to annoy, they couldn't resist the temptation sometimes. 'Will they send the Beatles into deep space? I think not. Proper music is what they'll send.' Apparently he'd been proved wrong on that one.

Still, there was something nice about pleasing him too – the very rare occasion that happened. He'd stopped the car violently one day, right in the middle of the road. Cars honked. Fists clenched at him. He leaned back to an unsuspecting Poppy. 'What was that sound you made?' She looked at her siblings. They looked out the window. Whatever it was, she was on her own. 'That sound – that sound,' he repeated, sweating with impatience. 'Oh, da da da – daa, you mean is it?' she asked. 'You see?' he said to the others triumphantly. 'Unbeknownst to herself, she's doing the start of Beethoven's Fifth.' They drove off with him bawling. 'DA DA DA – DAA. Fate comes knocking, kids. You can caterwaul yourself up the Cahas now, Kate Bush. Heathcliff how do.'

The small town didn't know what to make of him. They tried for 'character' but he was too consistently venomous for that. He never pandered. They tried for intellectual eccentric – an aberration of nature. But he countered that by behaving with stratospherical stupidity so often. They could not disown him, his stock was linear and too well entrenched. So they ignored him. He was avoided. Nodded to but rarely spoken to, he was the angry man with the cigar and dog, walking alone each evening. A nimbus of grey-blue smoke trailing in his wake. Lucifer himself.

He turned to her, swallowing a triangle of sandwich in one go.

'You don't have to love me, you know. Just because I'm your father. My mother was a cold, dark place. I hated her. We all did. I wasn't much of a father, I suppose?'

'I'll live.'

'Oh, I'm sure you will,' he said bitterly. 'Yuppies are well protected from the ordinary pain of living. Can I have some of the tea in that pot?'

'Help yourself.'

The good moments were indeed few and very far between. But like most unhappy families, when they were happy – they were ecstatic. The highs were spent on a razor's edge, everyone trying desperately to stave off the clouds which gathered above his head, threatening, threatening, until in an access of ecstasy, beyond his endurance, he had to rain on them. The books would come tumbling out –

'Read that let ye, stop the rot of ignorance.' Yeats, Swift, Beckett – film critiques, plays – it didn't matter what, he read *at* them. While they ate cornflakes or pickled corned beef or starched his butcher's apron. They learned to say bugger off but he never learned to do it. He gave them one thing though, Poppy, her sister, the punk their brother – the gift of speed. They left that small town like three sputniks.

He was pacing again. All the sandwiches gone. Poppy could barely catch the flow of his monologue. Still retracing steps. Perhaps he meant to do his entire life, but from what she could make out he was only on the journey to Dublin so far. She checked her watch. Dear God Almighty, he'd been here well over an hour already. He was checking to see if she was listening. Years of experience had taught her how to glaze her eyes, nod her head at appropriate moments. Say – 'Really?' While mentally she did her homework or blowdried her hair in advance. If you got real lucky and played your cards right, sometimes he would burn himself out, before he'd intended. The trick was to never ask a question, never voice an opinion, never argue and never, ever let that pity get to you. Because then he was human, and not the excruciatingly embarrassing father you had to laugh off with your friends.

But he had a way of sidestepping the barriers. She was there now. Upstairs, in Mrs Scully's good front room. Practising the piano, over Mr and Mrs Scully's small grocery store. Her father had insisted that they all learn, even though there was no piano at home, even though they didn't have one note between them. She went to a tutor and daydreamed her way through the lessons. Then she was to practise on the Scullys' old Steinway.

Doh-ray-mee-fah-so – it was too boring for words. That

was the only scale she actually could remember. So she improvised to pass the time. One afternoon, she got a bit carried away. Well, a lot carried away. She was twelve, with raging hormones and huge sweeps of sadness that came rushing over her. She began to play. Tunelessly pounding that piano, until her fingers ached and her feet were sore from the pumping. But for moments, she could hear every tune she wanted to hear. It was 'Climb Every Mountain', *Doctor Zhivago*, *Madame Butterfly* – all rolled into one. She was sweating. The music wasn't enough. She had to sing. She opened her mouth and for moments she was Madame Butterfly – the aria – soared heartrendingly to the ceiling. The piano was begging her to stop. It could not bear the pain. She was crying hysterically, pawing her cheeks, whenever the flying hands would let up. Finally, it ended, with a dramatic crash of her head onto the keys. She turned to take her exhausted bows, the crowd was hysterical. Baying for more. But she had no more to give.

It was on the way downstairs that she remembered where she was. Mr Scully would not meet her eyes from the kitchen, where he sat with his cup of tea in mid-air, untouched tomato sandwich on the table in front of him. The shop was full. Poppy tried to slink through, but all eyes were upon her. Mrs Scully, the bristles of her top-lip moustache standing out like needles, was making a great deal of trying to suck her butterscotch sweet as loudly as she could. Nyaa nyaa mm-hmm. Kindness itself.

'All right now, pet?'

And there was her father, head down, behind the phalanx of women, buffing an apple against his sweater. Poppy could see that his cheeks were burning. There was a distinct – it must run in the family – air in the shop. A mixture of contempt and pity in the eyes all around. And for the first time in her life Poppy saw what he saw, every day. She was scalded with shame and humiliation. She wanted to run away to Calcutta and live amongst the poor and the crippled for the rest of her natural. But she couldn't move. Her feet were glued to lino.

'And this great big shiny one – for the maestro here,' her father was saying, handing his purchases to Mrs Scully.

They had walked out of the shop together. And up the street, in silence, except for huge synchronized crunching mouthfuls. And if there was ever a time when Poppy might have slipped her hand into his that was it. But her friends were loitering by the corner.

'After that – I stopped in Bandon – only missing that other A,' he was saying. 'I had to see the floor of the pub where I smashed my front teeth.'

'I thought they were smashed for you.' Poppy sipped her cold tea.

'And then . . .' He sighed so hard she thought his shoulders would come off. 'After the tailor's in Cork – I went to the hotel, where I left my father's ring.'

'That was twenty-five years ago.' Poppy knew that she was breaking the rules. She was engaging.

'I wanted to look at the sink, in the jacks, where I left it.'

'And I suppose it still wasn't there?'

'No. Neither was the sink. A nightclub now, where the jacks should be, if you don't mind.' He looked at her. 'You know – I'm sure in my blood – I'd have been fine all these years, if I hadn't lost that ring. I'd have been fine, if I never came back from England to run that bloody shop. I'm a poet, not a butcher, for Christ's sake. I've been wasted.'

'Yeah.'

The men in white coats had come up with manic depression with such ease the family felt certain that anything that could be diagnosed that quickly could surely be cured that quickly too. Such was not the case. He had pills for this and pills for that, with whole bottles of whiskey in between. That such a small, wiry frame could withstand so much was a constant source of wonder to them all. He could drink litres, undiluted. And when he returned home at night, roaring and begging for a fight, the children would jump on him to keep him from their mother, who was in the kitchen, mashing sleeping tablets into his treacle coffee. Sometimes it took as many as six pills to knock him out. Finally, he would sleep on the sofa, splayed out like a starfish, and their mother would say, 'Ah little man, you've had a busy day.'

He was always threatening to kill himself. Telling them he was going up to the slaughterhouse for the humane killer. Their mother would hand him the breadknife – 'Save yourself the trip.' The ambulance came a number of times to ferry them all to the local hospital after he'd swallowed the entire phial of sleeping pills. Again. Still, he would dance around the hospital corridors, bellowing abuse at the doctors, punching his fists into the air – not a breath knocked out of him. The doctors would tell the family, in sombre tones, how they would have to pump him out. With a wink at her giggling children, huddled in a corner, twiddling their fingers, their mother would say to the white coats, 'Ah sure now, what's the rush – couldn't ye hang on a small while?'

She couldn't leave because he controlled everything. Toward the end of Poppy's time at home even his meanness had become a form of psychosis. Her mother couldn't afford a haircut. There was no such thing as a joint account or access to his many and varied deposit accounts. He hoarded, he stashed, he moved what little money there was around. He knew it was his power. And her mother knew that if she left no legal power on earth could get past his madness to give her her fair dues. She had no skills. Had never worked. 'Should I leave – penniless – with the kids, or penniless without the kids?' There was justice – then there was James. Poppy remembered her mother's tears of frustration. Great heaving sobs, going nowhere.

As it turned out, the days of pills and tears and ambulances were not the worst of the worst. Mere dusky afternoons to the long nights to come, when things would get really dark . . .

Poppy did not want to be there. Or here. Especially there, though, pushed into the past, by his presence now. She would not succumb to it. But her mouth was open and the cry was out before she could stop herself.

'It was a miserable, rotten, stinking childhood. And I hope you rot in hell!'

Silence. He relit his cigar with trembling fingers. Poppy closed her eyes. She was abandoning all the rules.

'Jesus Christ,' he said. 'You shocked me into a moment of lucidity there. Thank you.'

What could she say?

'You're welcome.'

A tentative knock on the door.

'Who's that now?' He jumped up.

Richard peered around the door. He was dressed in gold lamé pants, platform trainers and a sheepskin singlet. He nodded, surprised, to James.

'Poppy – the suite is all fixed up. Maybe you wanna take a look?'

'I'm sure it's fine.' Poppy said, fixing a smile. 'Richard – this is my father. Dad – Richard.'

They shook hands. Her father kept his eyes on his own shoes. She wasn't sure if Richard caught the murmured, 'Jesus Christ Almighty.' Richard checked his watch and eyed Poppy, silently enquiring.

'I'll be along shortly,' she said. 'How long have we got?'

'Well – thirty minutes, maybe? He might be early. I can stall him if you—'

'No, no,' she abruptly cut across him. 'No need for that. I'll be on time. You just see to the models, give the stock a last check. I'll be there.'

'Okey-dokey.' Richard spun on his platform heels. 'Good to meet you, Mr Fitzpatrick.'

'Oh yeah – you too.'

When Richard was gone, her father turned to Poppy with eyes like dinner plates. 'What was that?'

'That was Richard. My secretary.'

'Secretary? God Almighty – is that what secretaries are wearing these days? And correct me if I'm wrong, but wasn't that a male?'

'We're not all stuck in the past, like you,' Poppy retorted with pleasure.

In truth, she was a bit uncertain herself the first time Richard presented himself in full regalia for a showing. Hardly the appropriate image for such a derivative line – schlock, not to put too fine a point on it. Strangely though his antithetical approach seemed to work. It reassured the buyers that tongues were firmly in cheeks, and they could all maintain a discreet veil of irony – a foil to the enduring gullibility of the punters.

'What's this thing you've on later?'

'I'm selling to a Dublin store. What I've always wanted.'

'You want so little?'

'We can't all be grandiose,' she snapped. 'Some of us cut the cloth to suit our needs.'

'Falcons I wanted. Small muddy brown hens I got.'

She was about to lay into him, get it over with, sling him out once and for all. Good timing. Why should she put up with this crap? But he slumped into the chair and began a high-pitched keen, rocking back and forth with his head in his hands. Higher and higher, the notes quavered around the room. Scorching her heart. She remembered that sound. It seemed like only yesterday. When she stood with her sister, staring through a glass wall, at their father, the human violin.

Anywhere but there. She could not go there again.

'Help me. For God's sake. Help me.' He was moaning. 'Please – help me.'

Poppy stood up quickly.

'C'mon,' she said briskly. 'We'll go downstairs for a while. Look – you need more cigars. We'll get two cappuccinos. You'll like that. They might even have nice buns.'

'I've gone off buns a bit.' But he stood, holding on to the back of the chair for support. She watched his knuckles grow white and red as his hands clenched and unclenched.

'Can you check for me?' He indicated the table. 'Train ticket, wallet, glasses, handkerchief – cigars . . .'

Poppy ticked them off. 'Spectacles, testicles, vallet and vatch,' she said, mimicking her mother.

He lit a cigar as they left the room.

'It's the easiest thing in the world to leave your watch on a table. Or a ring by a sink, for that matter. It could happen to anyone. In fact, I'd lay odds that it has happened to everyone at some time or other. Try to carry as little as possible wherever you go, that way you've less to lose. Really, the best thing would be not to go anywhere at all. Then you'd have nothing to lose. You never said what you really thought of my suit.'

'You'll set off the fire alarms with that smoke,' Poppy said, waving her hands to disperse the grey ghostly spumes around him. 'It's a fine suit. Have you plans for it?'

When she turned to look back, he was standing in the middle of the corridor, with the cigar raised above his head.

'I hope I set the damn things off. I hate this place. No comfort here at all. Finbar my bollocks. I'd set off stars, if I could.'

*

Poppy stretched herself into a tautness to match his. So that she would be ready to spring into action, if necessary. But he seemed a touch more relaxed. They were sipping cappuccinos in Fiona's Bar, the long chrome and glass lounge. The party in the Irish Bar had picked up a pace. Rumblings of songs about to start, but no one quite drunk enough yet to carry them off.

She watched a shabbily dressed man in a raincoat stir a coffee by the bar counter. A thick head of greying tufty hair, but she could not see his face, he kept a hand by his cheek, like someone shielding himself from an expected blow. There was something vaguely familiar about him – for some reason, the words *the sky is chicken* came into her head. Maybe she was nuts too. Maybe he just reminded her of the quivering, knee-jiggling mess across the table from her. James was also studying the curious figure by the counter.

'Someone else's father, come to visit,' he concluded.

'I doubt it,' Poppy said drily. She held the patent on that one.

'No, look at him,' her father said. 'He's sitting there. Before he goes up. Wondering what he's going to say. He's thinking it all out. Look at the cut of him. He's in rags, worse than me. He doesn't know what to say, does he? He's afraid. Afraid he'll make a balls of it as usual. The poor gobshite. No doubt he will make a hames of it and all. Story of his life. I know him well. God knows, I wouldn't be surprised if he writes poetry too. Offer him a cigar, Poppy.'

'I'll do no such thing.'

'But look – he hasn't got any.'

'He probably doesn't smoke.'

'Have you no heart?' His voice was high-pitched again. 'Jesus Christ, there the man is – about to be crucified by some ungrateful wretch of a child, without so much as a smoke to see him through.' He stood up, knocking his cup to the ground. 'Give that man a cigar, I say!'

People were looking now. The man at the bar seemed to freeze. As though he knew he was the subject of attention. He slipped off the stool and made for the door, in a quick, practised glide. Poppy tried to grab on to her father's jumper sleeve but he swung his arm violently, managing to free himself, just as the stranger passed by, a hand still shielding his face.

'Here! Here!' Her father thrust a cigar at him. Rivulets of sweat ran down his cheeks. His eyes were beginning to roll horselike in their sockets. Poppy feared the worst.

'Please, Dad,' she hissed.

'Take it.' He pressed the cigar into the man's hand. 'Here, d'you want a light?'

The man peered through his raised fingers. Poppy saw one dark eye. His free hand curled around the cigar. Both men were staring at one another. Her father was shaking so hard, the chair by his knees rattled. There was a moment when Poppy thought the worried barman would intervene – then slowly, with almost reverential care, the stranger placed the cigar between his lips. Both hands cupped his shadowed face now. He leaned forward slightly. Her father flicked his lighter and held it to the tip. The flame bounced with his trembles. A stream of blue smoke issued from the man's mouth. Poppy saw the black eye meet her father's again. He nodded.

'Thanks,' he mumbled in a nasal American accent. 'I guess.'

'You'll be fine,' her father said. 'Fine.' He sat again, with a huge sigh of relief. The man smiled crookedly, a hand snaked out as he passed, and quickly squeezed her father's shoulder. He was gone.

'You see? He did want a cigar. Course he did. Don't tell me I don't know a man in want of a smoke when I see one.'

Poppy had to pinch her cheeks to stop herself from remembering. Another time. Another place. No cigar.

'Can I get you another coffee there?' The barman approached.

He was a young fellow with a cheeky smile and big flappy ears. Poppy felt herself relax for a moment. She was in Dublin after all. Nothing like New York – where you couldn't even smoke a cigar, never mind accost a stranger. She felt all her old affection for the city creep back into her bloodstream. The politeness of the hotel staff – 'yes madam' and 'no madam' and 'if madam would care to' . . . then a

quicksilver change on the phone – 'howya' to their colleagues. Always that gentle pisstake in their voices. Like the
barman now.

'Not at all,' he was saying to her father, who had stooped
to collect the pieces of shattered cup. 'I'll have that done as
soon as look at it. You'll have the other coffee so?'

'Will we?' James asked her.

'Why not?' She checked her watch and nearly left her
skin. Twenty to eight.

Through the glass doors she could see Richard talking
animatedly to the buyer in the lobby. Stalling, obviously.
The man was checking his watch and tapping a foot on the
marble floor. Karl Brown moved about in the other bar,
sampling the local atmosphere, carefully detached from
Richard's plight, leaving himself available to whatever might
fall into his lap. For some reason she had always found his
presence to be like a good luck charm. She could sure as hell
use one now. She scraped her chair back.

'There was an old man on the train,' her father was saying.
'Well, not that old. Shook enough, though. He was trying to
read a paper, just minding his own business, trying to read a
paper and hold onto his things . . .'

'Look, I just have to—' She tried to stem the flow.

'But these young punks wouldn't let him alone.' His face
twisted with bitterness. 'They were mocking him – right to
his face.'

'Yes yes,' Poppy interrupted impatiently. 'Just sit here for
a sec, drink the coffee. I'll be back.'

'He was terrified. Scared out of his wits. I couldn't do a
thing to help him. Then – then he wet himself. It was all
down his leg, dripping into his shoes. Imagine – the shame
of it – wetting yourself like a newborn baby.'

Poppy was standing. She looked down and saw the yellowed tidemark around his crotch. She sat again.

'We'll go up to the room again – maybe you'd like a bath or something.'

'I've no time for taking baths,' he hissed, clenching his fists.

'There's time for everything,' she said, guiding him up by an elbow.

He trotted along the lobby after her, like a chastened dog. She caught Richard's eye and drew him aside.

'Poppy! What's going on? He's getting mighty pissed, this guy. I can't stall him for much longer.'

'You'll have to start without me. Just say I've got jet lag or something. I'll be along in a few minutes.'

From the corner of her eye, Poppy spotted the dumpy secretary. Clearly she was finished in the Echo Rooms and was now furiously typing again, this time on top of a sofa. Suddenly she snapped the laptop shut and stood up quickly. Poppy instinctively urged her father toward the lift – she didn't want to share with anyone. But the woman was heading for the lobby desk.

'You'd better be along pronto,' Richard was warning her. 'He's not the type to give an order to a minion like me. Hey! I mean it. This guy is serious – he's not gonna like it, if you mess with him. Hi again, Mr Fitzpatrick.'

'Hullo.'

Richard was about to get needy, clutching at her hands. Poppy shrugged him off with a frown.

'Go on – shoo! You can handle him. I'm on my way. Really. Go go go!'

Richard gave her the full flounce. Petted lip and head turning a full circle. But Poppy saw the polished smile return as he approached the buyer once more. She didn't have much time. Then again – who did?

*

On and on, he went. Unfurling his life like a skein of cloth. Angry one minute, desolate the next. Silent for brief moments, while he sat, jaw jutting out, examining his splayed fingers. Poppy had to open the window, for air. As usual, he was taking more than his fair share of it and she felt like gasping. The Liffey rode by, uncaring. New blocks of apartments with wrought-iron balconies on the other bank. A siren screamed in the distance. From the window everything appeared new, until her eye caught crumbling red-brick ruins, still fighting shy of the developers. Pockets of Dublin out there, rank as the underbellies of long-dead fish. Children embracing their fates – unlike her great escape. You are what you eat? The hell you are, she thought. You are what you've been fed.

The phone rang, interrupting his flow. Richard to tell her that the buyer was halfway through the showing, with steam coming from his ears by now. What the hell was she playing at? There wouldn't be any orders if she didn't get her ass down there – pronto. Poppy listened, trancelike. Richard bleating in one ear, the stops and starts of her father's life journey winging by the other.

'You have to go? You have to go now?' her father asked.

'Looks like.'

'Fine. I'll be off. Just let me gather my things. Glasses . . . train ticket . . . where am I going? Yes. I'm going home now. No, no, Mrs Deasy. I think I'll leave the suit, if it's all the same to you.' He was pacing again, grabbing at things, dropping them in equal measure.

Poppy watched him, with a hand covering the earpiece.

'Poppy?' Richard was shouting. 'I know you're there. Tell me – what am I to say to this guy?'

'How will I get there?' her father asked. He stopped in the middle of the room. Hands hanging limply by his sides. Head down. 'What are you going to do for me?' He whispered. 'What are you going to do for me?'

Poppy closed her eyes.

'Richard?'

'Yeah? Yeah?'

'Tell the man from Del Monte,' she swallowed, 'tell him – we're all out of pineapples.'

'What? What the . . .'

Poppy clicked the receiver into place. She reached for the box of cigars, lit one and put it to her father's lips. He nodded gratefully. His hands were trembling so badly, she had to hold it for him to take a puff. When he had inhaled a couple of times, she touched his shoulder, guiding his backward steps to the chair. The phone trilled again. She grabbed it, ready to bawl at Richard, but it was her mother.

'Yes yes. He's still here.' Poppy nodded. She looked at her father, he was staring around the room, as though trying to focus. Not sure where he was. 'Look, Mam,' she interrupted her mother's flow, 'I'm sorry about earlier, OK? No – don't worry about all that. I'm sure Dublin will manage without . . . Just take care of yourself. Yeah. Me too. Bye.'

She was standing with her sister, squeezed into a small glass cubicle. Rows of beds, drill-like, filled the vast room beyond. The men sat or lay on the beds, staring at the ceiling or the walls. The male nurses said, 'There he is.' They turned within the glass chamber, and saw their father, trussed up like a turkey, staring back at them through hollow eyes. It was Christmas Eve. 'We've to keep him in the jacket, girls, or he'll do damage to himself,' a nurse explained apologetically. The sisters nodded, as though they understood. They were on their way home. A reluctant pit stop on the way.

Their father approached, pressing his face to the glass. A sane remnant of him smiled, to reassure them. They rolled their eyes, making a naughty child of him, just as they used to, throughout childhood. 'Cigars?' he mouthed hopefully. Poppy looked at her sister. How could they have forgotten? They had come with nothing. He frowned, not understanding. 'A fucking cigar?' he shouted, through the glass.

'He's getting agitated now, girls, maybe 'twould be better if you . . .' The nurses were kindly. The sisters didn't move. They watched another inmate, a young man with corkscrew hair, pass their father. He lit a cigarette and placed it between their father's lips. His exhalation fogged up the glass.

'They're not supposed to smoke in here.' One of the nurses rushed inside. 'Give me that.' He pulled the cigarette from his mouth, stubbing it on the ground. 'Now, now, James, you know the rules.' The emptied mouth opened and closed silently for a time. Like a baby working up for a cry. Poppy could never remember which one of them started it, but suddenly both sisters were laughing hysterically. Laughing laughing laughing. They couldn't stop. And the mouth outside continued to open and close soundlessly. The nurses shunted them toward the door. 'Best be heading off, girls.'

They had to pass him, twin high-pitched laughs still on their breaths. He eyed them hopelessly. Then he began to laugh too. In loud snorting sobs which seemed to echo up from his belly. They stood there, the three of them – braying – while the nurses shook their heads and looked away. He

stopped as suddenly as he'd started. An intermittent shrill
keen strumming on his vocal cords all that remained of the
laughter. While his black, despairing eyes pierced theirs.

'What are you going to do for me? What are you going to
do for me?' he keened over and over again, as the sisters
were nudged toward the solid oak door. But it was not a
serious request. His voice was flat, out-lived. He backed
away. Arms in a forced wrap around his body. At the door
they turned. He had made it to his bed, and lay with his
back to them, stretched out with his short, spindly legs
bouncing together. They knew he was still saying it – 'What
are you going to do for me?' They asked if they might return
with cigars, but the nurses declined another visit. They
would see to it that he had a cigar for Christmas Day.

'What do you want?' she shouted now. 'For God's sake –
what do you want?'

His shoulders collapsed. He had jumped to the middle of
the room once more. He lifted his head and she saw those
hollow eyes again.

'What can I do?' she asked in a softer voice. 'What do you
want?'

'I want . . .' His face crumpled first. Then the body as he
sagged onto his knees. He had to pitch the words through
his throat. 'I want – to wear my suit,' he said.

Poppy lifted the hanger. Picked at imagined fluff.

'Wear it, then.'

She guided him to the bathroom, lifting the suit onto a
hook on the back of the door.

'Can you manage?' she asked.

He nodded. The door closed behind her. Poppy waited
with hands folded on her lap. So he had brought her there,
after all. The place that had made her succeed in every other

place in life. The place where you had to laugh or suffocate with pity. The place where nothing could be fixed and men walked around without their skins on. She could dress continents – and yet was only beginning to learn how to wear her own past.

He stepped out. She made an appreciative sound.

'My hands,' he said, looking at the flapping birds, 'I can't – the bloody flies.'

She zipped him up. Recoiling from the unbearably tender intimacy of it. He checked himself in the mirror.

'Not bad.' He turned for more approval.

'Pretty damn fine, I'd say.'

'Well,' he took a deep breath. 'I'd better be going, so. Mrs Deasy – a formidable woman. I wouldn't want to cross her.'

'Look – there's loads of room here. The bed's the size of a football pitch – you're welcome to . . .'

'Ah no.' He slicked his hair back with spit. 'I'll stay on the road now.'

'Have you money for a taxi?'

'Oh, yes. That's it. I'll get a taxi.'

'Are you absolutely . . .'

'I'll get a taxi.'

She gathered his things, placing them into the empty typewriter case. He stopped her from bundling his old clothes inside. His head gestured toward the rubbish bin.

'I'll walk you to the lift,' she said.

'Ah, yes. The lift.'

All the way along the corridor, he checked himself in every mirror. Hitching the lapels. Running the trouser creases through his fingers. When he stepped inside, he looked blankly at her.

'What do I do now?'

'You press that button.' She pointed. 'Look, Dad, I just want to say . . .'

He put a finger to his lips.

'Lifts and taxis. Lifts and taxis,' he said, rolling his eyes, as though they were enjoying their own private joke. A muscle spasmed on his left cheek but he held on to the fixed smile, as the door closed. Poppy stood there for a while, with her cheek pressed against a wall. Then she ran back to the room.

She was just in time to see him leave. He strolled over to the river. She watched him light a cigar. Taxis passed but he didn't hail any. He was moving along now, stopping from time to time, to pat himself down. He turned and looked up at the building – staring up, as though he would take it on. Dwarfed by the height. She knew that he could not see her. She thought the tears coursing down her cheeks would surely leave tracks like riverbeds. She watched until nothing of him remained except for a swath of smoke where he had stood by the river. Not one pill throughout his visit. Retracing steps all right, and she had been the end of the journey. She understood then. He had made the only concession he knew to make. Draping across his body the words he could not voice. He wanted her to be able to say – to tell the others – that when she saw him, for the last time – he was wearing a suit.

The phone rang on and on.

THE DEBT COLLECTOR

Ronnie Ryan hated the car wash in the garage on the quays opposite Finbar's Hotel. It felt as if two bright green dead sheep were somehow savaging her mother's Toyota Starlet. But then she did want it to look good when she went to the airport next day. There was no point in spending a small fortune on her hair, her skin, her nails and her outfit if she turned up in a dust-streaked car. Tomorrow everything had to be perfect. That was why she was staying here in Dublin overnight.

Her mother had said she was daft. The man's plane didn't get in from Stockholm until lunchtime, couldn't she drive up in the morning and be there to meet him in plenty of time? It was three hours at the very most. Instead of throwing away money staying in a hotel in the city. But Ronnie was adamant. She didn't want to be stuck behind some fellow with a horse box going at nineteen miles an hour, or meet a diversion, or not find a parking place at the airport and arrive rushing and fussing. She was going to meet Chester. Chester Stone who was coming over to Ireland to marry her. Next week she would be Mrs Veronica Stone.

One week before her thirtieth birthday Ronnie, who had thought that no man could ever love her, would be a bride. If *that* didn't deserve a little celebration, a night in one of Dublin's trendy hotels, Ronnie didn't know what did.

She looked at herself in the car mirror while the dead

green sheep went on worrying the car windows with soapy foam. She saw big slightly anxious dark eyes, good skin and long straight brown hair. Tonight she would ask Deirdre honestly, utterly ruthlessly honestly, to tell her was she getting too old for long hair. Deirdre would say. Well, she might say. Maybe she might not want to be hurtful, say anything that would spoil Ronnie's wedding.

It would be a small wedding, family and a few friends. Twenty-six people to a buffet lunch at her parents' home, she had arranged it all long before her mother could try to wrest control of proceedings. Ronnie had organized a cream of tomato soup to be made by her sister-in-law, a dressed salmon, with a variety of salads, from the local supermarket and ice cream to be served with the wedding cake. She had hired china, cutlery and glasses long before her mother could say that there were plenty of those around the house and nobody looked at whether things were matching or not. The drink was on a sale or return basis and a reliable young fellow from one of the local bars would serve it. Chester's mother and brother would come and his friend Michael who would be the best man. The other twenty-two were from Ronnie's side.

She had no anxiety about the day. It was perfectly organized.

And that was what Ronnie was good at, organizing: sales conferences, trade fairs, exhibitions. This is what her life had revolved around for the past four years. Far away from home in the New York travel firm where she worked. Where she had gone to hide from all that had happened. She knew how to identify and marginalize possible trouble areas, isolate those who might be disruptive or negative, maximize the

strengths and self-importance of everyone who would per-
form better if they thought they were appreciated.

Ronnie was well experienced in seeing that the function
should end on a high, that they should quit when they were
winning. A car would sweep the bride and groom away just
before anyone thought that it was time for them to go. Plans
had also been made for Chester's mother, brother and best
man to be ferried back to their hotel lest too much exposure
to Ronnie's family prove mutually tedious.

Her own mother and father now believed they had set up
this generous and stylish wedding party themselves and were
actually looking forward to it.

Ronnie drove her clean shiny car out of the car wash and
headed across the bridge for Finbar's Hotel. Dinner with her
friend Deirdre in the Echo Rooms there as a treat, nothing
too boozy or raucous, an early night and a good sleep. Next
morning the hairdresser, the airport and then take Chester
home for the wedding and the start of a new life.

*

She parked the car and took the elevator from the car park
up to the foyer of Finbar's Hotel. She had been for drinks
there three weeks ago when she had come back from the
States with her amazing news and plans.

It was in Fiona's Bar that she had told Deirdre all about
Chester, and how it was like turning pages of a familiar book
getting to know each other. They had the same hopes and
dreams, a more equal society without resorting to revolution
to achieve it. They loved the same Ella Fitzgerald and Bessie
Smith numbers and Woody Allen films, they had both been
overawed by Arizona, annoyed by Paris, and happiest in

Amsterdam where they had met and walked hand in hand by the canals.

*

Deirdre, married with two small children, had listened almost unbelieving as Ronnie told her the tale with words tumbling after each other. She was to be the bridesmaid, or maid of honour. She would wear a beautiful jacket and skirt in rose-coloured silk with a trim of cream lace. The bride would wear cream lace and a hat trimmed with rose-coloured silk. They would knock everyone's eyes out, they promised each other.

'Imagine all this happening to you, Ronnie, after everything else that happened,' Deirdre said before she could stop herself.

But Ronnie wasn't upset. 'I know, after everything, isn't it amazing?' she had said.

And with a wave of her hand she dismissed the pain and hurt and humiliation which loving Neil Nolan for all those long sad years had meant. They had smiled brightly at each other as if a whole decade had not been taken out of Ronnie's life because she had had the bad luck to meet Neil Nolan on her twentieth birthday.

*

There would be no chat of Neil Nolan tonight or ever, she thought as she watched an elderly woman with caked make-up sweep through the lobby from the lounge in a faded emerald-green evening gown. Ronnie knew her face from somewhere. She never forgot a face. The woman sensed she was being watched and turned to give a small haughty wave to Ronnie, who walked towards her as if summoned. 'We all come down to this in the end,' she muttered, almost in a whisper, to Ronnie. 'Love is a bastard.' The woman looked pitiful as she tried to wink and edged closer to Ronnie, her voice even lower as she asked for a pound.

'I hope your luck changes,' Ronnie told her, pressing the coin into her hand. The woman turned, as if embarrassed, and yet as she stepped out into the evening light Ronnie saw the chauffeur of a long limo that had pulled up get out to open a door respectfully for her.

Neil Nolan was in the past, she thought, Chester was the present and the future.

There was no need to act and lie for Chester.

No pretending that she liked greyhound racing and boxing.

No being nice to dubious people who boasted of how they cheated the tax, got things without paying VAT and screwed the insurance companies by throwing away a suitcase of old clothes at the end of a vacation and getting massive compensation.

Chester worked in the travel business like Ronnie did; he specialized in Incentive Travel, holidays as rewards for sales teams who had achieved their targets. And of course Chester knew her as a successful person, someone who had worked hard to succeed in business. Neil Nolan had only known her as a loser, someone who dropped out of college before her degree to live with him and be his humble adoring slave.

Someone who had stayed on long, long after it was over, accepting the scorn and slow destruction of her confidence.

*

The woman at the desk was crisp and efficient. Her name badge said Máire Dermott. She had a touch of an English accent under her native Dublin one. Ronnie wondered what had brought her back to Dublin. She didn't look like the sort of woman who would have come home following some man. Much too independent and strong for that kind of caper.

Máire Dermott said there was a message for her and handed over an envelope. Deirdre was so sorry but young Cathal had a raging temperature and she didn't think she could make it tonight. Could Ronnie ring the moment she checked in? Maybe Ronnie might come around to the house instead?

Ronnie was very disappointed. She wouldn't go visiting to the house of someone who was worried about a sick child. And it wasn't just the thought of an evening on her own that upset her. She was well used to entertaining herself. It was just that this was going to be Truth Night. Deirdre who had been married for six years would tell her the good and the bad about it. Deirdre would be seriously truthful about Ronnie's hair. They would giggle at the fact that Chester would have to stay in a different bedroom because Ronnie's parents would never be able to accept that the marriage had been anticipated in any way. But still Deirdre was worried about the child.

Ronnie went to the phones beside the porter's desk and called her friend.

'No, no,' she reassured her, 'it's much wiser to stay with the child . . . of course it's not meningitis. But you have to be there. Won't I see you at the wedding. Nonsense, an early night is what I need.'

Pleased that she had reassured her friend, Ronnie looked at the clocks which told the times in different lands.

It was half-past six in Ireland, it would be half-past seven in Sweden where Chester was packing his bags to come to Ireland for his wedding. It would be 1.30 p.m. in New York where Chester's mother was still in shock that her forty-year-old son had decided to marry in an Irish country town.

Ronnie picked up her little overnight bag to go up to Room 103 on the first floor, suddenly placing the face of the woman in the limo. It was from an old ad they used to sometimes show on cable television, back in the States.

It would be 10.30 a.m. in San Francisco where Chester's brother Mark would be spending further time trying to get the court to reduce the alimony he paid to his ex-wife.

How amazing to think of all the different lives that people led.

*

Ronnie and Chester had often said that being in the travel business gave you insights into people's dreams. Clients frequently thought they would love five days in Las Vegas, but in fact they might much prefer time in the Scottish Highlands. Try to tell them that? Forget it, you were the very worst in the world.

She was heading towards where the lift doors were closing over on a panic-stricken looking man in a striped jumper when she saw him.

Neil Nolan coming out of the Irish Bar a drink in his hand and the same lopsided smile on his face.

It was over four years since she had seen him. She had wondered from time to time, had he run to fat, grown a beer belly – he drank a lot. But no, he was still achingly handsome.

To her.

She realized that other people had said that he wasn't handsome at all, with a small pointed face. A bit like a rat, according to Deirdre, who had hated him with a passion.

He always reacted very quickly, unlike Chester, who had a slow smile as things dawned on him. He recognized her now and adjusted his expression within half a second.

'I don't believe it,' he said mockingly. 'The dead arose and appeared to many.'

'No, I didn't die, Neil,' she said.

'Might as well have, no news of you anywhere. Your parents frozen in silence. Deirdre saying she'd call the guards if I asked for you again. That odd note you left. What was I *meant* to think except that you'd topped yourself?'

He sounded aggrieved and almost sorry that she hadn't.

Ronnie felt totally calm. 'Don't be so dramatic, I said in that note very clearly that I was going away.'

'Yeah, but the way you left everything in the flat, it was a bit obsessive, how was I to know what your state of mind was?'

She had played this scene over in her mind so often, meeting him again. Would she cut him dead? Would he apologize and say that he hadn't realized how good a person she had been? Would they realize that the separation had been part of it, something that *had* to happen, and would they take up where they had left off?

What she had never known in any scenario she had dreamed up for herself over the long years without him was that she would feel so indifferent.

His being there among the off-white pillars in the lobby of Finbar's Hotel wasn't nearly as important as Deirdre's not being there. His face was as nothing compared to the face she was going to see tomorrow when Chester flew in from Sweden. She laughed at him in an unforced way.

'Come on out of that, Neil, nobody knew what my state of mind was back in those days, not even myself. And how are *you*, anyway?'

He looked at her admiringly. She hadn't seen him look like that at her for very long time. Not since the very early days, before she had become obsessed and infatuated, turned herself into a tiresome encumbrance in his life.

He really did see that she was over him, and it annoyed him. He might even make a move to get her back. The thought thrilled her since it would never work. But it would be heady to have that power even for a few minutes.

'I'm fine, just fine,' he said, looking her up and down in that slow way he did, from her throat to her knees, deliberately examining her body.

She felt foolishly pleased that she was wearing a smart knitted suit in soft green wool, and a good silk scarf.

She had not got fat, those deep circles of anxiety and sorrow had gone from under her eyes, she looked well, and she knew it.

'And business? That going well too?'

She was polite, not overinvolved.

She couldn't be more pleased with the way things were working out. This wasn't even role-playing as it always used to be with Neil, it was for real.

And he realized it.

'Yes, my sort of work flourishes when the economy is good, people get greedy, they have to be put straight.'

'Indeed.'

'Are you meeting anyone here?' Neil asked.

'I was, but it's just been cancelled,' she said.

It was a factual answer, it wasn't angling for an invitation or setting up a drink. She looked as if she were about to say goodbye. And he seemed to realize this.

'Well, perhaps . . .?' he began.

She looked at him enquiringly. 'Yes?'

'For old times' sake if we could maybe . . .?'

Old times' sake! What could he mean, she wondered? A man who had slowly and systematically destroyed her confidence, her esteem, her hope for the future, any kind of future, by his taunts and criticism. He wanted them to have a drink or a meal to celebrate this process in some way. He was even more cruel and unfeeling than she had believed it to be possible.

'I don't really think . . .'

'Come on, Ronnie, it's been two years . . . three, even.'

She didn't say that it had been four years and two months. But she knew that was what it was.

She said nothing

'I'd like to hear how you've been, come on, it would be nice,' he pleaded.

She decided suddenly. She would talk to him. She might even ask him some of the questions she had been going to ask Deirdre.

'Sure, all right, which bar will we go to?'

Suddenly he looked shifty, wary even, as if he hadn't expected this. 'It's a bit awkward . . . I mean . . . there are people around, I don't want to be seen. You know the nature of the job.'

Ronnie knew the nature of the job.

Debt collecting. Fairly forcible debt collecting.

But that had never meant that Neil Nolan couldn't be

seen in public. In fact it was the reverse. The very sight of him and some of his colleagues was often enough to make people pay up quickly.

She looked at him quizzically without saying anything.

'So you realize the problems,' he said.

'Another time, then.' She turned to go to the lift.

'Ronnie?'

'Yes?'

'We could go up to your room, there might be a minibar, we could have room service even?'

'You *must* be joking,' she said.

And she knew she said it with such amused amazement that he believed her. It wasn't at all like the feeble protests she had made for year after year, when everyone knew she didn't mean it. Giving credence to the myth of women who say no when they mean yes.

'No, for God's sake, Ronnie, I don't mean . . . go up to your room for . . . nothing like that. No, just so that we wouldn't be disturbed.'

'Who don't you want to see?' she asked.

'There's not anyone in particular. It's just general.'

Ronnie looked around the suddenly empty lobby with its white sofas and its colourful pictures on the wall.

There was nobody around.

Even Máire Dermott had gone from the desk into the room behind. A foreign-looking receptionist was taking her place at the desk, not even glancing towards them. There was nobody else to see them talking.

'You were drinking here perfectly openly, Neil, it's just that you don't want anyone to see you with me, or with any woman. Who are you hiding from? Is it your wife again?'

He was married when she had met him first, married to

the dreaded Dara. Well, that's what Ronnie had called her. Dara Nolan, mother of two and aged twenty-five, the most hated woman in the world from Ronnie's point of view. Neil had never really left her properly, he had got a flat for his own space, the flat where Ronnie had lived with him, while the dreaded Dara was bringing up the children.

How much she had hated Dara then, a selfish hard unfeeling woman who could neither keep her husband nor let him go, but who made snivelling demands and told tales about children missing their dad instead of giving the children some kind of solid safe background herself.

They were three and four at the time that Ronnie had crossed their lives, nice little things with blond hair and their father's smile. It wasn't their fault, the whole terrible mess. Neil would go back to see them on Sundays, he was always bad-tempered and upset when he returned. It was impossible to please him those evenings, everything that Ronnie said was wrong.

Dara must be thirty-five now, the children thirteen and fourteen. He couldn't have gone back to them? Dara would never have taken him back, not after all that happened.

Neil looked embarrassed. 'The kids were having problems, bad age and everything you know, we made it up on the surface, so I hang about the house more.'

'Very wise.' Ronnie actually meant it.

She hoped that she and Chester would have children, it was definitely in the plan. What matter that they were nearly thirty and nearly forty now? Parents always seem centuries older than their children, even if they were young parents like Neil and the dreaded Dara.

'Yes, so you see . . .?' He indicated the lifts.

'You mean Dara might see us here?'

'A lot of her friends drink here, and I did sort of say . . .'

'That you wouldn't see me again?' she asked.

'Well, not you specifically. I mean you've been out of here for years, I said I wouldn't see anyone.'

'That must be difficult in a city jumping with life like this one.' She hoped she didn't sound too cynical. She needn't have worried, he took it on its face value.

'It is in a way, but I get out of town on a few jobs, and then the coast's clear.'

'That's nice,' she said.

'Well, it helps,' said Neil Nolan.

Ronnie knew she was never going to meet anyone less sensitive, courteous and protective to answer some of the questions she had about her future. This was the man who would tell her straight out her weaknesses, and since she didn't even feel the slightest twinge of regret or rekindled anything it would be quite safe to invite him to her room.

'Right then, so we go upstairs,' she said, and saw the surprise on his face and she walked ahead of him to the lifts at the back of the marble-floored foyer.

At the door he took her entrance card to put it in the door. He had always done this sort of thing, assumed a woman could do nothing. There had been a time when she liked it. Now it irritated her greatly. They went in and she laid her bag casually on the big double bed and went to the window.

'How long are you booked in for?' he asked.

'Only the night. Look, they *do* have a minibar, that's handy,' Ronnie said.

'Well, they do in most places now,' he said, voice scornful again, ridiculing anyone who would have expected less.

She took no notice of the tone, she was kneeling in front of it.

'Beer, wine?' she suggested.

'Come on, we haven't seen each other for two years, let's have something more special?' he suggested.

Suddenly she had an idea. In her overnight bag there was a bottle of champagne, a gift from her cousin, who said that it was useless giving people presents that had to be carried back to the United States, Ronnie should demand things that must be eaten or drunk here.

'A champagne cocktail?' she suggested.

'Go on, they don't have that?'

'They have miniature brandies in here, and I have champagne and we can put in two sugar lumps from the coffee tray.'

He looked pleased by this suggestion and made a great deal of fuss about getting the glasses out.

She remembered the time when she would have given anything to please him like this. Now when it didn't matter a bit it was all amazingly easy.

Ronnie sat on the chair beside the window, Neil sat on the bed.

The drinks fizzed up and they raised a glass to each other.

'Good luck,' she said.

'And no hard feelings?' he asked. Neil always liked to cover his back.

'About what?'

'We didn't part friends.'

'But that was ages ago as you said, tell me about yourself.'

And he did a bit.

A lot of wideboys in the city at the moment, people who couldn't wait until they got the proper gear and didn't know you had to set up some kind of deal. No, they just had to have the £400 jacket that very night to go clubbing. So what did they do? They went into a place and bought it, with a dodgy credit card, or a cheque that bounced. Whatever. Well, that couldn't go on. He sounded almost self-righteous about it.

'No, of course not.' Ronnie tutted with disapproval.

So more and more stringent debt collecting and warnings had to go on. A bit more stressful now than in the old days, some days these fellows travelled in gangs, you'd need three of you to face them down.

She had known very few of his friends, so there were not many names from the past to take out and examine. He had known none of her friends except Deirdre and that would not have been one to recall. Deirdre had shouted at him in public one New Year's Eve when he was out with Dara and a group of friends. 'You told my friend to wait in, you bastard, you told my friend Ronnie to stay at home and wait for your call. God but it would serve you right if she has her head in the gas oven.'

He had called of course shortly afterwards, saying that yet again Ronnie had managed to ruin a perfectly civilized night out by getting her friends to follow him and harass him and as far as he was concerned if the gas oven was her option then she shouldn't hang about. It was the lowest time of her life. She wouldn't mention Deirdre.

He looked at the television programmes listing. 'Look at that, *Terminator* is on,' he said, pleased.

'But much later on,' she said. 'You'll be well home and tucked up by then.'

'Not necessarily,' Neil said, pouring them a second drink.

'How are the children?' she asked.

'You don't want to know about them.'

'Of course I do.' She was pleasant, relaxed, interested.

'But you used to cry when I talked about them.'

'Oh, *Neil*, for Heaven's sake, that was then, this is now.'

He looked at her for a moment and seemed convinced.

It was a sorry tale.

The boy, who was fourteen and a half, had been in front of the children's court twice, nothing too drastic, the usual shoplifting, cruising the shopping malls with a crowd of other kids, getting into bad ways.

The little girl had what they called an eating disorder these days. Starving herself, eating in front of them under great pressure, then going upstairs and throwing it all up in the lavatory, they could hear her doing it.

'And is Dara able to cope with it all?' She sounded concerned.

'You used not to mention Dara's name,' he said in amazement. 'No, I remember, that was then . . . well she's OK, Dara, she really is. Her parents wanted her to get rid of me but she said no, for the children's sake, so I have to put in a regular appearance, do the heavy father bit to the one and the loving dad bit to the other.'

'But not tonight?' Ronnie said.

'No, I could be out of town legitimately, if you know what I mean.'

She knew what he meant.

He had asked to have a drink so that they could talk about her, about what she had been doing. He had asked nothing, he didn't know she had been living in America, he didn't know she would marry next week, he knew and cared nothing of the life that she and Chester would live. That she hoped and prayed she and Chester would live.

For somewhere deep inside, Ronnie felt it wouldn't happen. She wasn't worthy of such a man, of being married, of having a home of her own. She had known this for so long.

That was why she had lived for all those long lonely months in New York in just one room paid for by waiting on tables. She had tried to make no social life but spent the hours with her home study manuals, her part-time courses. She didn't even believe she was good when she came top of her group, when she could find her way around a computer program before the other students had barely begun to grasp it.

She knew she had to be a hopeless, worthless person. Otherwise why would Neil Nolan who was normal have told her this so many times? Tonight he might be able to give her chapter and verse. Point out her most irritating ways, guide her through a minefield of mannerisms which would irritate Chester and drive him away from her.

But Neil was suspicious about intense conversations. Unless, that was, when he initiated them himself. She must not ask him too directly. She felt he was uneasy talking about his wife and children, there were no glowing tales of success here, she should move back to the field of work. This was the area where Neil Nolan would shine.

'And is the picture still the same, the courts not being able to enforce debts?'

He warmed to the subject. 'Well, you know the way it is, it's not necessarily a criminal act to write a cheque when there are no funds to meet it. Like you could be putting in the funds in a few hours later. As if! Anyway most of the recovering of the money or goods has to be a civil action, and the length and cost of proceedings means that it's bloody interminable.'

'I know.' She was such a good listener.

'So the human presence, the little message passed over that it might be as well to get that bloody car back to such and such a place and in good nick . . . well, that usually works better than lengthy court applications.'

'And you don't have any violence, do you?' She looked pointedly at a scar on his forehead.

'Not unless they start first. Some of them do. Bastards,' he said touching the scar lightly.

'It hardly shows. It's just that I know you, well, used to know you so well.'

'Why weren't you normal like this back then? What was all the screaming and roaring about?' he asked.

'Was there a lot of it, then?'

She sounded interested in a mild sort of way.

'Jesus, Ronnie, you were like a bloody banshee, it was like Niagara Falls every night.'

'Then why did you stay with me?' Her question was light not loaded.

'You used to promise me that it would never happen again, and I believed you. Right eejit.' He smiled at her the smile that used to break her heart, she saw it now the way it turned on and off like a lamp.

'And what was it all about?' She seemed genuinely puzzled.

'Oh, search me.' He raised his hands to heaven. 'I never knew, I promise you.'

'What was most irritating about me back then?'

'The crying and moaning, I think. Jesus, after a hard day a man wouldn't want that. And the constant need for me to be admiring something.'

'What sort of thing?'

'I don't know, but, "Look, Neil, I made a cushion cover.

Look, Neil, you didn't notice I changed round the bread bin and the biscuit tin."'

'Was it as bad as that?' She laughed with ridicule at the person she must have been.

'Worse.' He was warming to it now. 'The really bad bit was asking me to guess. '"Guess what I did in the house today, Neil, look round and guess."' He made a mincing, lisping imitation of the way she used to speak. She forced herself not to get annoyed.

'And did you ever guess right?' she asked.

'I don't think so.' He grinned at his own basic blokeish desire to please. 'I tried, I know I did. I used to ask myself: Were the bloody curtains like that this morning or weren't they? But you know how hard it is to see things after a day's work. All I needed was a beer, a cuddle, a meal, then I used to get this desperate grilling. What was I to do?'

He looked at her, a fellow conspirator, both of them groaning over what Ronnie used to be like in the bad old days.

She hardly trusted herself to speak.

She had slaved over that flat. He had no money to maintain it, she had painted every inch of it. Though no seamstress she had struggled to make furnishings since they had no money to buy any. She had persuaded the landlord to let them live on there over the shop by helping out downstairs dragging in sacks of vegetables, and weighing them into bags for him.

And letting him pinch her bottom without crying so loud that his wife would hear. She could take some of the vegetables upstairs with her too.

Neil was well into memory lane.

'And God Almighty, Ronnie, will you ever forget those

vegetables, soups and stews, I farted my way from one side of Dublin to the next because of them? What possessed you to serve them? You weren't a bloody vegetarian, were you?'

'No. I can't think why.' She pretended to think. 'Could it be because we didn't have any money for meat or fish or things?' Her face was open and innocent-looking.

He saw no irony.

'Aw, come on, we'd have had enough for a bit of something normal, but you were so into this stuff, and lentils! It's a wonder my stomach's right at all.'

'And what did we talk about when we were eating . . . this awful stuff?' She was so eager to know what he would remember.

'God, Ronnie, you've got bloody Alzheimer's already. What did we talk about? This and that, mainly your plans, you were a great one for making plans. Next weekend we'll do this, next summer we'll do that. In five years' time we'll do the other. The day itself was never good enough for you, it was always on on on to the next thing.'

Bingo! Ronnie thought to herself. That was something she would have to watch.

Her long months of home learning had included books on how to behave in public, on social skills. She knew that people could irritate without being aware of it. Everything Neil had said so far had been entirely irrelevant. But this matter of advance planning might indeed be something which could drive Chester mad. It possibly hadn't so far because both of them needed planning in their work in the travel business. And of course they needed it also in their private lives to arrange when they could meet, before Chester went to Sweden to set up this incentive tour, after Ronnie came back from Pittsburgh and the Travel Fair. But it was something to note, perhaps she had a tendency to overplan in private life as well.

He went to use the lavatory in her bathroom. He left the door open as always, she had always hated it. It seemed so arrogant. But she wouldn't mention it. Neil Nolan had come up here to talk, not to learn any life skills.

She poured another miniature of cognac skilfully into his champagne glass and topped it up. Drink had always loosened his tongue, she would learn more. She would have a self-improvement course all of her own.

He flushed the chain and came out without washing his hands. Had she noticed such things years ago, and if she had noticed, had she cared?

'These are going down a treat,' he said.

'Glad you like them,' she said.

He looked as if he were going to ask something about her life, a world where she knew how to make champagne cocktails, a world which gave her enough money to stay overnight in Finbar's Hotel.

Just for a second he seemed poised to enquire about someone else's world rather than his own. But the moment passed.

'Well, at least you took my advice about keeping your shoes on,' he said with a laugh, indicating her feet. Ronnie wore plain black court shoes, with high heels. The articles that she had read on power dressing had suggested these for almost every occasion. They were essential for every work engagement and probably suitable for every social one apart from something connected with sports or the open country. They were just beginning to feel a little tight and she had been about to remove them.

'I beg your pardon?'

'You know the way you were always flinging off your shoes, putting your bare feet covered with corns and veruccas and things up on the sofa. I was always telling you what desperate feet you had, better to keep them covered.'

'Oh, I keep them covered nowadays,' she said with a tinkling laugh.

'Well, I taught you something, then,' he said, pleased.

Yes, Neil, she thought to herself. You taught me to hate my body, just as your thirteen-year-old daughter hates hers.

You taught me to feel awkward and unattractive. I was a fine bouncy twenty-year-old when I met you, with fellows fancying me, a future, a degree, a career ahead.

I was a weak frightened old woman of twenty-six and a half when I left you, or when you left me, I never know which it was.

It wasn't because you wanted to do this to me, you never set out to do it, I allowed it to happen. She wondered was this another *Bingo* about her feet. Something she should watch out for in her future life?

She had hardly ever been in a position where Chester could have looked at them and felt revolted. Either they were both barefooted on a beach, or by the fire toasting little scones together after a shower. Or else in bed. And he had said nothing against her feet or any other part of her in bed. In fact quite the reverse.

'What was my next worst bit apart from my feet, tell me?' she asked cheerfully.

'Come on now, Ronnie, don't put yourself down, you've turned out a fine-looking woman, I know it's a case of fine feathers making fine birds, but you don't look at all like you used to.'

'I had hardly any feathers in those days, if I remember rightly.' She was frowning as if trying to drag up a memory. But it was clear, only too clear.

The pair of stylish jeans she had stolen from a market stall which she wore any time they went out. They were all she had. Those and some T-shirts or blouses that Deirdre gave her, together with an earful of warnings about where life would lead her if she stayed any longer with Neil Nolan.

She had never stolen anything before or since and she still remembered the raw fear in her throat in case she would be caught. It went on for days, the agony that someone had followed her home and the guards were only biding their time.

'You must have had something, you weren't interested, that's all, you barely combed your hair.'

Oh, that was so wrong, she was very interested, she would have loved the clothes that she saw on other young women, on the television, in cafés, on the street. Clothes she could have afforded if she had still had the allowance from her parents as a college student, clothes she could have bought if she had got a degree and a job.

And he was so, so wrong about her hair, too. She did comb it, and brush it, and wash it in lemon juice when she could get any. She just couldn't afford to get it cut so she got into the habit of trimming it herself.

How strange of him to think she didn't care.

'That's youth for you,' she said lightly. 'What did I care about? I must have cared about *something*.'

'Oh, just crying, and planning, I think that was all.' He laughed and opened the little plastic pack of Digestive biscuits that was on the coffee tray.

'No, come on, I was in my early twenties, there must have been things I was interested in? Sex, even? How about that? Was I interested in sex?'

'Now, now, Ronnie, don't bring up things that you know will cause a fight. We're being very civilized here drinking grand things with a kick in them, why spoil it.'

When he was in the bathroom Ronnie had topped up her own glass with mineral water. She had drunk far less of what he called grand things with a kick in them than he had. Her mind was very clear but she let her voice get a bit slurred.

'No, that's not a fair question to ask you, I was interested, I know I was, what I should ask you is was I any good at it?'

'What's past is past, for all I know you can screw like a rattlesnake nowadays,' he said smiling.

'Do they do it well, do you think?' She sounded fascinated by the whole idea of it.

'I don't know whether they do it well or not, but they'd do it with a bit of enthusiasm and a hint of danger maybe.' He laughed.

'And that wasn't the way the two of us did it?' Again the innocent trying to remember.

'More like a sack of potatoes, you didn't really enjoy it, love, did you? You just lay there eyes closed until it was over. Which it was fairly quickly with such a response.'

She nailed the look onto her face, she wouldn't let him know how cruelly unfair this was.

She hadn't known that it was possible to rewrite history like this.

Sometimes they had lain for hours together with her trying everything he suggested. Long after she was tired and bruised. She thought his desire meant he loved her so she must strive to keep it alive.

He was smiling affectionately as if at the foolish antics of a hopeless puppy dog.

'Anyway, let's not go back on all that now,' he said in a magnanimous tone, 'we talked enough then, I tried to please you, to get you to know what it was all about, but you just couldn't seem to get it.'

'No, I suppose there *are* people like that,' she agreed regretfully.

'And others who expect too much, maybe.' He was meeting her halfway on this.

'It wasn't just being too tall and having droopy breasts, do you think?'

'No, there's was nothing wrong with you, Ronnie, believe me, just that you couldn't put your heart into it.'

There was nothing wrong with me.

He tells me this now.

So why did I hear over and over that I was ugly and that no man could possibly desire me, and that I was lucky that he could just manage to for a bit?

Or that it was tragic to look at those beautiful pictures of girls in magazines and then have to hold floppy breasts like mine?

And when she covered herself with her arms he laughed even more.

What could she learn from this? Was there anything to bring to her new life? A sack of potatoes who couldn't put her heart in it.

That wasn't what Chester said as he held her in his arms afterwards.

Nor could it be what he thought.

There was only one more question she must ask.

'Let's finish this, come on.' She drained the last little

miniature and the rest of the bottle into his glass. He was looking at the red-covered menu instead.

'Won't we order up something from this lot?'

He was reading it out aloud.

'Salmon, Chicken, Sirloin Steak. My God, look at what you can have here if you pay for it. Not for vegetarians like yourself . . . no, I tell a lie, there's a mushroom something here.' He was like an eager child.

She wanted to pick up his drink and throw it in his face. She wanted to shout at him: 'I'm not a vegetarian you stupid thoughtless senseless oaf. It's just that for six years I didn't eat meat to save us money.' But she still had a question to ask him.

She took the room service menu away from his hands and laid it on top of the television.

'We're not eating, then?' He was disappointed.

'No, I'm not hungry,' she said, and that sorted it. As it might have sorted it years ago if she had only had any sense.

'Why did I stay with you all those years, do you think?' she asked.

'Well, come on, you're the one who stayed, you must know.'

'I don't really, Neil, I was wondering, did you know?'

'What?'

'No, really, it was all long ago as you say, and we've been very frank with each other.'

'We have,' he agreed.

Her mind reeled. Did Neil really believe she had been frank with him? She had offered not a word of retrospective criticism. Not one.

'So why did I stay? Was it love? Or a crush? Or fear of going off on my own?'

'Jesus, I don't . . .'

'No, I'm sure you know, you know everything else. Truly, you know that you *let* me stay because you were a soft-hearted eejit, now isn't that what you said?' She was laughing, apparently delighted with it all now.

'Well, yes, a bit,' he grinned.

'So?'

'So you stayed because you were hopeless, Ronnie love, you hadn't the personality of a paper cup, you were kind of half-witted. I must say you've pulled yourself together a lot, and smartened yourself up. But you were a real loser then, that's the truth fair and square, since we are being frank.'

Only minutes more and then he would go.

There would be no room service, no more drink, no movie, no sex.

He would have to go.

Ronnie had done so much with her life in recent times, she could keep her temper for a few minutes, couldn't she?

She would not let him know that it was him who had taken away everything that the bubbly girl just out of her teens had going for her and left a lonely worthless shell.

'That's it,' she said brightly, 'I was a slow starter, that's all.'

'Well, you've done fine since by the look of you,' he said as if giving credit where credit was due.

'Oh yes, you must have been able to teach me a few things along the way.'

'Well, I hope so.' He was glad to have been of help.

'So will I let you get back to everything. It was really nice to see you.'

He had only to touch her arm in the old days and the

hairs stood up as if she had an electric shock. He touched her now and nothing happened.

'I don't have to go immediately,' he began.

'Ah, but I do,' she said.

'I thought you said your friend had stood you up.'

'I've more than one friend,' she smiled, moving him gradually towards the door. There were voices from next door moving down the corridor.

She opened the bedroom door slightly. She heard the lift closing over and then footsteps run back into the room as a phone rang on there. The corridor was now empty.

'Goodbye, Neil,' she said, opening the door fully.

'I can't believe you're not crying,' he said.

She shrugged. 'Oh, I don't do that any more.'

He still didn't want to go so she began to close the door.

He touched her, just a little stroke on the lapel of her expensive green knitted suit.

'Much too floppy,' she laughed.

'I never said that, perfectly shaped, from what I remember.'

'Goodnight, Neil.'

She shut the door fully and he was gone.

She sat still for a long time, she didn't know how long, and thought about the good man in a Swedish hotel room who would arrive tomorrow to marry her.

She knew she would take as lessons the fact that her bare feet were unattractive if too easily displayed and her advance planning could lead to irritation. She would take nothing else of the years of degradation. She wished there was a way she could make him pay for that sentence that left her so humbled and lacking in faith and hope.

He had been punished in a way, with his children turning out to be problems. But not enough.

She rinsed the glasses, wrapped the empty champagne bottle in a newspaper and put it in her overnight bag to discard somewhere tomorrow and was about to turn on the television when there was a very loud knocking at her door.

She went to see who was there but did not open it. The guards gave their name and station.

'What is it about, please?

'Are you Ms Veronica Ryan?'

'That's right.'

'May we come in, Ms Ryan?'

'As I said, can you tell me what it's in connection with?'

'We just want to know if you can substantiate an alibi for us, madam.'

She opened the door. Two young guards stood there. Further down the corridor there were other guards and the sounds of scuffle as if they were restraining someone.

'An alibi?' Ronnie asked.

'Mr Nolan claims that he was in your room between the hours of six thirty and eight fifteen this evening.'

'Mr *Nolan*?' Ronnie sounded eager to help but confused.

'Yes. Neil Nolan, he says he is an old friend.'

'And why does he need an alibi?'

'We're just checking the movements of several people, there was a serious incident not far from here. Someone got badly beaten. Excuse me, Ms Ryan, do you know Mr Neil Nolan?'

'I knew Neil Nolan yes, years ago,' she said slowly.

They looked back towards the lift and the sound of voices raised.

'And was he here tonight in your company?'

Ronnie paused.

Tonight he had not beaten someone in a car park. Tonight his knuckles weren't grazed or his face scarred as they used to be after an evening spent on business.

But there had been other nights when he had done this. Other nights when the guards had not been in the vicinity.

No, tonight Neil Nolan had been nowhere near the serious incident where some young man's face was rearranged because a debt collector couldn't wait for the due process of the law to reclaim what was owed.

Instead he had been here in this room knocking back champagne cocktails and telling a woman whose life he had destroyed that she wasn't bad now that she had smartened up a bit and that as an ultimate accolade he wouldn't mind giving her one. A woman so broken and humbled that she had hardly dared to face the future that was being offered to her.

Neil Nolan had been punished because his son was heading for a series of detention homes and his daughter was bulimic.

But he hadn't been punished enough. Not himself.

She thought back to their meeting in the foyer. It had been empty at the time apart from the foreign receptionist, who hadn't even glanced in their direction. They had not met anyone in the lift nor called for any room service. Nobody had seen them together.

'No, Guard,' Ronnie Ryan said, looking around the room which was innocent of any visitor. 'I haven't seen Neil Nolan for over four years.'

1☩4

GOD'S GIFT

In a chaste and milky light she sat on a long cream-coloured sofa in a secluded corner of the foyer, feeling strangely at home. Really, she thought, Finbar's Hotel was rather like a convent – admittedly not like any convent she knew but still oddly familiar.

There were palms in great clay pots that reminded her of views of the Holy Land in a child's prayer-book. The smooth marble floor was like the chapel aisle at home. In chic black suits, cool white vests to the throat, a couple of young women were moving about behind the reception desk, which was long and pale like an altar. Clients of the hotel sauntered through, big men and small women, big women and small men, bearded and unbearded. There was a dominant style among them, the loafer teamed with loose beige garments, so many of them wearing it that it could have been a uniform. She approved of this, the easy comfortable style. People's clothes were so often uncomfortable, distracting them. Foreigners probably.

Her own neat grey suit and white shirt fitted in here quite well, she was glad to see, though her brand of chicness had a more modest Irish stamp. She thanked providence that it was Finbar's he had named and not some busy lounge around O'Connell Bridge where she could have found herself in a colourful and flouncy crowd and been terribly out of place.

When she went to check out the bar, however, she was

confused. Finbar's had two. Which one had he meant? The one at the front as you came in, the Irish Bar, she found alarming. It was dimly lit, with candles set in bottles amidst hillocks of grubby wax on kitchen tables, not a practical design touch for the short-sighted such as she. Without her glasses she might not be able to make him out. To be obliged to wear her glasses was unthinkable. But the conventual aspect of Finbar's was reinforced when she saw a pulpit stripped of its plush standing bang in the middle of the floor. It had woody protuberances you would have to be careful of. And among the upright chairs with plaited seats there were pews for sitting on, not suggestive of comfort or relaxation. Though it was only early evening there were already a lot of men in there with red faces drinking pints who said, 'Sorry, love,' politely when she stepped around them but who, she feared, could be intrusive or even offensive as the night and the drinking wore on.

'Have a drink with me,' the man on the train had said. 'Tonight. Do. Why not.'

He was busy fastening the clasps on his briefcase but glanced up to give her a professionally engaging smile. That smile and the 'why not' she recognized – rather acute of her, considering her relative inexperience – as a sign that he too was illicit, married or something; and perhaps even had recognized her illicitness as well. Could he know? Could a man be as intuitively perceptive as a woman? Or even more? And for a moment she felt wearied by the compulsion to accept his invitation, a weariness it seemed impossible he too could not be feeling behind all that energetic bonhomie; obliged to ask whatever half-passable woman he met on a train to have a drink with him. Had he not come down the aisle, his eyes compulsively peeled for a suitable prey? It had been she who caught his carnivorous gaze. All the long sunlit journey to Connolly Station in the June evening, emollient and yellow and lax as butter, he had pawed and patted her, verbally speaking.

'I don't drink,' she had replied automatically, habit rearing its stupid head. And that was really very stupid because it wasn't even the truth, not any more. It was a habit with her by now to tell lies, to cover her tracks on this extravagant journey in search of holiness or heaven or whatever you wanted to call it. Hell and damnation, probably.

'Much,' she added quickly, seeing his shockingly anonymous male hands with black fur creeping down under the pale pink cuffs of his shirt. She was glad she knew so little about him. He had introduced himself only as Jim. That, she assumed, indeed hoped, was false. Julie, she had told him, was her name. 'Nice name, Julie,' he had responded, with a gullibility that was unexpected. In response to his question about why she was going to Dublin, she had told him the truth. She was attending a conference. But had been clever enough to switch its theme from 'Spirituality and the Sisterhood' to 'Nursing in the Community'. This, luckily, did not interest him at all and elicited no further questions.

'I was asking you for *a* drink.' Chidingly, he emphasized the 'a'. 'Well, maybe two. But now who's to tell you that you can't have a Ballygee if that's your poison.'

'Where?' she asked. The word sounded glorious to her ear, like 'heaven' had sounded once, an actual if postponed place of bliss. To Jim, it all seemed commonplace.

'How about Finbar's. The hotel. Do you know it?'

'I do,' she replied. She would find out, it would be in the telephone book. He was buttoning his jacket with a jaunty air, the deal clinched. 'South Quays,' he said, as if he knew she was fibbing. 'Near Heuston Station. Nice spot. Used to be a bit of a hole. But done up lately, no expense spared. By that Dutch rock star, what's-his-name, who was hooked by our own Fiona McNally. Sweet lady.' This he enunciated with a heavy irony suggestive of acquaintance with the same Fiona, whoever she was. 'He's loaded,' he went on. 'Finbar's is the new in-place, or so they say. Good spot for people-watching, if that's your buzz.' He leaned towards her with a theatrical intimacy, as if he not only wanted to but indeed could gaze into her soul. 'Not my buzz, not tonight. Tonight, I will have eyes only for you, Julie.'

'What time?' she asked faintly. She had begun to feel a little sick; nervousness, no more. Who wouldn't be nervous, falling in with a furry woman-eater? Thank You, Father, she mentally gave thanks – gratitude to the deity was her habit on most occasions – thank You that You did not present this Jim to me as my first on this unorthodox pilgrimage.

'Eightish? In the bar. That suit you?'

'Can we say a quarter past?' She surprised herself by putting the time back, but it seemed obscurely right, a necessary tactic. To be assertive, keep him interested. Leave him to understand that she too had important things to do in Dublin. This, unusual in her present phase, was not a lie. Her business here, taking the long view, was surely more significant than his could be with his little laptop and his reptilian briefcase. He would certainly be surprised, possibly even angry, to know that he was to figure as the currency in the transaction. But then he never would know.

Dallying on the platform, she watched him disappear into the crowds swarming under the vast grimy canopy, his dark hair showing bronze lights in the muted golden shades, moving quickly with the air of a man with money to make, rich brutal men to see. Then, still dawdling, she followed, among the straggle of the homelier and the unpressed for time, girls dragging suitcases, old couples heavily linking arms, and the lame propelled effortfully with the aid of sticks.

After a keen appraisal from a distance of the taxi queue, she joined it. It was lengthy if thin and he was not in it, she was glad to see. Must have been picked up. By a wife? No, the wife would be safe at home in Kilkenny while he roamed the aisles of trains and the byways of Dublin's Left Bank. By a business associate, she supposed, or at least a driver sent by one such, who would have held a card aloft with his name written in ramshackle letters, his real name. Another reason perhaps for him to leave her with such a show of busyness.

'Finbar's Hotel,' she told her taxi man. 'South Quays.' She liked to get the lie of the land, to maintain a sense of control, above all when control was likely to be slippery. Anyway she had a reputation for extreme punctuality.

Finbar's appealed to her very much. Especially when she found the second bar and recognized it at once as the place Jim had earmarked for their rendezvous. Called, rather incongruously, Fiona's, it was a long elegant room with a cool and airy feel; spartanly decorated in white and grey, lots of chrome fittings and pale green cushions on seats that she found exceedingly comfortable. A place that implied transparent drinks tinted like palely stained glass would be more appropriate than the heartier stuff being consumed in the Irish Bar. And there were indeed no red-faced men propping up the bar and knocking back pints. Perhaps the evening shadows would draw them in. But it seemed unlikely. She ordered tea, which came in a shiny chrome service, and sipping it considered her options.

Then she went to the Ladies' and counted the wad of notes she kept in the zipped pocket of her black briefcase and sighed. There was still such a lot. Although she was duly grateful that God had provided her with the means to facilitate her journey towards Him, she also occasionally wished that He might relieve her of it to show His disapproval of her actions. For instance, He could have arranged for a drug addict to accost her and grab the briefcase. In fact, when she was preparing for her trip to Dublin, where there were so many drug addicts stalking the streets, she had prudently transferred the papers for the conference from the briefcase to her overnight bag. The addict could have it and the money, enough to feed his habit for days, to his relief and probably hers.

The vow of poverty had been the first to go. Or had it been obedience? But obedience was such a moveable feast these days. A nun was expected to do her own thing, to use her initiative, to trust her inner voice. The lottery win had been unequivocal, her inner voice had told her – without some money she was unlikely to be able to resolve her predicament, her hope of salvation. And then, like grace wafted from heaven, it had fallen into her hands. Three thousand, five hundred and forty-one pounds. Paid out in cash – she had no bank account – by a bemused girl in the big post office in Waterford. It was His bounty, she decided, an answer to her inchoate prayers.

And it had led to the final rupture, the breaking of her vow of chastity. First in Galway, with a fisherman called Robbie. Then in Belfast with a mature medical student called

Macintosh, a Presbyterian by birth but Buddhist by conversion. Did that make the sin worse or better? Indeed, was it, considering the mitigating factor of her motives, a sin at all? It was probably an absurd question, too absurd to ask any priest she knew. And she could not ask Mother Martha, normally her guide in the matter of sins. It would give Martha too much pain to be asked. Martha found the widely reported transgressions of priests, bishops and cardinals in this area very painful, although she tried to understand them and forgave them and prayed for them. The transgressions of nuns were still a closed book. She did not want to be the first to open it up to Martha's hurt and bewildered gaze.

She had hoped the fisherman would be enough, that the experience would answer her question, restore her knowledge of the way that she had once seen so clearly. That after it she could walk with a sure foot the straight and narrow path again, her conviction and faith renewed. But no, he had taught her nothing except the comic if tender awkwardness of a disengaged human coupling. Little to do really with the fact that his gansey had smelled of fish. And Macintosh, more practised, had shown her its headiness; but nothing, on cool reflection, that she had not experienced years back, with Liam, before she joined up, and had relinquished. Now, at Finbar's, it might be third time lucky. But then again, it could be a case of once too often. What if she became addicted to the sweets of love? But she had always been able to resist temptation. As she had always been able to tell the chaff from the wheat. This was what she felt she could no longer summon, the ability to see the wheat.

It was impossible to explain, especially to Eileen. She had tried, after the episode with the fisherman, but really Martha would have been more understanding. Still, from her room in Finbar's, the first thing she did was to sit down on the bed and telephone Eileen. However much she might complain, Eileen was her sister, and had to be informed that she was spending the night in a hotel and not in Eileen's guest room.

Getting the room had been easy once she made the decision. And surely He approved, since a room was available, though Finbar's was the in-place and it was the tourist season. On leaving the Ladies', she had walked decisively up to the reception desk and requested a room. She was a decisive woman, as nuns were by and large – it was maybe what gave them that edge of intimidation. The virginal acolyte handed her a flat plastic card as the key to 104 without batting an eyelid. There had been a flurry of surprise when it became clear that she didn't have a credit card. But after a whispered discussion with the managerial-type woman who examined her with narrowed eyes from the far end of the desk, the acolyte had allowed her to pay cash in advance. Then her overnight bag had been seized by a slim young man wearing a badge that said SHANE on the lapel of his green-tailed coat. Shane led her to the lift and examined his reflection in its mirrored interior with obvious satisfaction until its doors opened with a smooth clunk onto the first floor. He had seized her key-card when she stood, confused, at the door, shown her how to use it, and remarked, 'You're not the first to be fazed, madam, believe me. But it does lend a clean line to one's pockets.' Then, with a last glance at himself in one of the room's several mirrors, he had left her alone. She went to the phone and dialled Eileen's number.

'Patsy. At last.' Already, Eileen was displaying signs of crossness. 'Where are you? Are you still at Connolly? Look, I can't come and pick you up, not now. You should have called me earlier. But your bed is ready . . . What do you mean, you're not coming? You're in Finbar's? Finbar's Hotel? Oh, Patsy, you're not. Of all places. Patsy, please, not again.'

There followed a lot of groaning from Eileen. 'Why don't you just leave? No, I mean the convent . . . I don't care where the hell you stay or what you do if you could be only honest with yourself . . . They'll expel you, you know. Martha won't have any choice when she finds out . . . You'll get Aids or something . . . I can see it, you'll be splashed all over the papers before you're finished . . . No, I don't need to calm down, but I will tell you what you need, Patsy. And that's a psychiatrist . . .'

However, calming down a little or at least curiosity getting the better of her, Eileen asked in a less quarrelsome tone, 'What's it like anyway, Finbar's?'

'It's nice. Although I don't think you'd like it. Kind of modern, quiet . . .'

'Quiet? But it's dead cool. Didn't you know? Have you seen any celebrities? Of course you wouldn't recognize a celebrity if one came up to you with Oscars hanging round his neck.'

'What's an Oscar?'

'Oh, forget it.'

'Yes, it's wasted on me, I suppose, that side of Finbar's. Eileen, please, don't worry about me. You know how sensible I am really . . .'

'Sensible? You?' There was a derisive screech from Eileen.

'I'm an adult, Eileen. I would like you to remember that. Now, I'll see you tomorrow evening, after the conference. I promise. I'll be in that well-made bed tomorrow night all tucked up safe and sound. If you'll have me.'

'I shouldn't, but I will. Anything to get you out of

Finbar's,' muttered Eileen. 'What's your room number? In case I want to ring. Somebody has to keep tabs on you, by tomorrow you might be a murder statistic, for God's sake.'

'An apt remark.'

'What remark?'

'You wouldn't understand. Eileen . . .' Patsy hesitated. 'Just one thing. If you telephone . . . could you ask for Julie Murphy.'

'Murphy? I don't believe it. The cheek. Using my name, my husband's name, as a cover for your carry-on. Raymond won't put up with it, Patsy, and neither will I.'

'Look, Eileen, you and Raymond don't have a monopoly on Murphy. It's the most common name in the telephone directory. That's why I'm using it. You wouldn't want me to use my own, surely.'

'If there's any more like you, all I can say is, God help the Church. Well, Miss Julie Murphy, I hope you don't get murdered.' With a crashing noise, her sister hung up.

Sighing, only a little ruefully, Patsy stretched out on the bed. She had been about to try to mollify Eileen by describing the room to her, the bed with its ends curved like the prow of a boat, the potency of the river viewed from its window. She was really too temperamental, Eileen, always had been. Too liable to fly off the handle at the smallest provocation, and so unwilling to allow her sister the right to her own personhood. For a younger sister, she was uncharacteristically bossy. The roots lay perhaps in the conflicts of childhood, the urge to compete, their similar natures expressed so differently; she quietly self-willed, Eileen vociferously self-opinionated. She would never think of apologizing, of course, for slamming down the phone like that. Oh yes, no apologies could be expected from Eileen. But tomorrow she would be all agog for an account of Finbar's, etc., etc. They would drink a glass of wine over their sisterly talk in the suburban kitchen while Raymond watched his soccer match in the den, and the whole thing would be elided, like all their conflicts.

Finbar's bed linen, she was pleased to find, was snowy and starched, more than a match for Eileen's guest room. The duvet, a deep jewel-like crimson, was a darker shade of the red and black carpet, patterned in squares to make a mock terrazzo. The golden evening sun, wrapping the buildings across the river in a slanted light, made her room dim, even gloomy, and oddly churchlike. A large painting, done in hard lurid colours by a geometrically preoccupied hand, showed rectangular masculine faces arranged haphazardly around a triangulated blonde woman in a blue dress raising a kind of metallic tumbler to her lips. Pondering this image, she decided the woman was a Madonna. Hard, modern, grotesque and profane, but a Madonna all the same.

Her imagination tended towards the ecclesiastical; what was churchlike was sublime. After all, it was in a church that she had experienced the most rapturous moments of her life, the afternoon when the mystical but mundane fact of her vocation had been revealed to her. It was a renewal of that revelation she was looking for now, what she trusted in Him, Jim and Finbar's to provide. Outside the first-floor window the river surged, dark and outrageously close as if it were only by whim that it did not overwhelm the room, the hotel, the whole of Dublin. She felt she was in a great ship, remote from land and the life of the city.

She tested the bedside lamps, shaded with small brassy horn-shaped hoods. Candles would have been nicer but in this world you couldn't have everything. She examined the facilities; the tapless fountain in the washbasin from which water flowed as if by divine instruction, the chunky bars of tangy soap, the mini-bar, well supplied, she was pleased to see, with little bottles of alcoholic drinks. He, more than likely, would wish to avail of them. She took out a bottle of spring water and drank it while she read the menu for room service. She had eaten a good lunch before catching the train – the nuns generally tried to lunch at midday to 'get a good run at the day' as they said half-seriously – but it was now past her suppertime.

The Fresh Mushroom Tortellini – pasta she supposed, anything ending in a vowel was usually pasta – seemed the most tempting – though she suspected this might be partly because at £11.95 it was the least expensive. Her habits of economy were ingrained even if she was loaded. Should she, on the other hand, go down and take a table in the restaurant, the Echo Rooms? she wondered. 'Perhaps the most elegant dining experience in Europe,' the menu asserted. A tall claim, surely, but one maybe worth exploration. No, she concluded, that was unnecessary. Such a gesture did not fall within the parameters of her quest. It seemed wanton, somehow, to position herself in public view at a restaurant table and be fussed over by foreign waiters to whose blandishments she might succumb and be obliged to eat more than her appetite demanded. She rang Room Service and ordered Mushroom Tortellini.

Then, kneeling on the floor by the bed, she murmured devoutly and fluently her evening prayers. Whatever about her vows, she was not about to give up on prayer, the respectful form of her communications with her heavenly guides.

In what seemed like no time her supper arrived, under a

domed silver cover on an enormous silver tray, borne in by Shane, the vain young man in his tailed coat. She gave him as a tip a five-pound note. He flashed her a honed professional smile and begged her to enjoy her meal. She did, what there was of it, as the tortellini turned out to be a rather meagre dish, decked up with white napery and too much silverware. There was also a small plate of leaves, tough, but all the more wholesome for that, she supposed. With it she drank another bottle of water from the mini-bar. Then, having placed the tray, tidily stacked, in the corridor outside her door, she took a bath.

Her hair, cut boyishly short, required little attention. While it dried, she had a look at the newspaper that she had started to read on the train when Jim sat down in the opposite seat and monopolized her attention. The news and opinions it contained had only a remote interest for her by and large but she turned the pages dutifully. It would give her topics to discuss with Jim when awkward silences occurred as they inevitably do when neither party to a conversation wants to talk about themselves. And it would not do to seem ill-informed about the affairs of the day. She should pass herself off as a woman of the world.

What to wear required no deliberation or trying on. Her bag contained only one change of clothing, a pair of jeans and a T-shirt, intended for weekend wear at her sister's. Worn with the jacket of her suit, it was an outfit that looked nondescript but quite acceptable. It had passed muster perfectly well before. But she had slight doubts now about whether in the more rarefied ambience of Finbar's something, not necessarily more glamorous, but at least that looked like she had tried, might be more appropriate. Would the nondescript look make her, paradoxically, stand out? But clothes bored her and this possibility did not worry her for long.

She made a face at her reflection as she applied some pale pink lipstick and a touch of 'barely there' mascara. These came from her sister's copious selection of cosmetics and had been pressed upon her some time before when Eileen assured her they were just what her pale complexion – looking a little washed-out, Eileen announced in her critical manner – needed. Eileen might not have been so generous had she known the circumstances in which they would be employed.

She didn't like make-up, neither the feel of it nor what it did to her face. All the same she could hardly make her entrance upon the hotel's night scene, dead cool as everyone seemed to be in agreement it was, with her usual natural – what Eileen contemptuously called the as-God-made-me – appearance. A touch of the super-natural was expected. Also, she should signal a certain amount of availability and keenness, otherwise the whole thing might end unresolved. Some form of costume was necessary to express the authentic and the essence. Rite and ritual, custom and tradition were a proof of that.

By now it was twenty minutes to eight. Eightish, he had said. The soul's test was at hand. How time crawls when one is engaged with worldly matters, she thought with a hint of distaste. And then pulled another wry face. What a nun I am, she told her reflection. Indeed, the sisters were often surprised at how gravely nunnish she could be, in comparison with themselves. Yes, Mother Martha need have little fear of young Sister Patsy. However, as the youngest nun in the convent, she was treated with an indulgence that came largely from an anxiety that she might not last the pace.

Eileen, who was quite sure she knew her better than anyone, had expressed her doubts about her staying power from the beginning. But, difficult as it was to explain (who could explain the mysterious workings of the soul and the conscience), she was quite sanguine about her purpose. All she required now, at the age of thirty-two, was to see the path as clearly again as she had seen it at nineteen. If it meant the thrusting of her head into the lion's mouth and risking everything, well, that was what a spiritual test took. She was well versed in the lives of the saints.

By 'eightish' he probably had meant a quarter to. Everyone, she tended to assume, was as idiosyncratically punctual as she was herself although she had often enough been proven wrong. It was time to make her way downstairs. As she made her way towards the lift, she knew she was nervous because her legs were suddenly a little unsteady.

Fiona's Bar was satisfactorily but not densely populated. A lot of bronzed foreigners, one and all drinking Guinness. Smartly turned out city executive types clustered along the bar, the women drinking shorts, pliant feminine gaze fixed on the men, belying their hard commercial careers. Eileen's and Raymond's kind of people. She went slowly down the long bar, blinking, in order to see better in the fashionably glaring light. He was not among the crowd, as far as she could see. She sat down at a vacant table by the wall which offered good views to right and left. After a little while she was offered a drink by a girl wearing a tiny pink-and-white-striped butcher's apron over a short black dress. Confidently, she requested a Campari and soda. She knew this was a suitable drink because it was Eileen's tipple. It cost £3.80. She gave the girl a fiver and murmured to her to keep the change.

He should appear now at any moment, pulling out the chair opposite and throwing himself into it with his impression of boundless energy. His eyes were sharp, he would miss nothing he didn't want to miss. And of course, she had amended his 'eightish' to a quarter past. He was certainly the sort of chap to whom 'eightish' meant a quarter past, not a quarter to. Twice, she reluctantly put on her glasses and peered around, replacing them furtively in her briefcase once she saw nobody likely to be him. When the girl brought her an evening paper unasked and gave her a vaguely sympathetic smile, she knew that she must look lonely and in need of diversion. It was eight twenty-five. Then she realized that he would be of course in the Irish Bar. He was a country chap, that was more his kind of place. With a firm purpose again, she finished her drink. Nothing for it but to go and find him.

The foyer looked different by night. It blazed with artificial light, though the soft mauve of the long summer evening sky was glowing through the vast glass dome in the roof. It had the look of a place gently lapsing into idle decadence. People were lolling in groups of two and three against the off-white columns with glasses in their hands. Joining them, she leant against a vacant column. She felt the need of a few moments out in its meditative languor before hitting the Irish Bar.

Opposite her column, the lift doors opened. Two uniformed gardai stepped out, grasping a limp white-faced man firmly between them. The whiteness of his face was deepened by the ugly scar that ran across it and as he passed and was frog-marched through the foyer she saw the look of horror that he wore. Well, naturally. On this blessed summer evening, to be one minute enjoying the delights of Finbar's

Hotel and the next, to be in the hands of the gardai . . . And nobody seemed to care or even notice. There was a woman seated on one of the cream sofas, her head bent over a laptop, and she was carrying on with her urgent tapping as if her whimsical words were more important than the drama of a suffering human soul a few feet away. Not of course that she herself was thinking of hazarding a rescue attempt. After all, the gardai surely had their reasons. But was it right that the man's plight seemed to elicit only a horselike snicker from two plump fellows in blazers? She uttered a quick aspiration for the poor criminal's spiritual welfare and early release.

It was bedlam in the Irish Bar. The numbers of red-faced men had been swelled by troops of their kind, along with a good sprinkling of women wearing bright clothing and scarlet mouths. A raggedly sung but emotive version of 'The Fields of Athenry' could be heard above the cacophony. Nervously hanging back, she found herself sharing the entrance with a weirdo in dark sunglasses. A born loner, she could see, definitely foreign, worn out from a life of drink and travel, down-at-heel with his shabby raincoat and limp tangle of greying locks. He was abstractedly holding a cigar which had gone out as if he were minding it for somebody else. Although he was the kind of man indeed who always had the butt of a cigarette dangling from hand or lip like a natural appendage. A great waste of health and money. From behind his glasses, he was inspecting her, she suspected, with a sardonic detachment. She had no wish to be drawn into conversation with him. Inserting her hands into the pockets of her jeans with a show of bravado, she made her way through the dense throng into the middle of the Irish Bar.

'Are you looking for someone, love?' A motherly woman

in a purple dress waved a pint of lager at her in a button-holing manner. 'Ah, it's himself you're on the lookout for. I can tell.' She eyed her with an arch and inquisitive smile. 'Who would he be now? There's not a soul here I don't know or who doesn't know me. The most senior of the lot, that's me, worked in Finbar's man and boy. Or lady and lass, to be exact.' She looked at her more keenly. 'Except for you, now. You're somebody I don't know, I have to say. And you don't know me either, I suppose.' She gave a peal of laughter. 'Well, I'm Mary. Mary Mooney.'

'I'm Julie,' said Patsy reluctantly.

'One of the fellas' girlfriends, are you, Julie?' Mrs Mooney suggested helpfully. 'You didn't ever work in Finbar's, that's for sure. Maybe you were related to poor Simon, were you, love? There's a few of his relations here. Though between ourselves, if it weren't for us, all the old staff from the old days, he'd have got a bad enough send-off.'

'I'm looking for Jim,' she replied distractedly, vetting the men near at hand, and then could have kicked herself. She had blown his and her cover. But why did he have to arrange to meet her in the midst of this convivial coterie? Everyone seemed to be on the best of terms. Maybe they were a wedding party. Surely he shared her view that anonymity was the point.

'Jim?' said Mrs Mooney. 'Ah. Our head waiter. Former head waiter, to be exact. There's Jim.' Watching her with a mingled expression of curiosity, delight and commiseration, she took a draught of lager. 'With Brenda. His wife.'

Apprehensively, Patsy turned. Of the men near at hand, none looked familiar. A little further off, she caught a glimpse of the dilapidated loner, his grey head bobbing. He seemed to be accosting the gang who had added a raucous finale to 'The Fields of Athenry'. They were shaking their heads in unison and laughing uproariously. Everyone here, she saw with increasing irritation, seemed to be in the mood to laugh uproariously at anything anyone said.

'There he is. That's Jim.' The woman swung her glass in the direction of a bald middle-aged man in a striped football shirt.

'Wrong Jim,' she told the woman and moved on.

'Look, lads, will you look who's here,' chortled a tall fellow, as she tried to make her way past an alarmingly merry group. A short woman with hooped earrings was breaking unpromisingly into song. The fellow who seemed to think she was his old friend gripped her arm. 'Terrible at names, can't remember yours, what is it now . . .?' She peered at him with a myopic hopefulness which made him chortle all the more. This chap was not Jim either, she was glad to see.

'Chambermaid,' he announced triumphantly. 'Am I right? You used to do out the rooms with Máry. Mary Brazil. Where's Mary? Is Mary here? Lads, was Mary Brazil told?' But there was little interest shown in Mary Brazil's whereabouts.

'Ah sure, I suppose Mary'd have no interest in wakes.' Her friend subsided into resignation. 'She was very fond of poor old Simon, though, God rest him.' The man's eyes took on a watery and distant look as he took a gulp of beer. Then he reverted to his old cheer.

'Are you not having a drink? Just give me a minute now and I'll tell you who you are.' He prodded her chest with his glass and then waved it gleefully in her face. 'I have it now. It's Hannah. Am I right, isn't that it? Hannah. You see now, I'm not as harmless as I look. What'll you have, Hannah?'

'My name is Julie,' she said.

'Julie, Julie, Julie,' he chimed. 'Sure of course it's Julie. What else. I could have told you that myself.'

'Who's Simon?' she asked, keen to change the subject.

'Simon was a fine man. A decent man. The night porter in Finbar's for forty years before they dickied it up. You'd never be stuck for a pint or a toothbrush or whatever you're having yourself with Simon on the job. None like him. This place will go downhill now he's gone. Don't make them like Simon any more. Here's to him.' He took a draught from his glass. 'He wasn't a pal of yours so, Judy,' he said commiseratingly.

'No, he wasn't,' she agreed.

'We buried him today. And came on here for old times' sake to have a drink to him. Ah, but the oul' pint isn't the same. There was a time when Finbar's had the best pint in Dublin. And to think that little jumped-up Johnny Farrell who sold the place out never even bothered to turn up today to see him off. But that would be no surprise to Simon. Simon always knew what little Farrell was made of.'

She had blundered into the aftermath of a funeral. On what would look like false pretences to all these people since she had no acquaintance with the deceased. Faintly embarrassed, she smiled her regret and moved on. 'Judy,' he called after her in dismay. 'Where are you going, Judy. Judy . . .' His tone changed, losing interest in her as he caught sight of someone else. 'Mary. Mary Brazil,' she heard him cry, 'for the love of God. You made it after all.' Then his voice was lost in the noise.

Dodging further intimacies, she kept going, weaving her way as unobtrusively as she could through the mêlée, looking to right and left with the pessimism of the short-sighted. The expression 'stood up' came into her head and once it did, remained obstinately stuck. How come she had not thought of that possibility. Lack of experience as well as a habit of certainty. Eileen used to accuse her of a habit of arrogance. She remembered now how it was. If a girl accepted a date she also accepted the possibility of being stood up.

There was a sudden lull in the level of talk and the strains of 'Danny Boy', sung in a warbling soprano, rose to fill it. 'Good girl, Molly,' a man next to her called out.

Jim had not given the impression of a man who would fling himself with joy into a bar where a funeral and a sing-song were in progress. Probably he had come, sized up the situation and repaired to the calmer regions of Fiona's. Many people were not punctual, the world offered delays, unfore-seen obstacles . . . She made her way to the exit, which was easier now as much of the crowd was making an effort to stand respectfully to attention with their heads bent to listen to the song. She passed by the loner in the raincoat. He seemed to be importuning the other Jim, the former head waiter. Was he too a member of the funeral? He could hardly be an old employee of Finbar's, like the rest of them. He looked like a man who had never done a decent day's work in his life. 'I'm sorry, sir, I don't,' she heard the other Jim say as she went by.

Returning to Fiona's, she walked its length twice. But the Jim she was expecting did not seem to be there. She caught the eye of the nice girl in the candy-striped apron who gave her a look of deep sympathy. Poor woman, she's been stood up, the look implied.

The foyer had more refugees now from the Irish Bar. She saw the man who had called her Hannah first and then Judy come out and eye up the scene with a blinking gaze. She saw the eccentric fellow in sunglasses, who had taken up his position again by the door, tug at his sleeve and say something to him in a questioning manner. The man listened intently, then laughed, shook his head and continued on with a slightly reeling gait towards Fiona's. Fearful that he was on the lookout for her, she shrank out of sight behind a column. The eccentric was asking people for money, she supposed. Sad, to be down on your luck in these surroundings. She must find a way of giving him some notes, discreetly, later on. He was not perhaps the most deserving of cases but then who was she to judge. That was God's task.

It was nearly nine now but the evening sky still loomed, an ethereal blue, above the glass dome. How nice it would be to be wafted upwards into its calm, to sit like a cherub on a column and survey things from on high, unseen and peaceful until Jim turned up. But she was beginning to come round to the fact that he would not turn up. If he did not, it was plainly God's will and she would have to reassess her goals. But to come all this way to Finbar's for nothing, could this really be His intention? She was not heartened by the prospect of reassessment. From the Irish Bar came the lamenting words of 'Slievenamon', sung in a robust baritone.

'Excuse me, ma'am.' She felt a hand on her shoulder and turned. The voice was a raspy American one that could not belong to Jim with his Midlands accent. All the same, she was a little disappointed to find that it was only the loner. 'Of course,' she said at once, reaching down to unfasten her briefcase, 'how much do you need? Have you a bed for the night?' She attempted to thrust some notes into his hand. 'Now, you won't go and drink it all, will you,' she heard herself say. Immediately she regretted it. If a person in need gave you the opportunity to earn grace by giving him a few pounds, you had no right to police his spending of it.

The man looked startled and stepped backwards. He waved his hands wildly in front of him as if she were slightly crazy and had to be kept at a safe distance. 'No, ma'am. No, put that away. I don't need your money. I have money.' He had a grating voice, almost hoarse. Then, maybe seeing her discomfiture, he said, though keeping well out of her reach, 'No sweat, ma'am. There's no call to be embarrassed. My fault, I guess. The customs are just different here. And, you know, you're proof it works. Skulking around in Joe Soap's gear, it really works, I guess.' He grinned, showing good white teeth. 'Though I ain't sure I want to look that much of a bum.'

He spoke in a slow grating drawl. 'You're American,' she said, for something to say. It was perplexing to talk to someone whose eyes were hidden behind black plastic and who insisted on standing a good yard off.

'Yep,' he agreed shortly. That line of conversation obviously did not interest him. All the same, he came up close to her again, if a little cautiously. 'No, I don't want your money, ma'am. I was only going to enquire of you whether you might happen to know the words of a song. I heard it once in Butte, Montana, sung by an Irishman. One of those great old Irish songs, I guess. And I've never heard it since.'

'You could get it from him.'

'The old Irishman? Naw. Met him in a bar. Ships that pass in the night, the both of us . . . Naw, he's passed on by now, I guess. That guy was in a bad way even at the time. And there's many a breeze has blown inta and outta Butte since then.'

'I don't know any songs,' she said. 'Well, only a few old ones. Quaint songs. Songs my father used to sing. Woody Guthrie. My father liked Woody. And when I was at school I used to really like Bob Geldof . . .'

She was getting into her stride. It was surprisingly nice to talk to some people. The guy stepped forward. She got a faint whiff of alcohol. A spirit, vodka perhaps. Briefly, he raised his sunglasses onto his forehead and peered into her face before lowering them again. But she caught a glimpse of raddled features and a penetrating glassy gaze. She had a sudden sense of recognition. Could it be? Of course it wasn't – but really this guy looked just like an age-ravaged dissolute version of a face she knew from album covers that lay around her father's stereo in dusty heaps years ago.

'This song I'm talking about was called "The Night Before Larry Was Stretched",' he said. 'And goddam, they're all singing songs in there but none of 'em knows that song.'

She broke into a smile. '"The Night Before Larry Was Stretched"?' she asked. 'I know that. It was my father's favourite party piece.' She began to hum the first lines. '"The night before Larry was stretched, The boys they all paid him a visit . . ."' Sensing his intense gaze, her voice faltered. 'It's long. Not an easy song.' She smiled apologetically. 'I'm not sure I can remember all of the words.'

'But you remember some of it?' He gripped her arm. 'That'll do. Hell, I don't know a damn word of it.'

He released her arm. 'Where can we go? I'll take it down. No, I'll tape it. How about the other bar? Let me buy you a drink. There's not the same degree of action in the other place.'

She was fed up with Fiona's and its pitying waitress. 'We can go to my room,' she offered, 'if you like.'

Again, he looked startled. 'Your room? You sure? You have a room here? Would that be OK, honey?'

She looked surprised. 'Why wouldn't it?' she asked.

He hesitated. 'No reason at all,' he said then, and took her arm.

Going up in the lift, she realized she had forgotten about Jim. Oh well, she could always come down in half an hour and have another mosey round for him. No call to waste any worry on Jim, if he was going to be so rude as to turn up at midnight. Meanwhile, this man had to get his song. After taking him for nothing more than a tramp – although in his shabby getup who could blame her – it was surely the least she could do.

As he stepped out of the lift, he made a small lunge for the corridor as a person might when they have a bit too much drink taken. But he seemed perfectly sober when, acting like a man who was quite acquainted with Finbar's rooms, he took the key-card from her when she fumbled with it and opened the door with practised ease. He pulled out the red-upholstered chair from under the writing table and sat hunched on it, impatiently jigging his right leg.

'Will you take something to drink?' she offered politely, going to the mini-bar.

'Water,' he said firmly. 'Iced.' If he had been indulging in drink earlier on, he was willing now to take a break from it, she was relieved to see, so he could pay full attention to her singing. She poured two glasses.

He drank his off in one go. 'OK,' he said then, like a man who expected to be obeyed, the man holding the gun in a film. 'Sing.'

He was waiting intently, his head bent. She decided, watching him, that even if he had a gun, he wouldn't be interested in using it on her. It was only the sight of the poor fellow being frog-marched through the foyer between two gardai that put the thought of guns into her head. The thought disappeared as she began to sing.

After she had delivered the first two verses, and was starting on, ' "I'm sorry, dear Larry, says I, To see you in this situation",' he raised his hand like a traffic policeman, signalling her to stop. 'Wow,' he breathed. 'This is incredible.' He stood up, took off his raincoat and flung it on the floor. In his black T-shirt he looked once again oddly familiar.

'Don't move,' he ordered. 'I'm going to get my guitar.' He pronounced it 'gee-tar' with a kind of abrasive tenderness.

'Where is your guitar?'

'In my room,' he said. 'I'll be right back.'

'You have a room?' She was surprised.

'I have a dive.' He spat out the word. 'I booked the penthouse and they put me in a dive. I'm fighting this famous Finbar's of theirs tooth and nail.'

'What's your name?' she asked, as he was at the door.

He paused, his hand resting on the doorknob, before he turned round. 'God,' he seemed to mumble sullenly, as if he were making a good-sized concession. The door shut behind him.

God? She had certainly imagined that, it was just the way her thoughts tended to run. She could be silly sometimes. But what was it he had said? Might it have been Gov? Not a name she had ever heard of, but then he was foreign and they often had the weirdest names. She sat musing on possible monosyllabic appellations. His inaudible mumble had definitely consisted only of one syllable. Rov? Short for Rover? But that was a dog's name. Rod? More likely. Could it have been Bob? That was even more likely. You could not say that Bob was the Murphy of Christian names, but it was certainly not unusual, especially among Americans. A bill-board she had been able to study from top to bottom when the taxi was stopped interminably at traffic lights on the Quays came back to her. Could he be . . .? Why not? He was sadly aged but that's what people did. Would he stay at Finbar's? Where else? Eileen would say. The music scene was a great draw, Eileen had told her, one of the best in Europe. He would hardly just fly in and fly out again in the early hours. He would have to stay somewhere, take in a bit of the city's nightlife. But such people attracted doubles as well, people who travelled around, living out their lives by impersonating their heroes.

A spiritual person, a seeker – that was how she thought of him. You could hear it in the yearning rasp of his voice. That was why she and Sister Renee liked his songs. She hoped she could remember the rest of 'The Night Before Larry Was Stretched' for him. But she had done all right so far and the rest would come to her as she went on. By the time she had hummed to herself the third verse, word-perfect she was sure, he was back, bearing his guitar.

He sat on the bed, one leg tucked under the other as musicians do, and patted the red duvet for her to sit near him. 'Let's run through it first,' he ordered. 'Then we'll tape it.'

'"For sure, when the gallows is high, Your journey is shorter to Heaven",' she sang. By then, he was strumming along, his face creasing with concentration. She was glad he had kept his dark glasses on, her concentration too was better as she sang into their black opacity.

'Right on,' he murmured when she came to a stop with

the traditional slow dirge-like note. 'Are you sure you haven't missed a verse?' he demanded then, sharply.

'That's all my father sang,' she said.

'Right on,' he murmured again. 'OK.' Suddenly business-like. 'We'll tape it.'

'I don't sing very well,' she said modestly.

'You sing fine,' he said.

He placed a small slick cassette-player between them on the bed. The red record-button glowed in the subdued light provided by the hooded lamps. Like a conductor, he raised his forefinger as a signal for her to begin. '"So moving these last words he spoke, We all vented our tears in a shower . . ."' Faultlessly, the guitar's heady notes accompanied her, leading her on. Closing her eyes, she let the music take her, making her one with it and the dry emotion of the words, that tell of the young rebel Larry who was hanged 'with his face to the city'.

'Perfect,' Bob – or Rod or Gov or perhaps even Don – breathed. With a reverent touch he stroked the off button. The red light went out. He placed the guitar carefully on the floor. Taking off his sunglasses, he wearily pummelled his eyes. Resting on his elbows, he sank back on the bed, as if spent by the intensity of the experience, and closed his eyes. The hollows around them were red and sore-looking from his rubbing.

'Can I ask you a question?' she asked.

'Shoot,' he said tiredly.

'Are you . . .?' She whispered a name, so low that he might not have heard. But he heard all right.

Opening one eye, he regarded her narrowly. 'I might be,' he said. 'And then again I might not.'

'Famous people,' she remarked after a pause, 'often like to go round anonymously. I do.'

He opened the second eye. 'Are you famous too?'

'No,' she said. 'I'm a nun.'

'A nun?' He sat up. His gaze was sharp. 'Is that what nuns are like? Do you look like a nun?'

She shrugged. 'I don't know. Do I?'

'Now you're asking,' he said, examining her with a new-found interest. 'I never met a nun before. Well, I never sat on a bed with one before, that's for sure.' He appeared, after some consideration, to be delighted with the situation.

'I'm up for a conference,' she explained helpfully.

'If you're up for a conference,' he grinned, 'honey, I'm up for it too.'

His keen gaze was bent on her. He leaned forward and roughly rubbed her neck. His fingers, guitar-string shredded, rasped like his voice. She drew back out of his reach.

'What I mean is,' she said frostily, 'I'm up in Dublin for a conference. I came up today, from Waterford. On the train. I live in Waterford.' You had to spell things out for Americans, clearly. 'The conference is starting tomorrow.'

'What's your name?' he asked.

'Patsy.'

'Sister Patsy,' he repeated with a slow grin. 'You a Sister of Mercy by any chance?'

'I am not.' She was not going to tell him her Order, no way. That would be going too far. Holding all the nuns up to disrepute, Martha would regard it as. Absolutely the last straw

'There's a good song,' he said wistfully, 'about the Sisters of Mercy.'

In an agile movement he was beside her and had grabbed her hand. 'Sister Patsy,' he announced, raising it to his chest, 'I want you to come to bed with me.'

His tone was that of a man who would not brook a refusal. Not that this would influence her in any way.

'Why?' she asked. She had no idea why this wish had suddenly occurred to him. The idea of going to bed with this man had not – surprisingly enough, seeing as he was, in his tired and shabby way, of the masculine gender – entered her head.

'Why? Goddammit, you're a nun. What could be more inspirational than a nun?'

Inspirational? Other people, she knew, wanted to sleep with each other for various reasons, attraction, lust, loneliness and so on. But for inspirational reasons? And yet she saw at once exactly what he meant. It was her own reason, though it had not appeared to her in that light, or at least the word had not come to her. It was what she had hoped the fisherman and the Buddhist and the guy on the train could provide, though they hadn't come up to scratch. No fault of theirs, of course, they just hadn't been compatible. But inspiration. The veil of reality to melt away and the real sublimity leaping into view. With this common purpose their union might be blessed, a fused wire sparking its way like a lightning-rod heavenward.

'OK,' she told him.

'Wowee,' he whooped. He laid her down boisterously on the red duvet. 'Let's get that habit off,' he rasped, whipping his T-shirt high into the air over his head. She kicked her shoes off.

As he burrowed inside her, she looked into his passionately dissolute face. It was the sad face of a contrite angel.

And the bed seemed to float on the dark swell of the river and she knew with a warm ecstatic knowledge, for the second time in her life, that she was one with the world of Finbar's and all the people in it, with all the fishermen and all the Murphys in the telephone book . . .

'Mystical,' he murmured.

'Right on,' she breathed ecstatically.

And then they were both drifting in the same blissful dream, as if they were ferried down the river in a gentle boat to the sea, a shadowy, nameless, but benignly familiar boatman to guide them standing at the helm. He lay beside her and they slept.

As angels do, he slipped away, sometime around midnight, after his pitted face had brushed hers roughly in farewell. 'There's somewhere I have to be,' he murmured. 'That place on the water.' He pronounced 'water' with a soft American 'd'. 'Have to be there, pronto. Gotta go, honey.'

In the morning she found his sunglasses lying on the floor. There was a tiny white sticker on the inside of the frame. 'J. P. Gaughan. MPSI. Tullamore,' she read aloud. People like that really got around, she mused. She put the glasses in too when she was repacking her overnight bag. Martha liked to wear sunglasses while driving but she was forever losing them. She was always glad of an extra pair.

The telephone rang.

'So, Miss Julie Murphy, you're alive, I'm relieved to hear. But next time, look, I don't want to know, OK? I have enough on my plate without worrying about you.'

'Who said there's going to be a next time?'

Eileen ignored that. She wanted to go on at some length about the stressfulness of her job and the extension to her kitchen which had revealed unforeseen problems with the drains.

'Anyway, tell me. Who was he?' she asked finally, curiosity getting the better of her.

'He was an artist,' Patsy told her. 'We experienced the revelation of a mystical union. I have been blessed with divine grace.'

'Patsy,' Her sister's voice rose. 'You're really losing it. Come on, who was he?'

She whispered the name. Well, the walls may not have ears but you never knew. And he had been so keen not to be recognized.

'You're mad,' groaned Eileen, 'you'd believe anything.'

'Well, he may have been an angel,' she said hastily, regretting her confidence. But that possibility seemed to have an even worse effect on her sister.

'Don't tell anyone at the conference about this,' urged Eileen. 'Don't say a word. Not to a living soul. Patsy, are you listening? We can talk about it tonight.' She rang off.

What was Eileen thinking of? Of course she wouldn't tell anyone at the conference. If anyone was mad, it was surely Eileen.

As she strolled along the Quays to get a bus – her obsessive punctuality seemed to have abated in the night – bag in one hand, briefcase in the other, a small dark thin woman in a flowery headsquare stepped into her path.

'I need the money,' the woman was crying out to all and sundry in an imperious foreign accent. 'I am sick, I am hungry.'

The passers-by walked on, averting their gaze. Patsy came to a halt. The woman confronted her, the dark eyes peering into hers. 'I am hungry, I am sick, I need the medicine,' she cried.

'Sure,' Patsy said, reaching to open the briefcase. 'Don't worry any more. I have money.' The woman, as if she had not heard, continued to chant the misfortunes of her life. She beat her stomach with her fist like a gong striking a hollow bell, as penitents beat their breasts.

'I am Romanian. I need the money. I am hungry.'

Patsy arrested the woman's fist in full beat and unfurled the fingers and placed them around the handle of the brief-case. 'Here,' she said, 'here is money. Take it. There's lipstick too. Some make-up. You might like it.'

The woman clutched the briefcase and looked from it to Patsy. The anxious lines on her face uncreased into a distrust-ful smile.

'God bless you,' said Patsy.

'God bless you,' echoed the woman warily.

By the time Patsy had reached the Four Courts she saw that there might be something in what Eileen had said. Yes, she was indeed perhaps a little mad. She had forgotten to keep back her bus fare.

THE MASTER KEY

'I'm afraid of heights!' protested Detta to the receptionist, a frisky blonde who looked like a pony. It was a lie and Detta enjoyed telling it; creative manipulation of language was one of the joys of her middle age. For a moment she felt as if a heavy bag, a schoolbag perhaps, had lifted off her back and flown on leather wings to the sky. 'I must have a room lower down.'

'Lower than the fourth?' The receptionist arched her eyebrows for the second time in two minutes. The egg-smooth plain of her forehead became a thundery ploughed field. One day, Detta knew, that ploughed field would be all she had left: all furrows and no forehead. Character forms the face. Beauty, at least in its later stages, is not in the eye of the beholder. It is the sum product of its owner's experience, and attitude. So is ugliness, and everything that lies between.

A man of youth and beauty waited by the desk as Detta sulked and lied her way to a room on the first floor of Finbar's Hotel, a room she had reserved a fortnight ago. The corner of her eye caught a blur of burgundy, a snowflash of white, but did not register the fact that he was dressed more like an actor in a costume drama on the BBC – Tom Jones, perhaps, or Wolfgang Amadeus Mozart – than a guest in a modern Dublin hotel.

'The first-floor rooms are all taken. There's nothing I can

do. I'm sorry!' The receptionist threw up her hands and snorted like an angry little stallion.

Detta's winged schoolbag of anxieties descended from heaven and began to attach itself to her shoulders once again. She puffed back at the girl. Annoyance spurted from the pair of them, invisible mushrooms of smoke.

'You can have my room!' The burgundy man dismissed Detta's problem with a wave of an elegant hand. He had a delicious American accent, comforting as minestrone soup. 'It's on the first floor. Room 105!'

Detta did not accept favours from strangers dressed for BBC costume dramas as a rule. But she was desperate.

'OK!' she said. 'Thanks very much!'

The receptionist tossed her blonde ponytail contemptuously and whinnied at her computer.

'I'll take your key!' The man seized Detta's slippy white card. 'And you take this!' He pressed his tenderly into her hand. 'Simple, really!' Picking up Detta's tiny suitcase he indicated the lift.

'Hey, Karl!' an American accent called from one of the white leather sofas which dotted the lobby like daisies in a meadow. Detta turned and saw a young American with cropped bleached hair holding a mobile phone. Even though he looked harassed he managed to be so in a way that still suggested he was rich, invincible and very, very trendy. 'Karl, you klunk! You can't just walk away from this with Poppy going AWOL.' But Karl did not look back.

'Detta Hanema.' Detta shook his hand. 'I'm from Amsterdam.' She scrutinized him. Close up, he reminded her of a chocolate, one of those wrapped in golden paper that you buy at airports in Austria or Germany. *Mozartkugeln*, they're called, or something like that. The man bowed slightly. 'Karl

Brown.' He didn't say where he was from. But all the culture, kindness and courtliness of someplace like Rutherford, New Jersey, was in the rich roll of his consonants, the generous breadth of his vowels.

'You're American?'

The doors of the lift parted and a middle-aged couple emerged, awkwardly, the woman first, the man stumbling shyly after her. They were so curiously mismatched in dress that Detta turned to stare at them as they crossed the lobby, slightly separated, as if they were reluctant to acknowledge their obvious connection. The man – he had to be the husband – looked as if he was on his way to a football match, while his wife seemed bound for a cocktail party or dinner dance. He wore a striped jersey and trainers; she was dressed to kill in a brilliant crimson frock pinched at the waist with a broad gleaming belt, the sort which had been called a waspie in Detta's youth, and still was, for all she knew.

'Come in!' Karl Brown smiled patiently, his finger pressing the 'Keep it open' button.

'Goodness! Sorry!' Detta jumped in. 'I got carried away there!'

She stepped into the lift.

'Here on business?'

'My grandfather, great-grandfather, came from Cork. I'm here to work on my roots, you know?'

He prepared to disclose the thrills and spills of his genealogical research as they were elevated.

The door opened. 'FIRST FLOOR,' sang the lift, in a swooning female voice that sounded mildly drunk.

'He came over on the *Titanic*, actually.' He picked up the case again. 'I just found that out recently. He tried to keep it under his hat but these things always get out in the end.' He grinned, embarrassed by the guile of his Irish ancestor. 'Don't they?'

'I suppose so.' Detta, who kept plenty under her hat, giggled. It was her first Irish giggle in almost thirty years.

'Sorry! I just wanted to . . . er . . . turn down your sheets.' A bellboy backed out of a partly opened door. It surprised Detta that they still performed this antiquated ceremony. The female voice which replied to the bellboy sounded even more surprised than she was. Detta could not hear any actual words, but the tone resounded with shock, guilt and terrible disbelief – the unmistakable tone of one caught in flagrante something or other. Actually, the disembodied, frustrated voice might as well have shouted 'Here I am, committing adultery!' for all interested parties to hear. Detta glanced at her companion. The glaze of his blue eyes told her that he too recognized that panicky tone of voice, and understood precisely what it meant. He looked as if he understood, as well, the special quality of whatever illicit pleasure had been intercepted. He knew what the guilty couple had been at. A man who looked like Karl Brown would probably be a specialist on sex.

Detta was surprised by a stirring, a tricky little twitch of desire. She sneezed, as she always did when suddenly aroused.

'Stop!' Detta warned her body. 'Down! You've known this man for two minutes! For God's sake!'

Karl Brown smiled knowingly at her. In guilty silence, they walked along the hotel corridor, which was not sexy at all. It looked like the inside of a pipe, or an artery in the human anatomy. It was like strolling through the alimentary canal.

'And you?' With a sigh he reverted to small talk. 'What do you do?'

'My job? I own a flower shop, as a matter of fact.'

As a matter of fact.

'Tulips?'

'I sell other kinds as well. But yes. Tulips.'

'Tulips are the best flowers,' he said, in his chocolaty, musical voice, a voice designed to accompany the most delicious pleasures.

Detta felt their drooping damp thick petals, their turgid stems.

'Oh yes!' she replied. 'They are.'

Actually her favourite flower was the narcissus. But who could ever admit to that?

The walk to Room 105 was all too short. They reached it in seconds. Silently, Karl Brown took her key-card from Detta and opened the door. The room spread before them, dim and seductive in pale mushroomy light. Its red and black carpet was thick and soft, and its enormous bed, shaped like a medieval longship, beckoned them to its fluffy bosom. 'Try me!' called the sirens of the bed.

Detta turned a deaf ear to them, and so did he.

He floated swiftly to the wardrobe and pulled out a suitcase and a bag of golf clubs.

'This is very kind of you.' She could barely speak.

'Don't mention it.'

'No really. I really did want very much to be on this floor.'

'Different folks, different strokes! The fourth floor is much quieter, as the lady said! And I'm used to heights, of course!'

He looked at her for a second. A question bright as a cornflower shone in his eyes – or did it?

She looked away.

Then he was gone, her Mozart chocolate, seductive as a sonata, gone before she could say, 'Well maybe a drink?'

Detta pulled back the heavy curtains. The room, facing towards the railway station and the river, filled to the brim with clear northern light.

She smiled, kicked off her shoes, and then pulled off her other clothes: her stockings, suit, bra. Her skin sighed relief, as her body expanded to its natural size – fourteenish going on sixteenish – and resumed its real, loose shape. She walked across to the bathroom, the soles of her feet relishing the thick woollen pile of the carpet: in her flat in Amsterdam the floors were all wooden.

After peeing, she gazed at herself in an enormous wall mirror.

'Not too bad!' she said, aloud, into the cool silveriness of the perfect little bathroom. 'Considering!' What she saw was a short woman with a perky blonde bob, no waist to speak of, small hands and feet. Her bottom had ballooned, then deflated, over the last few years, and there were pepperings of brown moles and freckles and pimples in places which used to be snow white. She sighed and cradled her single breast, imagining, for a second, Karl's touch there. Her hand brushed a slab of shivering thigh. She sneezed again. A tiny disappointment stabbed the inside of her groin.

'This can't be happening!' She grabbed a fluffy white dressing gown from the back of the door and wrapped her treacherous body in it, knotting the belt viciously. 'Cop on, cop on!' Angrily, she dashed to the minibar, and snatched a tin of tonic and a miniature bottle of gin from its well-stocked shelves. Sitting against the white pillows in the prow of the bed, like the Lady of Shalott, she mixed her drink and swallowed half of it in one gulp.

Alcohol could take the edge off any attraction, as well as the opposite.

Relieved, she relaxed and surveyed the room.

Although warmer than necessary in temperature it was cool in colour. In the pale evening sunshine it was translucent as the inside of an iceberg: many shades of white and pale blue; sudden glimmers of silver. Everything was blue now, it was the colour of the nineties. Even the Dublin gin gleamed like a luminous sapphire in its tiny bottle. They used to say blue was too cold for rooms. When Detta had last been in Finbar's Hotel, brown was the favourite colour. Chestnut carpets with swirly brown leaf patterns on them, gently muted by dust and sun. Fawn-flocked wallpaper, embossed with elephantine roses, covered many of the rooms. There were variations, of course. Endless variations. Rooms had been redecorated by the old owners, the FitzSimons, according to necessity, not choice, so that by 1970, when Detta was last here, almost every room had evolved its own distinct character. They had numbers, but to the staff they were known by individual names. The Wine Room. The Piano Room. The Room With the Creaking Board. Mr O'Hanlon's Room.

Mr O'Hanlon's Room was the one she remembered. Was this it? She couldn't recall its number – if she had, she would have demanded it for the night. But all she recalled was that it was on the first floor. Her memory was eclectic in the extreme. Some memories, the significance of which she could seldom fathom, remained firmly embedded in the consciousness, while others were shredded. Thus she remembered the creaking board very well – it was the sixth board from the door of Room 203. And the wallpaper in the Green Room, which was white with a green sprig, lily of the valley, very pretty and feminine in a hotel which did not, on the whole, boast many feminine touches or even many women. (In those days, guests, and staff, in grade two city hotels were mainly men. Probably the same was true of every other grade of hotel, as well.) But she couldn't remember, at all, the colour of the corridors, or even of the dining room, although she retained an impression of its shape and contours. Was it wallpapered, like the bedrooms, or painted some 1960s colour. Magnolia? Mint green? The tables had been draped in white cloths. But then almost all hotel tables had been, and still were, so recalling that was not much of a feat of memory. What kind of cutlery did they have? Gone. Crockery? Or 'delf' as people called it? White with a gold rim? Willow pattern?

'You're making it up, Detta!' she said aloud again. 'You haven't a clue. It's all gone from your head and perhaps from everybody's head.' Sunk, like the *Titanic*, into the bottomless ocean of the forgotten past. Mental waste. How much of it the minds of the human race has generated, millions of tons of forgotten facts, dumped at the bottom of the ocean, crushed or shredded or melted.

Gone. And in physical fact the Finbar's Hotel Detta once knew was now archaeology. The place had been renovated over and over again, and practically rebuilt just recently by these new owners, as, no doubt, generations of houses on this site had been built and demolished, built and demolished, over the centuries. A layer cake of human lives lay under the edifice now called 'Finbar's Hotel'. Forgotten, half forgotten, but inescapably there, inescapably here, making their mark, ever since the Vikings first erected some wooden turf-topped hut in the place whenever they came here. The founders of Dublin. Where's my Carlsberg? What a bunch!

Detta felt her head begin to protest. She swallowed her drink and poured herself another. The pressures of the present, and of her personal history, were all she could deal with at the moment: she couldn't cope with the Vikings, and all that went before and came after, just now.

Brown, the chocolate American, popped back into her mind momentarily. She pushed him out again, almost laughing aloud at herself, at the pointlessness of her desire. The sort of love her body still yearned was firmly consigned to her past. You'd think it would know that! What interested her anyway, now, were other forms of love, less physical but not less intense. She was still learning them. Even if she'd had confidence in her body, she wouldn't want to muddle up her new kinds of love with the old, messy kind, the kind she had been such a mistress of once, in a life – and a body – that seemed as foreign to her now as if it had belonged to someone else.

She glanced at her watch. It was still early. She should eat something, before the meeting. But there was plenty of time. Stretching her limbs, she luxuriated in the springy newness of the snow-white duvet, and allotted herself another half-hour's daydreaming.

The owners of the hotel were Dutch. She hadn't known that until the receptionist downstairs told her, while they were still on friendly terms. Coincidence? Not so much of a coincidence, really, as it would have once been. Dublin was becoming more cosmopolitan by the minute. Or more European, rather. Its relationship with the rest of the world seemed tenuous. Irish people still seemed to believe that

Europe was the whole world, the only world they had to conquer. America was a sort of laughable, rich relation, benign but too familiar to be taken seriously. You couldn't imagine anyone in Ireland aiming to be more American, whereas becoming more European (as well as aiming to loot Europe, while giving as little as possible in return) had been the national pious aspiration for decades. And the rest of the world was still just the rest of the world. Irrelevant.

Detta found herself writing a letter to the paper, or a short article, as her mind wandered over this topic, generalizing wildly about the Irish and the Dutch and the rest of them. A column: that's what she wanted to write about it. She realized that she had been writing columns in her head since she boarded the plane, since she started thinking in English again. In Dutch she tended to think about business, what she had to order, whom she had to pay. She thought about buying flowers and potatoes, about which friend's birthday was coming next and what would be a suitable present. Her language was the language of work and domesticity, as her life was. In Dutch she was a stereotypical Dutchwoman, practical, down to earth, mistrustful of speculation. In her native English her speculative Irish mind could wander at will, solve the problems of the world. In English she could do anything. Except, perhaps, what she was supposed to be doing.

She had wanted to be a journalist. She reclined on the puffy pillow. When she worked in Finbar's Hotel that had been her ambition. She had not thought of this in years.

*

Detta – her name was not Detta then, but Bernadette – had worked as a chambermaid, the summer of 1970. Finbar's had two permanent chambermaids, Mary Mooney and Mary Brazil, but for the summer the Count, as the man who did the hiring and firing had been called, took on an extra. Not that there was that much extra in the way of additional guests. Finbar's Hotel was patronized by commercial travellers, and was always more or less full anyway. If anything there was a slight falling-off during the summer. But Mary Brazil had her fortnight's holidays to take in August. So had Mary Mooney, although nobody, especially not herself, seemed sure whether she would take it or not. Anyway the summer clientele was more demanding than the winter. In the summer the hotel got more couples, people from places like Clonmel or Ballina, on their honeymoon for a week in Dublin. Occasionally a family, Irish emigrants from Manchester or Liverpool or somewhere like that, stayed at the hotel, still bonded enough to want to visit their Irish relations once a year, but rich enough, at last, not to have to actually live in their dour and chilly houses. These people, with their lively, confident English children – dismissed by most Irish people as impossibly bold and cheeky – were much more troublesome than the winter clientele, who did nothing in their rooms except smoke and sleep. (No hanky panky: the rules, pinned to the back of the door, stipulated clearly NO GUESTS IN BEDROOMS UNDER ANY CIRCUMSTANCES. The other rules were about drinking in the bedrooms and vacating the rooms before ten o'clock on the day of departure. The times of breakfast and dinner, and of daily Mass in St Paul's and Adam and Eve's, the nearest churches, were also listed.) These men barely dented their beds. It was a shame, Mary Mooney remarked, to have to change their sheets after only one night. You had to, though, even in 1970, even here. But otherwise all you had to do was empty the ashtray.

Commercial travellers had a gift of not making any dust or any crumples. They were a godsend! Not like the ones that came in the summer. Oh gonny!

Detta's job was very badly paid but very easy. She had to visit twelve rooms every morning, make the beds and tidy them up. Then in the evening, at seven, she had to come back to 'turn down the beds' – what that bellboy had been trying to do this evening. It was a strange convention, presumably based on the customs of servants in rich houses: turning back the bed, brushing the mistress's hair, laying out her clothes for the next day. It always struck her that the logical next step would be to return when the guest had slipped into the opened bed, and tuck them in. But this was not required.

Detta had loved her work. She loved visiting the rooms, every one of which was different, and seeing what the guests had in them. There was usually plenty of time to snoop around, to look in the drawers and wardrobes, examine the contents of suitcases. To her, at the age of seventeen, person-alities seemed infinitely varied and fascinating. Her curiosity about humankind was still insatiable, and her experience thereof nil. The tiny differences between guests thrilled her. Although these were nothing more than minor distinctions of gender, financial and marital status, they seemed to her, empty jug that she was, profound. She believed she was gaining illuminating insights into human nature in all its wondrous variety in the bedrooms of Finbar's Hotel. To her these contained God's plenty. Inside their faded brown walls were locked the psychological secrets of the universe, and in the pocket of her pink nylon overall the master key. One guest travelled with a pair of pyjamas, a razor, and a rosary beads. How wonderful that was, how wonderful! Another had two dressing gowns, three nightgowns, a dozen dresses and pairs of shoes, four different kinds of perfume, boxes of chocolates, bottles of lemonade, Mills and Boons books, copies of *Woman's Own*, *Woman's Way* and the *Irish Press* and the *Evening Press* every day. The things they carried! Some rooms were filled with the heady aroma of glamorous perfumes, rich soaps – aromas of which Detta was exceedingly fond. Others had one bar of Lifebuoy, or even nothing at all, relying on the tiny tablet of dryish, acidic white soap the Finbar's Hotel supplied, one a week per guest and no more – if the guest had a bathroom, that is. (If you didn't get your own bathroom you didn't get your own soap either.) Some guests probably never did wash, while others spent half the day doing it. Some slept till the last minute, dashing down to breakfast at nine thirty, while others were up and off, to Adam and Eve's probably, for seven o'clock mass or some other form of 1970s masochism (nowadays the notice on the back of the door advised that the gym was open from 6.00 a.m.). 'I don't know which is the worse,' the cook was prone to say. 'The early birds or the late worms.'

During breaks, of which there were several in the course of the day, Detta retreated to the kitchen, her master key in her pocket and her bucket, mop and trolley of sheets abandoned on the corridor. There she drank tea with the two Marys and other staff. Mary Mooney, who was aged about forty, and shaped like Mrs Skittle in the Noddy books, round in the body with tiny high-heeled feet and a rubber ball of blonde permed head, regaled them with stories of her health and that of her family, or their ill-health. She had ten children, and lived in one of the new tower blocks in Ballymun. Her husband, Eddie, suffered from nerves, chronic shingles, angina, and arthritis. Not surprisingly, he had stayed in bed most of the day for most of his life. Her children had a variety of problems. One of them was in prison, two were expecting, one had spina bifida, one was mentally handicapped. In addition, the lift in the tower block was always broken and Mary had to get herself and these children up and down ten flights of stairs. None of this was funny, Detta knew. But somehow Mary herself made it seem hilarious.

'It's one thing on top of another,' she sighed and giggled, as if it was all great gas, designed to provide her with good stories and a bit of a laugh. 'Sure what's the use of complaining?'

Detta's own mother said that but she meant the washing machine had packed it in and on top of that the clutch was gone in the Anglia again. Whereas Mary Mooney meant Jim was back in jail for a year on top of Monica having an epileptic fit on Dorset Street and Sharon getting venereal disease. 'Does she make it up?' Detta once asked wide-eyed Mary Brazil, who was twenty-three and whose exclusive topic of conversation was her boyfriend, Michael.

'Oh gonny no!' said Mary. 'I met them, at Mary's mother's funeral. They're just like she says.'

'How does she survive?'

'She gets a lot of tips,' Mary Brazil replied. And she added 'Plus, she does nixers. She's a handywoman.' Detta did not know what a handywoman was. 'She lays out dead people,' Mary Brazil explained nonchalantly. 'And she delivers babies as well.' Detta was shocked. Mary Brazil stared at her and screwed up her nose. 'You know,' she said, impatiently. 'Some babies. Babies that don't get born in hospital, like.'

'Most of them do, don't they?' Detta was embarrassed. She knew just what Mary Brazil meant but pretended innocence; it was a technique she had used for years to deflect embarrassing confidences.

'Yeah.' Mary Brazil had had enough of Detta for one day. She shook her head and turned on her Hoover.

This was the first week in July. Detta had been working in the hotel for two weeks. She had saved ten pounds out of the twenty she had earned, towards college in October. Her mother had taken eight for her keep now that she had got a job and she had spent two on bus fares. The sun shone on the quays every morning as she ran along by the river. The air was champagne, the water danced a jig. The old houses, white and yellow and purple and green and pink, smiled like grandparents as she ran along, and the spires of Dublin soared confidently to the enormous sky of her whole waiting life. Her blood raced and her skin glowed and her eyes shone with hope. Every dapple of sunlight, every sweep of spire, promised her that something extraordinary, amazing, stunning, wonderful was just about to happen. The light clean air told her that she was stepping into her future, right now, as you might step from the grey concrete of the quay onto the bridge of a white ocean liner. She was on her way to adult life – a magic island, a treasure trove of riches.

*

She zapped on the television set. Sports results. The reporters looked very formal, suits and ties, short hairstyles. They spoke excitedly, as if reporting from a war zone. She zapped. An Irish-language thing. Drama or soap, with English subtitles. She let the strange sounds sink into her ears. Everyone spoke at breakneck speed. Only an odd word was comprehensible to her. She had always been bad at Irish. Her mother had hated it, because it was a useless dead language, and because she had been forced to speak it at her old school, Golden Meadow. Her firm belief had been that Irish children should be taught a useful modern language, unburdened by history, instead. Modern meant German. That a knowledge of German was the key to success and happiness was her firmest conviction. When Detta had told this to Piet, her Dutch husband, he had screamed with laughter. Not screamed, he never screamed. He'd had a good laugh, at the idea that German was untrammelled by historical burdens. But he didn't care much about it one way or another. 'A language is just a system of communication,' he said, in his logical way. 'I do not think a language should be regarded as a war criminal, or a hero!'

Detta, who had been a silent, subdued girl, was now a fairly assertive chatterbox in German, Dutch, and French as well as English. She was more European than her mother could ever have dreamed – too European, her mother had suggested, on her infrequent visits to Amsterdam, which she had, after all, hated. Europe was not all it was set up to be, when you actually got there. Mostly just poky apartments, not enough Masses, and overpriced cups of coffee.

Detta zapped. *Boom boom, boomboom, boomboom!* screamed the signature tune of the newsroom. Here we come with our tales of disaster!

Drama, drama, drama.

She turned it off. What she loved about Holland was what she loved about her husband: its quiet efficiency, its low-key tolerance of human diversity, its reluctance to dramatize everyday situations. 'What happens is silly enough,' Piet said, frequently. 'There is no need to embroider reality.' In Ireland embroidery, often of a very complicated kind, had always been all the rage.

154

Piet was an electronics engineer, working in a computer firm. Sandy-haired and short, he was as Dutch as a tin of cocoa. He tried to manage life with a light-hearted sense of control, as if it were a rather elementary computer program, or a football match. The past was over. He did not forget it but grudges were a waste of time. Piet lived in the present, kept his eye on the ball. The only real problem was, he said, over and over again, indecision. 'Decide, decide!' he said impatiently to Detta. 'It doesn't matter what your decision is. Just decide and stick to it.' Kick the ball when it comes your way.

Detta couldn't. For her life was complex, mysterious and unfathomable. Unlike Piet she believed in the existence of one right answer. It was not on the pitch, but somewhere else, far away – hidden in rolling, electric clouds or buried deep in the radioactive earth of some dark northern forest. Her task was to find it. She seemed to believe that if she worried enough she would. Then her questing would be over. She'd be happy.

Piet and Detta had no children. They seldom went to bed together now, but they loved one another as deeply as is possible for a man and a woman. Detta believed this as firmly as she believed anything.

*

On the tenth of July Conor had come to Finbar's Hotel. Even though he, too, had just completed the Leaving Certificate examination, he'd taken a break with his uncle, playing golf in Kerry, before starting his summer job. He would be the still-room waiter.

As soon as he joined the staff, a rift developed between Detta and the two Marys. They had tolerated her, as one of

them, a chambermaid, even though they found her tire-
somely secretive, childish and snobby. The fragile solidarity
of sisterhood crumpled under the pressure of the much
stronger bond of shared Dublin geography: Conor and Detta
were from the south side, the Marys from the other bank of
the river. Conor and Detta had done the Leaving, they were
summer workers, they spoke in the narrow, cautious accents
of their side of the city. The Marys dumped Detta on Conor.
What difference did it make, that she was a girl, a chambermaid, like them? She was only pretending anyway. Come
October she'd be off to her real life.

Anyway they hadn't quite known what to make of Detta,
who was almost pathologically reserved in those days. Conversation had to be dragged from her, word by word. She
never volunteered a single bit of information about herself.
'Slippy tits,' Mary Brazil called her. Mary Mooney, being
older, was less judgemental; she had met other Dettas in her
day. 'She's quiet,' she said, summing her up in one Hiberno-
English word.

Conor was a different kettle of fish. Everyone loved him.
He was a good-natured, good-humoured extrovert. He chatted to all and sundry about his family, his past, his plans, and
was quick on the draw with witty retorts. But he was a good
listener, too, attending to the Marys, the Count and even old
Mr FitzSimons with eager ears and eyes full of sympathy and
interest. In short, he was just the type of fellow any hotel
would be delighted to have on its temporary staff.

In looks he was extremely attractive, but in such an
unostentatious, inoffensive way that nobody noticed: they
believed they liked him only on account of his personality.
He had a big-jawed, blue-eyed, JFK kind of face, and his
body was well-knit, coordinated, not gangly or loose like

many young men's bodies, and not too tall. Even little men like the Count felt secure beside him. Pleased with life and with himself, he had the gift of disseminating a sense of well-being. He could have been a chat-show host, or the manager of a successful football team, or one of the more popular presidents of the United States. (Or he could have been Detta's father, whom he strongly resembled: she realized this years later.)

'He knows what he wants!' Mary Mooney said, with her chuckle cum sigh. 'Oh, go way outta that, he's cute enough!'

What Conor wanted was to earn two hundred pounds towards his college expenses for next year, and he wanted several honours in the Leaving and some sort of special distinction, a scholarship or a prize, as well. Then he wanted to get a place in medicine and become a doctor.

Acquiring two hundred pounds was not going to be easy, or even possible, as a still-room waiter. The pay was ten pounds a week. No tips came the way of still-room waiters, which is even more of a backstage job than chambermaid – indeed, Detta had not known such a job existed until Conor arrived in the hotel. Soon Conor persuaded the Count to let him work in the bar at weekends, for a few extra pounds and tips. Before long he was working there most nights of the week.

Detta had never had a friend who was a boy before. In fact she had never had a conversation with a boy, at least not a conversation lasting longer than about ten minutes, the time it takes to drink a Fanta lemon in the cloakroom of a school hall. She'd danced with many boys but you couldn't talk much, while dancing, especially when you didn't know what you were supposed to say to them anyway. Thinking of conversational topics while clenched in a tight embrace and assaulted by very loud music was daunting. Anyway, even when there was no competing band or disc jockey people usually seemed unable to hear what Detta was saying. A lot of her slow, low comments faded into the air, as ears turned the other way, eager to catch brighter, louder conversation from mouths which were quicker-witted, and more in tune with the preoccupations of the moment than Detta ever was.

Conor's ability to listen was his greatest and most astonishing gift as far as she was concerned. He could open her up, turn her on as if she were a radio, and out poured all this guff. In his presence she was transmogrified from being one of the quiet ones to being great gas, from being a bore to being a wit. He asked interesting, intimate questions and actually listened to the answers. Detta had never met anyone like this before in her life.

She sat for hours with him in the kitchen, soothed by the intermittent hissing of the silver still, in the quiet evenings between after-dinner tea or coffee and ten o'clock, when Conor knocked off or went to the bar. Talking. They had an ideal subject for openers: the Leaving. A detailed postmortem of the various examination papers led them through the first stage of their romance. By the time they had analysed Latin, the last exam, Detta was up to her ears in love with Conor. Then they moved on to more thorough discussions of the hotel: the guests, the staff, the food, the architecture, the owner, the future, the pay, the exploitation, what they would do if they ran the place. A week of this and Conor was in love with Detta. He asked her to the pictures on his night off, Wednesday. *Anne of the Thousand Days* was the film. They saw it in the Savoy. Conor saw it. Detta couldn't concentrate. The images hopped before her eyes as print does on a page when you are excited. Conor was holding her hand, right through the film. It was the first time she had been touched by any man with whom she was in love. This experience she was unwilling and unable to dilute by concentrating on anything else.

Conor was very quiet after the film. On the way home, he continued to hold Detta's hand. He hummed 'Greensleeves'. Detta wondered whether she could afford to buy a hairband that looked like Anne Boleyn's sweet tiara. She wondered if Conor had noticed that she looked just a little like the doomed romantic queen. She wondered if he would kiss her goodnight.

He didn't. Not that night.

*

Detta drained her second gin and tonic and resisted taking a third from the minibar. She should stay sober, at least until after the meeting. But her appointment was not for another two hours yet. She decided to go for a walk and a bite to eat.

She picked a striped blouse, blue and white, and a loose denim skirt from her suitcase. She rubbed her face against the cotton: the fresh shop smell of new clothes always delighted her, and it was a smell you only got before the clothes were worn. Quickly dressed, she slipped her feet into flat open sandals and set off.

Down the pipeline of corridor a youngish, smartly dressed woman was ushering an elderly man into a room. The old man looked terrified, as if he was about to meet some kind of monster. He must have been the girl's father – browbeaten father, apparently. Adult children could wield enormous power over their parents, for better or worse. Detta's own mother, dead for two years, slid into her mind: a ghost bearing gifts of guilt, love, confusion.

She felt something dropping inside her. And her courage, the ordinary quotidian courage which got her out of bed in the morning, got her into the shower, onto the plane for a holiday, deserted her. It shot out like tea from a flask and this cold, piercing fear rushed in to replace the vacuum. Agoraphobia. But it was not agoraphobia. It was Dublinophobia. Hibernophobia.

The ghost of her mother told her a terrible story, as it tended to do from time to time. The story, recounted in her mother's strong, cynical voice, concerned an event from her mother's childhood. Her mother had been privileged in her day: her poor parents, small farmers in Clare, had sent her to boarding school, at great cost to themselves. The school was in an old grey manor house, set in woodland in the middle of Ireland. It was there that her mother had spoken Irish. Golden Meadow was the name of that school – a lovely name. But it was not a lovely place, her mother explained, sighing. It was not lovely, but hard and cold and cruel. And she told her story to illustrate these qualities. The names in the stories changed: Edel Moloney or Annette Finn, Marie Byrne or Rita Darcy. But the story was always the same: a story of beating or starving, the ritualistic humiliation of some child. The children's parents, like Detta's mother's parents, paid fees for this, condoned the abuse. Asked for it. Detta's mother, now dead, had condoned it too, retrospectively. She had condoned it by her silence. Only Detta heard her stories. Her mother told them, not in public, not to protest, not even to her friends or Detta's father. She told the stories when she wanted to hurt her daughter. She must have known that such stories never go away. They wait for their chance in the corners, under the stairs of the mind, jumping in when the good stories flee, at cold moments on thresholds, in the heartbreaking time when the day is ending.

Moments like this. On the steps of the hotel Detta heard the screaming of Golden Meadow. She heard her mother crying. This was the sound of Ireland, Detta thought, drowning out the roar of traffic along the quay. Keening and weeping, children wailing. A longing to flee seized her. In two hours she could be safe in Amsterdam – she could be back in Holland. In Amsterdam she felt safe as she had never felt in Ireland, where the screams of children were mixed with the clay in the parks, were mortared into the faded bricks. Amsterdam had shed its own tears, as she knew well enough. But they were not hers and she couldn't hear them.

A hand alighted on her shoulder.

'Hi!'

It was Karl Brown.

She was pleased to see him.

'Oh, hello! How is the fourth floor?'

'I can see the Phoenix Park from my balcony. The biggest park in the universe, it says in my brochure. You might have liked it!'

He had removed his burgundy jacket. Now he was wearing purple. He looked more like a chocolate than ever.

'Well . . .'

'Of course, you're afraid of heights!' He laughed.

'Yes.' Detta looked closely at him. 'I sleep-walk sometimes.'

'Ah!' This impressed him. 'Settled in, then?'

'I'm perfectly happy.'

'Any plans for dinner tonight?'

'As a matter of fact I have an appointment.'

She felt apologetic, and mildly disappointed. Apologetic that she couldn't have dinner with a complete stranger because she had an appointment with her own flesh and blood! Karl put that hand of his on her arm. Her confusion evaporated. He'd got the gift of touch, this man.

'That's great. Who with?'

She wanted to tell him. But she held back.

'An old school-friend.'

He smiled, calmly but too knowingly. He could see through her, he knew everything. Men like that over-whelmed her. Her ego toppled for them because they appealed to it, her libido rose to meet them.

'I'll see you around,' he said, without rancour.

Detta watched him for a minute as he moved across the bridge, a purple blob against the blue sky. Two fat seagulls hovered over his head. It seemed to her that he was flying lightly above the footpath, floating on a swath of misty air.

Some of her courage had returned. She stepped into the street and strolled across the bridge to the north side of the river. A Mozart air was filling her head as she walked. She seemed to hear the music, although she was not musical, could seldom recognize any piece of music, as some people – Piet for instance – could. 'What is it?' he would ask. 'It's Haydn,' she would reply. 'It's Grieg. It's Beethoven's Ninth.' Guessing. Sometimes she hit on the right answer and if she did Piet glowed with a profound, genuine delight which Detta found amusing and puzzling. More of Piet's games: he was such an innocent, by comparison with her. Was that the difference between men and women, or between Dutch and Irish people?

Without him to help her, to quiz her, to inform her, she was unable to name the music in her head, as she sometimes was unable to remember the titles of books she had read in her dreams – aloud even, according to Piet. But a piano pounded in her brain, anger and drama alternating with slow acquiescence. Allegro, andante, allegro, went the symphonies. Piet had drummed it into her. Allegro, andante, allegro. Like life. Like a story. Like a river.

Detta walked along the footpath on Arran Quay, a walk she had not taken since she was eighteen. Changes? Yes. And no. Apartment blocks, red-brick, with dusty curtains in the windows, had replaced old warehouses and tenements. Otherwise the assortment of pubs – the Croppy Acre, the Legal Eagle – and shops – Heather's Shoes (*Ladies' up to Size Eleven*), Bargaintown – seemed familiar, if smarter than she remembered them. The blend of elegance and vulnerability which had always characterized this particular stretch of the river had not changed much, although the details were different.

Few people were about. She met an occasional man or group of men, all of whom eyed her up and down, as if wondering who – or what – she was. Women did not seem to walk along the river, not alone anyway. She pulled her cardigan around her body, the merest frisson of fear galling her stomach. She wished she'd left her bag at home in the hotel.

Arran Quay. St Paul's. How could she have forgotten it? A grey hunk of a city oratory, it had, attached to one of its walls, like a pocked wart, a huge stone cave. In a niche high in this cave stood the calm blue figure of the Virgin, hands outstretched, her smooth face smiling sadly at a smaller brown figure kneeling down below: Bernadette – the saint. Not Detta.

Bernadette of Lourdes enjoying a vision of the Virgin.

From the angle of a passer-by, Bernadette was a little brown-veiled girl, on her knees, adoring and supplicating the Virgin. Mother of Divine Succour come to my aid!

She'd need all the supernatural aid she could get, in the Ireland Detta knew.

By a happy, ironic accident of Dublin planning, or lack thereof, the next door neighbour of the fake Grotto of Lourdes was the Four Courts, where the secular powers of Ireland sat and judged – their brand of wisdom heavily inspired by the Roman Catholic Church for most of the twentieth century. A statue of a woman representing Justice stood, austere and stiff, brandishing the weighing scales of objectivity in the yard of the elegant courthouses; the judges might more honestly have placed the Virgin on their threshold, the Virgin with her meek sad smile and her arms haplessly spread, empty of any balance. But at least they had her as a next door neighbour. (The only Protestant church in the vicinity was the medieval cathedral of Christchurch, thoughtfully concealed from view by the glass and concrete edifice that housed Dublin Corporation. Out of sight out of mind.)

All that old state-religious stuff had changed, according to report. Ireland was getting more liberal, the fundamental Catholicism which had underpinned its every law for most of the twentieth century diluted by the march of time and by the revelations of flaws in the divine structure itself.

Could you believe it? Detta was sceptical.

You're out, you're just a tourist now, she argued with herself. You escaped from the last bastion of Catholic Europe. You don't need to worry about it any more. Let the Irish fend for themselves – they always got precisely what they asked for.

What most of them asked for, anyway.

Filled with a longing for the solace of water, she crossed the street to the riverside.

When she remembered the Liffey it was a rippling blue-green river, musically dancing under the blue skies of Dublin. She remembered silver and gold, ripples and dapples of merry light. Riverrun, riverdance, riverfree. Riverlaughing. Annaliviaplurabella and all that.

What she had forgotten was that the Liffey was tidal. Just now the tide was low. Between staunch granite walls the river was the colour of bottle green, grimy wellington boots. Its surface was covered by a film of oil: reflections of cloud, tree, houses were filtered through greyish blue whirls and rambling virulent rainbows. A pelmet of dirty ochre kelp dangled from the walls at the high-tide mark. Otherwise there was little sign of any natural flora – or fauna. No swans or ducks, not even a seagull hovered over the thick opaque water.

It improved as she moved downstream. On Ormond Quay the intimidating wall which barricaded the Liffey for most of its journey through Dublin, hiding it from view unless you were right beside it, was replaced by a white classical balustrade. The gentler architecture encouraged nature: sprays of buddleia sprouted from crevices in the chalky stone of the twisting pilasters here; right in the middle of the river a sooty cormorant swam towards the white curve of bridge, its wings outstretched in the stupid way of cormorants – like the Virgin Mary's arms. It looked lost, far from the sea rocks where it belonged. But the water must be salty, witness the kelp. A tang of ozone caught Detta's nostrils, a dark, heart-breaking smell.

Inns Quay. The Winding Stair. The Woollen Mills. The Tanning Shop.

Bachelor's Walk was just as she remembered it: pink and yellow, blue and cream, cheerful, redolent of pleasure and glamour. The Knightsbridge Hotel. There were plenty of people here. Young men in blue jeans and shorts – that was new. They usen't to wear shorts in the old days. Girls looked the same as always: long haired, they teetered along the path in groups or couples, their feet imprisoned in strappy dramatic platform shoes – beautiful shoes, gleaming black, brilliant crimson.

Surely I never wore skirts so short?

Surely I did.

But tighter, over a curvier figure, and in the flamboyant colours of the sixties. Shocking pink and brilliant green. Yellow. Gleaming brown with snow white. Girls gleamed and glowed and shone then, with our long plump brown legs, our pointy breasts, our curtains and veils of gleaming hair. All shine and flash and gloss and bounce, a veneer over the terror that lurked inside.

That was before Conor.

*

Conor hated brash, displaying clothes, loved soft romantic things: misty days in the west of Ireland (preferably on a golf course), traditional music dropping slow into the bleary grey smoke of uncomfortable public houses. Conor liked girlish women – slim and modest, noble and strong, long haired and beautiful, mysterious but subservient to him – like the girls in his favourite novels by Walter Macken. The feature he loved most about Detta was her Irish colleen hair; well, he wasn't alone in that. Deep red, of a colour often striven for by hairdressers but seldom achieved, it curled and waved in gleaming cascades down to her waist. Conor liked to bury his face in it when he was tired – as he frequently was. Then he would sniff it as if it were opium, and tell Detta she was beautiful.

What he liked best in the way of clothes, Detta soon discovered, were flowery blouses with drawstring waists, flowing green skirts. Shepherdess smocks. And in the way of conversation he shared with her a predilection for long serious anxious discussions about sexual morality followed by long passionate necking and petting (as it was called in the agony columns, although not, of course, by the people doing it, who didn't need to name their activities).

After *Anne of the Thousand Days* the relationship deepened. Detta felt herself descend into love as into a warm, teeming ocean. Further and further down she went, losing sight of everything that floated on top of this sea, losing all sight and all memory of common dry land. She transformed, girl to fish, girl to mermaid. The surface of life, a few weeks ago so all-important, demanding, was gone. She was in another dimension. The dimension of love, a dimension which changed her completely. The reserve which characterized her relationships with almost every other human being vanished. When Conor looked at her, he unlocked a different Detta, a Detta who normally hid inside the skin of the polite, friendly, obliging Detta, the Detta who was diligent and nice, but seldom brilliant, never sparkling. He changed all that. She felt herself glowing and dancing, jokes tripped off her tongue, trite details grew into riveting stories.

He was in love too. Locked into it, as she was, so that every moment of their lives, every possible moment, had to be spent together. But his personality did not change as hers did. She was recreated by him. He remained what he always had been. So it seemed in retrospect. At the time none of

this occurred to her at all. All she knew was she was ...
somewhere where she had not been before but where she
belonged. Home in love. It was a great gift, she knew it, for
the first summer of her grown-up life. The glances of the
Marys, of everyone in the hotel, let her know that she was
blessed. Shy, amused, awed glances, they were. Not envious
in most cases, unless envious of youth. In some situations a
young couple in love are irritating, arousing jealousies and
other kinds of hostilities. It says much for the atmosphere of
Finbar's Hotel and its staff that Detta and Conor endured
none of this.

It was partly due to their modesty. At that time, and
perhaps at all times, ostentatious displays of sexuality would
have irritated people profoundly. Good children of the sixties, Conor and Detta restrained all their natural impulses
for physical contact when in public. In private they
restrained them too, but not much: broom closets, linen
cupboards, empty bedrooms, even the yard – full of beer
crates and junk – provided them with spaces in which to
give vent to their passion. Their love was so physical it made
them cry, as they kissed and hugged and pressed their bodies
together. His golden skin, the smell of his arms, the crunch
of his hair, filled her with amazement. She ground her teeth
together, caught her breath, just thinking of him.

They didn't, of course, have intercourse. That is the word
they would have used: the word itself was enough to put
anyone off. A cross hostile word, like barbed wire, a concentration camp. Interrogation. Cross-examination. Coursing.
Mothers wagging their tongues, of course of course of course.
Of course not.

Contraception. The very word made Detta feel sick: it
was so taboo. At that time if a customs officer caught

someone trying to sneak a condom, or even a book on what were called artificial methods of family planning, into Ireland he could confiscate it on the spot. That was the law.

So Conor and Detta kissed and petted and their bodies fought, valiantly, for what was their natural due. But Conor and Detta had clever, determined minds, trained in denial. No.

Conor's training had been more intense than Detta's; she could see this from the start. He was more conscious of his natural desires but, in inverse relation to that consciousness, more frightened of them. Boys, especially boys like him, were, in those days. Detta did not know what they had been taught, but they had been taught something – unlike the girls, who had been vaguely told not to get pregnant, but given no details at all referring to how that disaster might occur. Conor probably knew how. Thus he saw the body as a real enemy, a sort of guerrilla fighter, clever and wily, which would ambush the unwary. He never was unwary. He managed to be in love and on guard at the same time.

Detta knew this, unconsciously, in her mermaid's heart, and her mermaid's heart resented it. But the real Detta, chambermaid and journalist *in spe*, was perfectly content with the way things were. She was getting everything a young girl would want: love, kisses, and what was known as respect – another word the mermaid regarded with sneering distaste.

*

She crossed the big bridge, O'Connell Bridge. A boy sat by the parapet, a tin box in front of him. He practised a gentle style of begging, passive as a Buddhist monk, his head bowed, his eyes wide and hurt. A note written in a shockingly perfect hand on a neat square of cardboard said *Homeless*. The boy was about twelve years of age. At the traffic light crossing at the south side of the bridge a woman wrapped in a blue silk shawl pressed a magazine on Detta: 'Buy one, I'm a Romanian refugee,' she supplicated in wheedling voice. She was sallow-skinned, thin and miserable. Wrapped in her shawl was a sleeping baby with a smooth, sleeping face. Catching her breath, Detta gave the woman five pounds for the magazine. She beamed magically, all pearl-white teeth, and said, 'Thank you,' with feeling. Not 'God bless you,' like the tinker women with the babies used to say long ago.

After a coffee and cherry bun in Bewley's, Detta walked back on the south side of the river, moving as briskly as she could. Aston Quay. Wellington Quay. Temple Bar – thousands of summer sandals flowing over cobbled alleys; incense, wine, the smell of cumin. St Winifred's Well. The Poddle.

The cormorant was still in the river at Ormond Quay. But now he was almost submerged in the greasy water. Only his head and big beak protruded. He wriggled his head frantically, and seemed to grin, as he ate a wormy-looking fish – an eel, maybe. Then he dived under. Perhaps he knew what he was doing, after all, marking out this uncontested stretch of Liffey as his own territory?

Wood Quay, Ussher's Quay.

Ussher's Island – a quay, but on a slight elevation, a hill above the river.

That's where the Ocean Club had been, next door to Number Fifteen, the house of the aunts in Joyce's story 'The Dead'.

It was not there, of course. Number Fifteen was falling down. In place of the Ocean Club a new apartment block stood. UNAUTHORIZED CARS WILL BE CLAMPED. Behind the apartments the higgledy-piggledy assortment of smoking buildings that was Guinness' Brewery loomed, comfortingly. The sweet maternal smell of hops drifted from its brick chimneys down to the river.

*

Cliché of clichés, they did it on the night the results came out, in the middle of August. It was not a big night in Dublin then, as it is now. People were anxious about the results, of course, but nobody queued all night waiting for them. Students called to their school in dribs and drabs, at eleven or twelve o'clock in the day, and the head nun handed them their envelope. Then they smiled and said, 'I got six honours,' or 'I got it.'

Conor and Detta got seven honours each. Some of them were Cs but nobody had to find out: a respectable veil of discretion covered the finer details. Conor would get his place in medicine, she would be admitted to the journalism course. There was no hassle, and hardly any reason to celebrate, since they had known all along that this would probably be the outcome. Nevertheless they took the night off; the Count insisted, although Conor wanted to work (he'd still got to earn seventy pounds, with five weeks to go).

They went to a film – *Airport* – and afterwards, instead of going home, dropped into a nightclub: the Ocean Club, on Ussher's Island. They had never gone to such a club before. Once or twice they'd been to Dr Zhivago's, which was a sort of series of linked white underground caverns, a whirlmaze of psychedelic lights and loud music. There they had felt silly: it was pointless being in the club if you were a couple. The disco was for people on the hunt, not for those who had already found their mate. They had been lonely, awkward,

171

disappointed. Conor had sneered at the dress of the girls, who tried harder than he approved of to be sexy. Detta had laughed, pleased to be demure enough for his good taste, in her flowery smock and long green skirt.

The Ocean Club was not like Dr Zhivago's. They had to knock on the green and blue swirly door to be admitted. Once inside, they found themselves in a dark cave of a room, its walls painted like the outside, swirled and waved, with shells and mermaids and fish, its lights very low. A small jazz band played, deep throbbing tunes that quickly caught Detta under the ribs, jagged her heart. The clientele seemed old; no teenagers, women in skin-tight dresses, jumpsuits, men in shiny purple shirts, bell-bottoms, white shoes. Some couples danced, slowly, on the little dance floor. Most sat at tables eating or drinking: the places was rich with the smell of fried food.

Conor and Detta sat a table. A candle flickered in a wine bottle, on which an avalanche of red wax drippings had accumulated. She fingered the wax, basked in the flicker of the candle. The smell of fish and chips, overlaid with a faint tinge of wine, thrilled her. The smells were not unfamiliar. The hotel reeked of them. But the ambience was. This place was different from Finbar's Hotel.

They ate fried scampi and French fries. Conor drank his favourite tipple, milk. Detta considered ordering her usual Fanta lemon, but on a whim said Babycham to the cool, sleepy waitress. Conor started, straightened his back, but relaxed when the music entered his bloodstream.

They danced not just close, which they had done hundreds of times, but dirty – that's what they would have called it. Detta wished she had worn her short skirt and T-shirt, instead of this floating gown. She put Conor's hand under the waistband, let him caress her bottom as they swayed around on the floor. She licked his ears. She pressed so hard into his groin that she came, silently, deliciously, in the middle of the dance floor, her lungs full of the smell of cigarettes and chips, her ears twanging to the jazz.

She'd bridged a gap. Swot to Slag. They were swots, swots from the tips of the toes to the crowns of their heads. In those days, the division existed, unspoken by the girls – usually – but tacitly recognized by most. On that night they transmogrified, as men become swans or monsters or beasts, and became what they normally were not. She did anyway. And he, if not transformed, at least acquiesced. He allowed himself to be carried along on the wave of her wildness. He permitted himself to be seduced.

Afterwards they sneaked into the hotel, into Mr O'Hanlon's room, using Detta's master key, and made love on the bed, on the floor, on the chair. There were no problems at all, for either of them: in all ways, they were ready. The room embraced them. Its chestnut swirly carpet and cigar air encouraged them, its dark uterine redness cradled their first intercourse. (It can be like that, if you are young and healthy, if you are in love. If you have also had the foresight to become a mermaid.) It was the first time, and the best time, for Detta. Perfect sex and perfect love.

Of course she became pregnant. They were seventeen, in peak condition. Of course of course of course of course.

*

Forty-five minutes to go. Detta was back in her room. She was more critical of her appearance now than she had been a few hours earlier: she had changed from being a compassionate reviewer to a Ku Klux lyncher. In the interim her face seemed to have had it. Face it. *Finito*. How had she deceived herself? She'd held on fairly well, to her tight skin, her youthful complexion, until a while ago: her face had lasted longer than most other parts of her. Even her illness and its terrible treatment had left that bit of her unscathed. But now it too had changed from something smooth and elastic and alive to something like putty-coloured custard. No amount of expensive make-up could ever disguise its jellyish texture, its repulsive puffiness.

Of course it could disguise quite a lot of other flaws so it was worth putting it on anyway.

She took off her wig and rubbed make-up into her skin: no problem getting up to the hairline when you could take off your hair. Cancer, dare she think it, had some advantages. Carefully she applied eyeshadow, a bit of kohl, lipstick. No mascara: she might be crying later, one way or the other.

She replaced the wig and surveyed herself again. The result was satisfactory: a little slap could work wonders, even on a crock like her, who lacked several crucial bits: she, who had started off believing that life was a tray of jewels waiting to be rifled, had moved through it, losing and gaining, losing and gaining. Losing. Allegro andante allegro. Most days she felt the balance was even. On bad days she railed against the unfairness of it all. On good days, her heart could still sing.

Paul.

Paul.

Paul.

A solid name. Upstanding, handsome. A curly-haired name, a name of a straight nose and white teeth. A frank open smile of a name. Ships towers domes. Soaring cathedrals and dauntless megalithic temples. Rocks steadfast in storm. Horizons. That's what Paul said to her.

Honesty transparency decency.

A good name for a judge?

Paul had written to her, asking to meet her, a few months ago. The request frequently came from the child, she was told at the adoption agency. It was up to her to comply or not but . . . they suggested that it would be normal, and kind, to honour it.

Detta had not thought of him for fifteen years, not since she had married Piet. It was not that she had deliberately blocked out the memory. She hadn't needed to: it had simply drifted away from her. Some mothers constructed barriers staunch and elaborate as the Berlin Wall; their psyches worked hard at trying to block painful memories. But Detta hadn't had to work at it. She'd forgotten all about him, her first child, within years of giving birth, without even trying. As if he were a school-friend who'd floated out of her life, or any scrap of the past.

The truth was that even now her mind was not on Paul but on Conor. She was about to meet her long-lost son, and all she could dream about was his long-lost father. Paul, poor little baby Paul, had spent years tracing her to her refuge among the tulips. And instead of looking forward to seeing him, wondering what he was like, she was secretly, stupidly, hoping that somehow she would encounter Conor. By some perverted miracle she hoped that when Paul walked into Finbar's Hotel Conor would be at his side, sturdy and tough as he had been in 1970, grinning all over. Her heart, her soul, her body, yearned for him: she had a picture, a feeling, in her, somewhere in her, of a jumper he usually wore, a pale green lambswool jumper. Her yearning to bury her head on that jumper was intense. A jumper from 1970. That was what she was thinking about on the day of her first meeting in twenty-seven years with her son Paul, who didn't even know that Conor was his father.

And Conor did not know either. She had never told him about the baby. After the night in the Ocean Club he had grown distant, not because of the sex in Mr O'Hanlon's room, but because of her transformation. Detta the slut. Conor did not want a slut in his arms, in his life. All his conditioning warned him against that. What he wanted was his career, and a wife who would be vivacious and modest, chaste and girlish, good-humoured and demure. A Walter Macken girl. Controllable. Predictable. All those able things. Not a wildcard. Not Detta, of the two characters.

When she found out she was pregnant, she had, however, asked him to marry her. His answer was that he loved her deeply; she was a marvellous girl. These were his very words, spoken in his mellifluous, seductive voice. *Marvellous girl.* When Detta heard them she felt sick. She knew there was no hope. She was a marvellous girl and he would always be grateful, eternally grateful, for knowing her. Tears were in his voice as he spoke. Something in Detta turned to ice. By the time he was telling her that he planned to become a priest all she wanted to do was run away from him, run faster than she had ever run before. She wanted to swim in a tempestuous ocean, or jump from a cliff into a deep cold snowdrift. She wanted to be as far away from him as she ever could be.

Later she considered her options. It was clear to her that she could force him to marry her merely by telling him about the baby. He would not have a moment's hesitation; if she told him, the marriage would occur at the first opportunity. The choice was all hers. She could probably have forced him anyway, by insisting on the rights of her love. He would have given in: that business about wanting to be a priest was probably a whim. In a month he'd change his mind.

But she didn't go back to him. There was something in the arch of his back, the distancing of his glance, the cold terror of the phrase 'marvellous girl', that prevented her. It had all been easy for them: they had found each other and existed in a shell of understanding. Once they had had sex, the understanding had vanished. She had already seen it, before she knew about the pregnancy. She knew he did not like her any more, although sometimes he fell, fell into her, longed for her, longed for sex with her. But it was against his better nature.

His better nature was what she no longer wanted, not on its own, with its critical apparatus polished and honed, ready to hate her if she fell into lasciviousness – if she reverted to the Ocean Club.

Sulking, she turned her back on him.

She told her mother about the pregnancy. 'This is the worst thing that could ever have happened to me,' her mother said. She had cried angry tears of shame. 'What will I say to people?'

Later her mother regretted her reaction. She tried to help Detta. Detta punished her, accepting the minimum of assistance. She, too, was ashamed. Also arrogant, proud, and independent. Damage had been done. She was in no hurry to forgive.

That her education would be postponed or ended was accepted unquestioningly by herself and her parents. She took a job in a solicitor's office, as a receptionist, and rented a tiny bedsitter in Ranelagh, much to her parents' upset. When she was seven months pregnant and the bump couldn't be hidden any longer her boss called her into his office. He asked her if she expected to marry shortly, and explained that he had a policy, in common with the Civil Service and most organizations, of not employing married women. Detta said she was not engaged or intending to marry. 'I am asking you to resign anyway,' was what he said. 'I will give you a good reference.'

Ever after Detta wished, more heartily than she wished most things, that she had replied, 'Don't bother.' But she had accepted the reference silently, and left.

There was a Mother and Baby Home not far from where she lived. Instead of going home to her mother she went there. The idea of approaching Mary Mooney never crossed her mind.

At the home, a friendly reverend mother talked to her. This nun advised Detta not to take a place in the home, not giving any special reason: Detta, thinking of the institution as a kind of hospital, got the impression that there were no vacancies, just then. If she called some other time, perhaps . . . Instead of taking her in, the nun gave Detta away, to a family, a kind of charitable foster family of a type which flourished in Ireland at that time, specializing in this exotic form of charity: putting up unmarried mothers while they waited to have their babies in secret. The family, Yvonne and Mick Clancy, lived in a yellow bungalow outside Athlone: their garden, where Detta hung out washing, since housework by the unmarried mother was part of the deal, sloped down to the Shannon. It was May then, the garden was ablaze with forsythia and laburnum, intoxicating lilacs. Detta had sat there, in the sun, drinking tea and chatting with Yvonne. Later, when Detta heard about the Mother and Baby homes, the cruelty of them, the ill-treatment meted out to the girls, she felt an overwhelming guilt. She could have been washing dirty clothes and scrubbing floors (a bit like Finbar's Hotel, only with shame and pain instead of fun and the Marys, money and Conor). Instead she sat among the lilacs, listening to the blackbirds, watching the sun dance on the shirred blue water of the Shannon. She never found out why this was her fate, while other girls got the dirty linen and harsh words. Luck, perhaps – or perhaps her seven honours, which she had mentioned to the nun, and her new cream bouclé coat and her Clonskeagh accent?

She could now remember the Clancys' riverside garden better than her own baby, whom she had, after a painful labour – muscles too strong and none of the hope for the birth which can transform normal labour to an adventurous challenge. The birth itself was a release rather than the moment of great joy mothers speak of. It is true that Detta felt a great rush of love when she looked at the baby, a sort of love she had never known before (or since). She started to cry at that moment. She had never wept so profusely. A splashing, exuberant fountain of maternal love gushed out of her. 'You're exhausted,' the midwife said, brusquely, fearing the joy in Detta's tears. 'You'll feel better when you get some sleep. We'll look after this big bruiser!' Bruiser. Detta winced. She wept on, but her tears became thin and bitter, and gave her no relief.

A week after the birth she handed him over: Conn, she called him, after his father. The adopting parents were allowed to replace her name for him with one of their own choosing. They did.

Detta was eighteen. The two big loves of her life were over. That is what she thought. She went to England, to London, where she got a job with one of the new computer companies: the excellent reference from her former boss helped. There, more than ten years later, she met Piet, who was over demonstrating new programs. He was older than her, and divorced from his first wife. She fell in love with him and after a while returned with him to Holland. That is her official biography, neat as a complex sentence.

*

At five to nine she bounced downstairs. Karl Brown was in the foyer as she passed, looking at a woman who sat on a sofa, opposite the entrance, writing busily on a laptop. Detta nodded to Karl. She would have a drink with him tomorrow. She promised herself this in order to put what was about to happen into perspective. Whatever the outcome, this was just one night in her life. Tomorrow would come along. Tomorrow would include a drink with Karl, if nothing more, as well as whatever else fate had in store for her.

She supposed the Irish Bar was the right place to wait, and went in there. It was less Irish than the name suggested, but warm and comfortable: through stained-glass windows coloured lozenges of light fell, dappling stiff wooden seats. Wallpaper Celtic mist music keened in the background, but its witchy moaning was all but drowned by a tumult of happy human noise, coming from a crowd gathered in the corner – one of those Dublin stag nights that even the Dutch had heard about? She looked more carefully. All the members of the party looked elderly. It must be some sort of old folks' celebration – a retirement, perhaps.

An arrow pointed to Fiona's Bar at the far side of the dining room. Detta went and had a look at the elegant length of it, with its sense of space and light – the place seemed to be modelled on an Italian or French café, which Detta always found mildly intimidating, probably because dozens of curious male eyes looked up from their drinks or their dominoes or their cards and stared at her whenever she walked into one. Only a few people sat in Fiona's Bar and none of them paid any attention at all to Detta. But she decided to return to the Irish Bar, where the plaited seats were comforting.

She sat as far away from the crowd in the corner as she could. They were a noisy lot, however, and impossible to ignore for long. Her eyes wandered from them to the doorway, from the doorway to them. Two or three of them looked familiar, but she could not place them. Then a woman shaped like a round skittle, with a small head of yellow pin curls, walked across the room to the corner and said, 'Howareyez! Sorry I'm late but . . .' Detta blenched. It was Mary Mooney.

She looked at the crowd in the corner more carefully. Other faces began to swim into focus, find their eternal structures, their names. There was Mary Brazil.

She had thought everything and everyone had disappeared, had sunk into the rubble of the old Finbar's Hotel. But the opposite was the case

Maybe she should go somewhere else? She didn't want to meet her long-lost son in full view of Mary Brazil and Mary Mooney. What had possessed her to select Finbar's Hotel at all? How could she have believed that all the old staff would have gone, just because time had passed and the hotel had been rebuilt and was owned by Dutch rock stars or whatever they were? Well. Because she couldn't imagine a Dutch rock star, or any other Dutch person, employing the likes of Mary Mooney or Mary Brazil, perhaps, or any of the old crowd? That some sort of reunion was going on the very night she had picked to visit was a horrible coincidence, that was all. Don't exaggerate!

She couldn't move from her spot. This was the spot Paul had meant. If he really came, if the meeting happened, it would have to happen right here, with Mary Mooney and Mary Brazil and goodness knows who else viewing it from standside seats.

Her eyes swung around to the door again. No sign.

Nine thirty. Conor was always late for things, she recalled – that was his style. The Irish way, different from the Dutch. Piet called when he said he would. Nine meant nine. If Paul was late it was because he was Irish, not because he was unreliable. You had to accept these cultural differences.

Nevertheless she was anxious, so anxious that she had a cramp of nervousness in her stomach.

She went to the bar and ordered a glass of port. While she was there Mary Brazil came up and said: 'Excuse me! Don't I know you from somewhere?'

Detta looked at her. She had seemed so much older than herself in the past, but in fact she was almost the same age. Her black hair was still black, her sallow skin unwrinkled. Had she married that boyfriend, Michael? Detta would have liked to find out but she said, 'No. I don't believe you do.' Her blonde cap of hair protected her privacy. Mary Brazil smiled uneasily, gave Detta a scrutinizing look, and returned to her corner.

Nine forty-five.

It struck Detta that he might not come. Cold feet at the last minute. It wouldn't be easy for him either, meeting his long lost mother. What resentments he might harbour against her! When she 'gave him up', as they expressed it then, it seemed for the best. It wasn't as if she was giving him up to an orphanage, although the place where she had the baby reminded her of the orphanages, of the terrible school her mother had told her about, the dark hatred of children which had characterized Ireland's past. She knew from the moment she gave him up that he was being placed with a good family. She knew their names, their occupations: the man was a librarian, the woman a teacher. You could ask for nothing more respectable, more humane, it had seemed to her. They had a house in Bray, close to the seafront. She felt the sacrifice was all hers, something she was doing purely for the sake of the baby.

But the baby might see things differently. Maybe he hadn't liked his adoptive parents? If such things did not work out, it would be easy to point the finger of blame at the mother. Who else could you blame, especially in this case, where the father did not even know about his son?

A pang of guilt caught her there, as well. Fathers. They had changed completely now, them as well as everything else. In 1970, it would not have occurred to her that Conor might have wanted to know he had a child. She had assumed that a child would spell disaster for him, for any young man. All she had heard was of how young men bolted, deserted, cried that the child wasn't really theirs. The idea that young men would demand paternity rights, would want to have the child, would have seemed laughable. Why would they? Young men don't even want to get married was the attitude her mother had inculcated in her. As a girl she would have to snare them into it in some way. Mothers fretted that all this free love would let them off the hook entirely. Detta's own mother predicted that men would never get married at all if they didn't have to. Why would they, if they could have sex for free? Without paying for all that with wedding rings and jobs for life and mortgages and babies? The society was misogynistic then; that was recognized by the budding, despised women's libbers, who already then were creating a flutter of protest against the deeply ingrained disparagement of girls and women in Irish society. But the same society hated men as well, in a subversive, mysterious way. The women, resentful of all other women, often mistrusted and derided men. They were regarded as belonging to another species altogether, lacking all human feeling, childish, boorish creatures to be tricked and manipulated, then reeled in and ruled for life. That was what Detta's mother had taught her. Detta's mother did not believe that true love was possible, and forced Detta to share that belief, in spite of all evidence to the contrary.

Being a martyr to men was what Detta had been taught she would be, and she fulfilled her mother's expectations. Being an abandoned unmarried mother was the ultimate fulfilment of her mother's expectations – so ready was Detta for the role that that she failed to notice that it was she who had done all the abandoning. What a martyr she had felt, living in her pathetic bedsitter, going off to the place in Athlone when she was in the eighth month. What a heroic, saintly, put-upon Irishwoman! Everyone she met encouraged this point of view. Yvonne, in Athlone, had gloated in Christian sympathy. It dripped from her like the honey-flowers from her laburnums. 'You poor love,' she gushed. 'It is all very hard for you, pet, but it will soon be over, and all for the best.' She fell short of calling it a 'learning experience' but only because the phrase was then unknown, at least in Athlone.

Detta could have just married Conor. He had not, as she'd anticipated, become a priest. She'd found out that he left the seminary after two years, and studied medicine. He could have managed that, married to her, with a baby. Conor was the kind who would have coped, and so was she. She had done well in spite of every obstacle. People survive, and prosper. Most people – the Romanian woman flashed through her mind, a reminder that there were exceptions to this rule.

She should trace Conor. Merely to satisfy her curiosity.

It wouldn't be hard. He was probably listed in the telephone directory. She could ring him after meeting Paul. She promised herself she would. After meeting Paul. Another task for tomorrow.

Nine fifty-five. Detta got up, her stomach still aching, and went to the door of the bar. The woman with the laptop was still sitting in the foyer, although she had stopped typing. She was looking furtively around, obviously searching for someone herself. For a dark and terrifying minute, Detta wondered if she could possibly be some emissary from Paul, sent to give his excuses. His adoptive mother, perhaps? Clenching her stomach, she walked in front of the woman, giving her a good view. But the woman got up and walked away, completely ignoring her.

'What happens is silly enough,' said Piet's voice, lightly mocking, in Detta's head. 'Don't paint the devil on the wall.'

Piet had encouraged her to come to Dublin and meet Paul, but urged her not to take the whole thing too seriously. 'Of course I won't!' Detta had retorted. 'You know me, carefree as a butterfly!'

Piet was Jewish as well as Dutch, or had been. His mother had given him to a childless Gentile couple when he was born, in 1944. Later that year she died, in Auschwitz. Abandonment by his mother had been Piet's salvation.

None of this seemed to have marked him. He was without bitterness. That is why Detta loved him, or one of the reasons.

She returned to her seat in the bar, deciding to give Paul another fifteen minutes. Then she would decide what to do: ring Piet and ask him for advice, comfort herself with his sound common sense. Or ring Karl and suggest that they have dinner, after all, and take the risk that involved. Or go back to her lonely barque of a bed, and cry herself to sleep.

Then Conor walked into the bar.

Conor, exactly as he was thirty years ago. Taller, perhaps, but with his sandy skin, his thick reddish hair, his JFK eyes and jaw. He was wearing jeans and a blue shirt, a waistcoat. He glanced around the room.

Detta's eyes widened, when she saw him. He opened his arms. She stood up and he moved quickly, running, towards her.

She stood up, extending her hand.

'It's Paul?' she asked, stupidly.

'Don't you know me, Mother?' He laughed and took her in his arms. Detta put her head on his shoulders.

In her head the crying of the children quietened.

Paul was smiling. He was handsome, easy, smooth skinned, smiling. Competent: Conor's son. He knew how to handle a situation, even one as awkward as this.

'You look beautiful,' he held her away from him, at arm's length. 'You're just like I imagined you!'

This is too easy, Detta began to think. There should be hesitation, misunderstanding. He should be disreputable, impoverished, mean. And disappointed.

She saw Karl Brown at the bar, looking quizzically at her. He raised his glass, a shining flute of champagne.

She heard Piet's voice in her memory saying, 'Everything turns out for the best!'

Keeping her hands on Paul's elbows, she moved back to gaze at him.

Karl was observing her and Paul with shameless curiosity, as, indeed, were most people in the room. Detta's eye wandered, uneasily, to the old folk in the corner. Mary Mooney was staring over, smiling sentimentally, taking it all in: she probably guessed everything. Detta grinned and Mary winked. Mary Mooney! She'd go over and talk to her later insofar as later existed any more.

Later and then became now.

Detta holds her baby up. She counts his eyes and his ears and his fingers and his toes. She turns him round and looks at the strip of fair hair on his back. She puts him to her breast and lets him suck.

'Oh, I love you!' she says. She says. She says.

This is it.

This is the moment, the moment the mothers talked about: the lightning flash of heaven, the blissful glimpse of eternity. Twenty-seven years late, but she is getting it again: the happiest minute of human life. Couldn't she find a more original way to express herself, to give voice to the amazing burst of emotion that washes through her, stronger than anything she has ever felt? But she can't find better words. She can speak English, Dutch, French and German. A smattering of Italian. But none of these languages help her. She would like to compose a symphony, or even a song. She would like to burst into a passionate poem.

Someone is singing an Irish song at last, some old air jazzed up to suit the new mood of Ireland, the Ireland where it's OK to be Irish, where it's the cool thing to be. Mary

Mooney is joining in in the song: she always had an astonishingly sweet voice, Detta remembers, it used to soar down the corridors as she moved around, mop and bucket clinking. 'I dreamt I dwelt in marble halls' she would sing, in her high soprano. 'My young love said to me my mother won't mind' used to float out from the downstairs toilet. 'Oh Danny Boy!' accompanied the Hoover, the notes dipping and swooning as the machine roared.

Karl Brown is smiling from the bar, sipping his champagne, his purple jacket glowing. A golden light shines from him and beams across at Detta and Paul, at Paul and Detta, at Detta and Paul, at Paul Detta's son and Detta Paul's mother. Mary Mooney sings with joy and surprise isn't life gas who would have thought and is that what's his name the one who was going to be the priest he hasn't changed a bit and neither have you Detta who used to have long red hair and two breasts and a boyfriend and a baby, Detta who once was young with all her life before her, Detta who once was a chambermaid called Bernadette.

Detta closes her eyes.

From the tight shells of her closed eyes warm tears fall and from her mouth fall the tawdry, overused tepid words, the only words she has.

'I love you too,' Detta's son, Paul who once was Conn, says. His body is warm, his voice is warm, his hug is warm around her.

*

The tide is in. The river prances busily under the spanning arches of the bridges. Capel Street Carlisle Matt Talbot. Louisa Bridge. The Halfpenny Bridge, a generous arm languidly spreading from bank to bulwarked bank. Blue slates, black slates, grey slates. Red steeples, green domes. Silvery spires. Nimbus clouds toss across the sky, careless as pillows in the warmth of the day. The air is sultry, the streets are woozy, drunk on summer. The tide is in. Water, green as bushes, dappled, speckled, sun freckled, rushes full forward, under the grey bridges, down to the sea.

*

I love you too! I love you too!

Detta's soul explodes. In a million singing fragments it rockets to the stars.

THE WEDDING OF
THE PUGHS

Emily Pugh, as prim, it seemed, as her name suggests, tippy-tapped on her laptop.

It was difficult to balance on the mushy white cushions of the sofa in the lobby of Finbar's Hotel. She had to sit right out on the edge, where the cherrywood frame – Mrs Pugh prided herself on her knowledge of furnishing woods – cut into the soft thigh flesh.

She glanced at the clock behind reception. Four minutes past five in Tokyo. Just four minutes since it was three o'clock in New York. She caught the receptionist's eye, sent her a dazzling smile and shrugged in complicit amazement. Was that the time? Time flies when you're busy! The foreign-looking girl in her black and white outfit, uncaring, did not smile back. This embarrassed Mrs Pugh who had spun out her dinner for well over an hour in the strangely named Echo Rooms across the lobby, picking at a salad, taking delicate mouthfuls of profiterole, teeny sips of espresso, until she really could not justify taking up her table for another minute. In fact the slow service, commented on in an exasperated manner by the couple at the next table, had suited her greatly.

She returned to her little screen. Taking the laptop to Dublin with her, even into the Echo Rooms, had been a good idea, greatly facilitating the complicated business of loitering with intent. Now. What was that she had been writing?

This was what she had been writing: as;dkjf jka;sdkfj jkl;aido io'ioa' eiog hi'

Mrs Pugh stared at the letters as though they had done her a great disservice. She deleted with deliberation, considering one keystroke at a time. This took maybe forty seconds. She blinked towards reception again. A momentous decision in the offing. Started again. Fingers flew, brows furrowed. A multinational corporation could depend on this text.

The laptop had been a Christmas gift from Mr Pugh. 'Might as well join the twenty-first century, pet,' he'd said, 'you could use it to make notes, anything you like. So powerful, that yoke, you could run a global enterprise with it, really you could.'

Emily, heart thumping nervously, had stared at the sinister flat thing, grey as a thundercloud. After Christmas dinner, which they always ate alone, she had set to with the manual which weighed twice as much as the machine, frowning at it through the canned laughter of some comedy special on the television. Ever after, when Mr Pugh had enquired as to how she was getting on with the information superhighway, she had laughed airily. 'I'll surprise you all one of these days. Look for me in the Cayman Islands.' Luckily, he had never asked for a demonstration. He was always very busy.

ido;gf id;ajkdl;a ejif;jid;a kdl;ak;ghi;ak;k.

Sitting here in this lobby where the smell of newness should have exhilarated with possibilities, Mrs Pugh felt as though she was an actor in a big new play. For the very first time in her life, the world was turning around her. When she checked in four hours and eleven minutes ago she had waited for curtains to part, a hush to descend. Some small cognisance, a little suspense of breath perhaps, from her expectant audience.

Yet no one she had encountered seemed to feel that what was happening was out of the ordinary. Not the porter, the girl behind the reception desk, the sour-looking blonde woman who, by the way she was behaving, could have been the owner and should *never*, in Mrs Pugh's opinion, wear tight leather. Even the nice uniformed boy who took her vanity case and wheelie bag up in the lift had behaved as though the arrival of Emily Pugh in Finbar's Hotel was just an ordinary event. And when the boy had unlocked the door of her room on the fourth floor and showed her in, he seemed not to notice how the curtains on the thick windows stiffened in anticipation.

io;qhu   i;hi'   I   gh   uri;   hir;hio'orp'   hi'hi'o hio'\poe8 . . . .

She deleted again, lowered her head, thinking deeply. Picked a speck from her new linen skirt. Proud of her appearance, yes, at least that. Clean hair, court shoes, pussycat bow at throat, shins sheeny in tights built to trim from waist to toe. A cotton gusset, of course. Comfort the motto these days.

Or was. Emily Pugh's heart had split. Like two-way armour, keep out, keep in, she wore these clothes, this hair, not only to repel sightseers – for she was sure everyone in the town knew her to be an object of sympathy – but to corset the matter spilling from her ruptured entrails.

She risked a look at the people who, wineglasses in hand, had come out into the reception area. A woman wearing a jacket over her T-shirt hung about in the doorway of the lounge, looking furtive as though she was waiting for an illicit encounter. Dublin was obviously full of this kind of thing. Mrs Pugh found herself glaring with naked hatred at the woman, then, remembering her mission to remain incognito, hastily transferred her attention to a pair of bespectacled, bewildered Americans, who, bum bags bulging over ample stomachs, were across the way, staring together at a lurid painting. The wife, who really should never have worn sleeveless, had surreptitiously eased off her sneakers and was cooling her feet on the marble tiles. Bewildered or loud, there never seemed to be a middle ground with Americans, thought Emily, who surprised herself with the observation. A worthy observation. One could drop it into the conversational lacuna which frequently fell across the table in the staff room during lunch hour.

Not that Emily had encountered all that many Americans. Her town was one of those found only by intrepid Swedes and Finns determined not to go to the West of Ireland. She was just surprised that any thought at all other than that concerning her present circumstance could arise. She saved it onto the laptop. Americans. No middle ground.

The lift opened and the stocky man she had seen stride into it flanked by two policemen a few moments before, now emerged with his arms pinned by the officers. Although she knew the impulse was ludicrous, Mrs Pugh hoped that he was being taken away to be charged with adultery.

Get a Grip, Emily, she thought then, surprising herself freshly with a vernacular she had so often excised from her pupils' essays. She concentrated again on her laptop and checked her work so far:

ido;gf id;ajkdl;a ejif;jid;a kdl;ak;ghi;ak;k.

io;qhu   i;hi' | gh   uri;   hir;hio'orp'   hi'hi'o hio'\poe8 . . . .

Americans. No middle ground.

The glass entrance doors whooshed open. Emily lowered her chin, thinking deeply. Actually she was checking from under lowered lashes who was coming in. She noticed that the furtive girl in the T-shirt was watching too. It was not Mr Pugh.

So where was Mr Pugh?

Out. Out to dinner. But not with whom he had said he was going out to dinner.

At two twenty-eight that afternoon, Mr Pugh had telephoned his wife in their house to let her know he had checked in. Yawning. Tired from London. 'Hello, pet. Going to have a nap. Then a quick shower and a bloody dinner with a client.'

The never-ending bore of life in the fast lane.

She had asked him about the hotel. Was it nice?

The hotel was, wearily, all right, you know, the usual. Trendy. Didn't sound it, of course. Finbar's, what a bloody name, eh? Mr Pugh would be back in the morning. He'd go straight to the plant, see her at six or seven tomorrow evening? Maybe she'd like to go out to eat, to save her cooking? Mario's as usual?

'Why not?'

'Right, then. It's settled. Cheerio, love you.'

'Love you too.'

'Talk soon, 'bye now.'

'Bye.'

She had telephoned straight back, first having had to get the number from Directory Enquiries. And when he had answered in his room, she'd said, 'Sorry, pet, I forgot to tell you that I might be a little late tomorrow evening. I promised I'd help Breda with her new curtains. It's a big job.'

They had said goodbye again and after she had hung up, Emily, heart flooding with a surge of adrenaline, had looked at the receiver. He was in Finbar's all right.

What poor Mr Pugh didn't know was that when he had telephoned, his wife's car was already out of their double garage and, tank full, doors unlocked, was facing the open gateway in the driveway of their bungalow. His wife was herself dressed and waiting. Until she knew the name of the hotel in Dublin. (It was a different one every time.)

Finbar's was a new one.

Now the policemen had left with their reluctant and bewildered-looking captive. The silent Americans, who, eyes bulging, perhaps thinking that this was part of a floorshow put on by Finbar's every evening, swivelled in unison as the door slid open again to admit a party of youngsters bound for the noisy bar. Androgynous boys and girls, black tank tops, tiny earrings, those lovely narrow bracelets on slim tanned arms. Wasn't it amazing, Emily thought, that in the state she was in, she could think of the word androgynous.

She shifted her gaze towards the elderly porter, who spent most of his time staring out into the breezy street when not standing behind an incongruous wooden pulpit. Seeing stories written in the sky above the river. If she had some sorrow to spare, she might have spent it on him. While his assistant buzzed around, he was tired, beaten. She happened to know that he walked on the side of his feet because she saw him doing so. They didn't give him a chair, just left him standing by that desk that looked like it had been ripped from an old Protestant church.

She had been in the lobby for an hour now. She couldn't spend much more time here. They'd get suspicious, especially that blonde owner-woman who frequently emerged from her office as though searching for slackers. Already there was another woman, foreign-looking like the receptionist, coming out to the doorway of the lounge to stare at her. Or was this one foreign? Emily stared. Memory stirred, lurched toward recognition. Twenty-five years ago, maybe more. Mrs Pugh had been for a time a substitute teacher in Athlone, had integrated somewhat with the locals, as one does. This was a face seen for a few months around the town, one of maybe a dozen such faces, some forlorn, some filled with bravado, who had come and gone, staying with the Clancy family in Athlone, with local people too polite to mention why. She could see that the woman did not remember her. Mrs Pugh's face was not memorable. She would have to get out of here.

tio;q ig 'u,,,,,,,,,,,hi' hiu;y ir; yu;rhi; hjagfd.

Emily placed the last full stop with the flourish of a magician. She read the dot, stared at it. Highlighted it. Changed the font size so it became a small boulder.

Yes. That was definitely it. She pressed Control Quit. Saved when requested. Shut down and carefully folded over the laptop until the slow click of the catch satisfied the tips of her fingers. She glanced at the girl behind reception, expecting acknowledgement for A Job Complete—

Still the girl cared nothing, talking on the telephone now, hand over the mouthpiece, head bent low so that a wing of polished hair sheathed the intensity of the discussion. Emily was disappointed, she found she had been counting on the complicity of the girl. All in this together. Women.

Then, remembering why she was here, Emily almost laughed. Very amusing actually, that she might, even for an instant, entertain the notion of solidarity amongst women. Quickly, while the girl was still talking on the telephone and the woman with whom she had crossed paths in Athlone had gone back into the bar, Mrs Pugh, heels clicking on the tiles, crossed to the reception desk and asked for Mr Pugh's key by room number. The girl, attention focused inwards towards the subject of her own conversation, reached underneath the counter and handed it over without missing a syllable.

'Thank you.' The smile at the girl's unheeding hair was for the benefit of the audience all around, in the bars, the Echo Rooms, the lobby, the street, the city, the universe, the pantheon which was registering and judging Mrs Pugh's every move.

With her own room key bumping against her hip through the thin lining of her linen pocket, Emily crossed the lobby and pushed the lift button. Fish-eyed, she stood watching the descent through the floors. The doors opened, she depressed the inside button (Braille too, wasn't that thoughtful!), she lifted off.

Emily knew very little about the woman who was undoubtedly glowing by now in candlelight paid for by Mr Pugh. She would have known nothing at all if it had not been for a nod of fate in the direction of 4 Canaletto Close.

That day, 29 May, Mr Pugh had been away with the other executives from the plant on the Spring Golf Tear. This was a biannual event; spouses and partners, as they say nowadays, were invited to the Autumn trip but the Spring, held at the end of May, was purely business, when the executives travelled solo to some distant leisure complex, Killarney, say, or Cavan, or Waterford. They stayed overnight, the idea being that thrown together like that without outside distraction they would bond, thrash ideas and come back to the plant eager for the summer sales push. Or so it was hoped by the top brass in Ohio.

Emily had come home from school on that Friday to find men from the gas company digging up the road outside her gate. A mundane event but as it turned out, a pivot on which the Pughs' life was to rotate.

Almost three months had elapsed, yet she could remember every pulse of the pneumatic drill, could see the yellow earpieces the men wore to protect their hearing, the cones and flapping tape which cut her off from her driveway. They did allow her, heavily escorted, to go into her house for long enough to pack a small bag. They were apologetic but adamant. She would have to find somewhere else to stay for at least one night.

Outside again she was pulled this way and that with indecision. What to do? What would Terry think if he telephoned to find no answer? Yet he hated to be telephoned at work or when he was away. He had warned her frequently. Only dire emergencies. And since both sets of parents were dead, she herself enjoyed rude health and they had no children, neither could foresee a single reason why she would ever have to telephone.

Did a gas leak count as a dire emergency? Hardly. Yet suppose he himself made an unscheduled telephone call – which he did occasionally – would he worry? Would he think she might have been carted off to hospital with acute appendicitis?

Her friend, Breda, the domestic science teacher, was surprised to see Emily on her doorstep but happily showed her to the spare room of her chaotic house. When the two of them (Emily feeling hugely naughty and adventurous) were ensconced at the kitchen table eating scones and drinking tea, she started again to worry and placed the problem between them for discussion. Breda's attitude was straightforward. For God's sake, Emily was just to ring the place in Cavan and be done with it. She didn't even have to talk to the great man himself if he was that pernickety, she could leave a message at reception.

Emily wasn't all that sure about the word pernickety but she took the advice and went immediately out into Breda's hall. Breda had a novelty telephone in the shape of a football. One had to detach the top third of this football which formed the receiver, and Emily had to put on her reading glasses to be able to make out the numbers on the brindled buttons.

She nevertheless managed to get the telephone number of the hotel from a very helpful person at Directory Enquiries and as she pushed all the relevant buttons subsequently, in her head was already forming the clear, unambiguous message she would leave. Mrs Emily Pugh would not be at home this evening but was staying at the home of her friend, Mrs Breda McLoughlin.

The operator answered and put her through to reception, as requested. Emily began with her message but was interrupted. 'Is he a guest at the hotel?'

'Yes.' Emily was patient. 'He's with a party from—' and she named the plant.

'Just a moment, please—'

The line went dead and Emily could have been irritated but she was not. She supposed the procedure for taking messages was well laid down and the girl was only doing her job.

'I'm sorry, what did you say the name was, McHugh?'

'Pugh.' Emily spelled it carefully. 'Mr Terry Pugh, he's with—'

The line went dead again and this time Emily allowed a small bubble of vexation to form behind her tongue.

But when the girl came back on, the bubble burst under its own weight. 'I'm sorry, we've no one of that name staying here.'

Emily held on and this time spelled out the name of the plant.

The girl was definite. She had checked that list, along with all the others. There was no one of that name, or of any name remotely like it, staying at the hotel.

Emily thanked the girl and fitted the wedge of football she held back into its circle. She stared at the football for a minute or two. There had to be some dreadful mistake and it was all her fault as usual. She had misheard the name of the hotel—

But then the niggle. The girl had recognized the name of the plant. She'd had a list. She'd checked it.

By the time Terry Pugh came home from his trip to Cavan, his wife had decided that she would not challenge him. She had the flimsiest of proof, after all, easily explained away. The receptionist could have made a mistake, for instance. Half of Emily wanted to laugh the whole thing off with her husband, for him to say, 'That girl? That dimwit?' And then for him to add, 'Really, Emily!' with that half-pitying, half-affectionate husband/wife shorthand which excavated the archaeology of a long marriage. The other half, however, the insidious second half, warned her to lie in wait. To watch. To listen. To stay alert.

And when he handed her his gift of a Cavan Crystal clock

– he usually brought her some little thing – she demurred that he was too good to her and put it with the other souvenirs in the crowded china cabinet which glittered now with insincerity from its alcove beside the fireplace in the lounge.

During the next few weeks, Emily Pugh's personality changed, but largely within. Outwardly, she dealt with school exams, end-of-term essays, meetings with parents, seeming as composed and sensible as she had always been and if anyone noticed that on one day she wore brown shoes with a navy suit, or sported the same blouse two days running, no one commented on it. And when the holidays finally dawned she was able to say her goodbyes and see-you-in-the-salt-mines to her colleagues with her customary quiet cheeriness.

At home, the succeeding summer hours, weeks, months dragged. She would be snipping the heads off the spent lobelia, or dabbing creosote on the trellis-built structure they liked to call the pergola, when something close to pain would clutch at a spot between her heart and her stomach. She began to read more and differently. *Cosmopolitan*, *She* and *Company* instead of novels, or *House and Garden* or *Interiors*. She turned first to the horoscopes, poring over her own and Mr Pugh's forecasts, brooding over any word or warning which seemed in any way significant. For the first time as an adult, she read the agony columns too – and seized on any piece which bore a title such as 'How To Tell If Your Man Is A Cheat . . .'.

Tiny episodes from the past began to make sense to her. For instance, the time her husband had dropped the tele-phone when she returned unexpectedly early from bridge.

(When she questioned him, he simply muttered that she had startled him.) Then there was his resurgence of interest in certain popular music. Inclined to haggle and shop around for deals on the smallest purchases, he now paid the full and unquestioning retail price for a boxed set of Nat King Cole love songs on CD.

The woman concerned was not his secretary. Emily knew this for sure because on her husband's last absence she had telephoned the office and the secretary had answered. That was one relief because she quite liked the girl, having met her twice during two Autumn Tears. There was such a thing as class and appropriateness and doing it with one's secretary was a cliché she doubted she could have forgiven him for – when the time came to forgive.

Even as her brain beavered on – she realized, for instance, that he always telephoned her before one of his client dinners and never afterwards – Emily strove not to act differently around her husband. During his absence on business, although her fingers itched to telephone him, she never did. Until she absolutely had to before embarking on her present mission.

The strain, however, was dreadful. Sitting across from him at their regular candlelit table at Mario's, her tongue frequently filled to bursting point with accusations and questions. She would watch him, head bent contentedly over his steak or salmon, while rage – an emotion heretofore completely foreign to her – boiled in the pit of her stomach. She wanted to snatch the steak or fish knife from his podgy hand and rake it across his cheeks and chest, again and again, damaging his skin and sinews so they bled and spewed all over his plate, the table, the world.

And then, unexpectedly, he would look up and, still chewing, all unsuspecting, smile at her. 'What's wrong tonight, pet? You're not yourself.'

And Mrs Pugh would laugh lightly, relating some new outrage attributed to the school scallywag, now freed for the summer months to terrorize the town. 'It would wear you down, sometimes, it really would.'

Sometimes, looking at his paunchy frame and balding head, she wondered what it was that the other woman found so attractive. Yet here was the absurdity. Somehow since her momentous discovery Mr Pugh seemed to have emerged in blade-sharp relief from a swampy milieu of habit, comfortable as a featherbed, in which she had lost sight of who he was. Who she was. Why they had married in the first place.

This was a very large question which had come to occupy Emily Pugh's mind when she wasn't picking over the traces of Mr Pugh's perfidy.

She had been Emily Crosson when she had met him first. Fresh out of teacher training, she and a friend had cast aside their books and gone on a walking holiday in the Scottish Highlands. When they came down to breakfast on their fifth morning, Terry Pugh was at the communal table. As soon as they all said their good mornings, the mutuality of accents became clear and the slow northern English intonations of the other couple at the table were drowned out with the customary Irish, 'Where were you from? I don't believe it, I've a cousin married there! And do you know so-and-so?' Terry, it turned out, was from a village less than sixteen miles from where Emily's friend was born and reared.

Thinner then, with longer hair and all his own teeth, he chatted pleasantly of this and that. At present he was travelling, he told them, for a firm selling shoe polish, but his future plans included an attempt to get back to Ireland. He'd heard things were looking up there and his mother (then still alive) was always at him to come home.

After breakfast, they exchanged addresses and went their separate ways.

Two years later, Emily, by then in a temporary post in Dublin, was surprised, astonished even, to receive a postcard, forwarded by her father, which informed her that Terry Pugh had indeed come back to Ireland and by a strange coincidence had taken up a salesman's job in the newly opened plant in her very town. *Don't know where you are now*, he'd written, *but you might get this and you might not. Just getting in touch. Cheers.* He'd signed it *Terry* and added a PS, *Give us a ring, sometime*, with the telephone number of his digs.

In Finbar's Hotel the lift stopped on the first floor, the door slid open and Emily Pugh found herself walking without licence towards her husband's room.

The card-key fitted and worked first time – without incident and without any security men descending on ropes through the ceiling to pounce on her – and Mr Pugh's wife found herself without authorization in her husband's room. The handle of the laptop grinding into one slippy palm, she closed the door and leaned her back against it. She waited. For something to happen.

She could hear the thump and wash of her heart. Redolent of him, the air was still in this room, stiller than it had a right to be. His briefcase lay, unsnapped, on a chair, his Samsonite suiter – a present from her – sprawled on the webbed stand beside the door leading into the bathroom. He'd left one of the reading lamps alight. On the right side of the bed. Her side.

Emily continued to wait. So did everything in the room. The bed, with a dinge in the red duvet where her husband had obviously sat for a time, watched her. The Cyclops eye of the television watched her. The new wood of the fitted furniture developed a thousand stares, as did the red and black squares of carpet. So many watchers and waiters that Emily was abruptly frightened and almost fled.

And then she noticed that he had discarded his electric shaver on the bed, wire curling over one of the pillows. He had shaved before he went out. To meet the woman. His assignation.

Emily was no longer nervous. She put Mr Pugh's key in her pocket, placed her laptop carefully against the wall beside the door and began to prowl. Briefcase first. A quick, careful rifle. Papers for meetings, product catalogues, pens, batteries, an invitation (command really) to a management seminar. Business cards in the leather slot designed for them. Terry had always been organized and neat. The only items missing were his Filofax and his mobile telephone, both of which went with him wherever he did. Nothing incriminating, no clue here. She went back to the business cards. This was a selection only, he acquired so many that he had a separate, alphabetized box for them on his desk in his home study.

The ones from the briefcase were mostly names she recognized. Only two women, and neither was a suspect in this case.

Or was she? Emily, about to replace the cards, changed her mind and sat on the bed, staring at the two small rectangles. One of these women was from the parent company in Ohio. She had come to Mario's with them during her last visit. Loud, quite pushy. Brassy hair. Terry disliked her intensely. Or so he had said.

The other woman worked for a firm in Cork. A girl, really, early twenties, petite, small eyed, sharp featured. She and her husband had been guests of the firm at last year's Autumn Tear and Emily had thought her unremarkable, although when she had said so later to Terry he had remarked that sometimes appearances and manner could be deceiving. The girl was a marketing whiz.

But early twenties? Married? All the way from Cork? To see Terry?

Emily replaced the two women's cards and went around Room 106 dowsing the secret life of a stranger. She stopped, understood that this was exactly what she was doing. Who was Terry Pugh, anyway?

Their courtship had been far from whirlwind. She had not telephoned him at his digs although, lonely in Dublin, she had often thought about doing so. But when, nearly four months after receiving the postcard, she was home for Christmas holidays, she literally ran into him in Nan Cunningham's grocery shop (since then grown into a thriving supermarket, video and hardware emporium with a side business in hackney and formal dress hire). On leaving the shop she was not watching where she was walking and cannoned into Terry as he was coming in. He helped her pick up her basketful, fruit, bread, tins and so forth, but it was only when she was thanking him and saying goodbye that they recognized one another. He asked if he could buy her a cup of tea and she agreed.

And that was the end of that, or so it seemed, although they exchanged Christmas, Easter and St Patrick's Day cards and again ran into one another from time to time during school holidays. Then, two years later, Emily managed to get a post in the local school and at a Macra dance, to which she had been dragged by her friend, Breda, she and Terry Pugh reacquainted themselves. He was now on the road a great deal, he told her, but from then on, when he was home and at weekends, they began to walk out, as people still called it in those parts. They went to the pictures, on picnics, to charity functions. They became a social fixture in the town, as in: 'Will we ask Terry and Emily?' They never actually discussed marriage until, to their mutual surprise, it seemed impossible that they would not get married. Everyone expected it, it seemed, and so they did.

And up to now, they had rubbed along well together.

Emily took the Samsonite suiter and laid it on the bed. Looked over her shoulder towards the door of Room 106 as though fearful of a sudden battering ram, being led by the leather-clad blonde woman. She quickly crossed the room and double-locked the door. Back at the bed, she unzipped the soft blue luggage and rifled it. Except for a duty-free bag bulging with dirty shirts, socks and underpants, the case was exactly as she had packed it for him three days ago.

With one addition. Probing into the outside pocket, Emily's hand encountered the cool smoothness of a magazine. She had a premonition about it. Little hairs stood on the back of her neck.

She withdrew it slowly. Expelled her breath. A long sigh of relief. Premonition absurd. He was bringing it home for her. *Vogue*.

Absurd, absurd, absurd. She panicked now for a different reason. What if he was really out with a client tonight? What if she had been wrong all along – and there was no third party? What if she had become obsessed with a phantom just because one snippy little girl behind a reception desk at a conference centre hadn't been bothered to check her lists properly?

What if he came in and found her here, playing detective? He'd never forgive her. She saw his accusing face. 'What were you doing here? Trust? What happened to trust, Emily?'

Frantic now, Emily replaced the magazine – hoping against hope it was the same way up she found it – zipped up the suiter, placed it back on its platform, raced to the door and hesitated with her hand on the lock. Had she left any traces? The briefcase looked undisturbed but there was a ruffle on the duvet cover where she had rested the suiter. She raced to smooth it out. Then had to try to recreate Terry's dinge where he had sat. She did it by sitting there herself and rocking slightly. He was much larger than she was.

Safe in her own room, to which she had made her way blessedly without being seen by anyone at all, Mrs Pugh lay on her own duvet and tried to concentrate on becoming calm. Through the double glazing of the windows, she could hear the muted city. Cars, a shout. From somewhere in the hotel itself, a regular thumping sound. A disco, perhaps. Or maybe a karaoke or just loud guests in their room. Nearer at hand, from overhead in what, on checking in, the reception-ist had told her was the penthouse, she heard a sudden, muffled roar. Mrs Pugh did not like to eavesdrop but one could not avoid hearing: the sound, obviously of passion, had been quite animalistic. Now she could hear a thump, as though two bodies had rolled heavily on to a bed. She covered her ears.

She uncovered them again. All relatively quiet.

Now what? Mrs Pugh refused to think about her own predicament just yet. She needed a little rest from thought and conflict. She would watch some television, yes, that always worked like Valium.

The remote control device, considerately to hand on the bedside table, was different from her own at home, although easy to master. She aimed it at the television and clicked. The screen filled with two men beating at one another with boxing gloves. Disturbed, she clicked again, getting some sort of inane American film with indecipherable dialogue. Click: now it was deafening noise. Huge spaceships.

Mrs Pugh clicked off the television. She liked *The Late Late Show* and *Kenny Live*, a nice documentary, provided there was nothing in it about sexual abuse. She loved David Attenborough.

She was mad to have come here. What had she been going to do anyway? She had become so obsessed with the springing of the trap, she had neglected to make any plan about what she was going to do with the prey. Now she saw that the only thing she'd had all along was a vague image of herself wafting in the open doorway of a hotel bedroom, incandescent as Camille, with her husband and his scarlet trollop covered in confusion, not to say sweat, in their tumbled couch of sin. The image had never got further than that. She could not even imagine what any one of the three would have said, or who would say it first.

The question now was how was she going to get away? She was fearful of simply checking out, in case she would run into her husband in the lobby. She could hardly steal out the back way, she would have to pay her bill. Wildly, she cast about: had she anything in her wheelie bag which could disguise her?

She pounded the bed in despair then slipped into something close to catatonia. She had made a complete mess of everything. Dull eyed, she propped herself against her pillows and stared into space. All over this city, people were dying, mating, having babies, drinking, having rows, making up rows, thrilling to the touch of new loves. Here was Emily Pugh, wasting the good life God gave her. There were no words adequately condemnatory for her actions.

And it had been a good life until now, it had really. Everyone said so. She was lucky, they were lucky. Free as breezes, they could pop off on holiday, any time Terry could get a few days together, without worrying about babyminders or kennels. They had enough money to eat out a lot. Terry's expenses bought them all kinds of little luxuries. They were planning to add a small conservatory to the back of the bungalow when Terry had time to organize a few quotations. (July was the sale season and they had missed this July, but what harm, wouldn't there be another sale at Christmas.) And now with both of them looking forward to lump sums and nice pensions, to the envy of the whole town, they would travel a little, maybe enjoy a small cruise. And there was the china cabinet sagging with the weight of all the little presents Terry had brought her from his travels. Considerate. All Emily's friends used the word. Terry was considerate.

If Breda bucked the trend sometimes by using words like pernickety, well that just went to show that she didn't choose to know what Terry was really like.

And who outside knew what went on inside a marriage in the first place . . .

Emily and Terry's wedding day had been perfect. The sun shone, the reception ran like clockwork, the speeches were so far from embarrassing they were almost anodyne, no one got drunk. And when they left on honeymoon (for sentiment's sake to walk again in the Highlands, plus Terry had managed to get a very good deal from the travel agent in the town) Emily was satisfied that no one could ever augment the ragtag folklore of the pubs with stories from the wedding of the Pughs.

As for the honeymoon itself, that had not been perfect, but they were sensible about it. Both Emily and Terry were adult enough to know that expectations of honeymoons were seldom fulfilled. So they wore themselves out with hiking and contented themselves at night with making plans for the next day and falling asleep comfortably in one another's arms.

And somehow, that state of affairs had stretched out and on, long after they came home. Until it became a permanent arrangement. They slept together in a double bed. They loved one another with cuddles and hugs. But neither seemed to need anything more.

Frequently, almost guiltily, Emily thanked God that this was so. She was contented. She did not miss children. And never having known it, she certainly did not miss sex. Particularly when, as frequently happened in the staff room, she heard about the goings on in other marital couches, spelt out in the most appallingly gory and ribald manner. She felt clean and neat and self-contained. Inviolate. Glad she did not have to be party to the type of thing that was obviously going on in the penthouse suite overhead. (Which now sounded like purring. Raucous purring. What did people get up to these days?)

Mrs Pugh was not stupid nor backward and sometimes, at the beginning certainly, she worried that Terry might not be as satisfied with their quiet state of affairs as she was. Timidly, she questioned him about it from time to time but he always brushed aside her misgivings. 'Not at all, pet. Sure, aren't we grand? And aren't we a bit over the hill now to be thinking along those lines?' She and Terry had both been over thirty when they were married. They were now in their fifties.

Mrs Pugh sat bolt upright in the plush new bed in Finbar's, so quickly that the television's remote control device slid to the floor and made not a sound on the thick carpeting. She forced herself to face a possibility she had up to now brushed aside as being too ridiculously full of psychobabble to be taken seriously.

All her magazines, her new magazines, were filled with articles about the male menopause. It did exist, screamed the headlines. It rendered men, scraped off veneers of content- ment and maturity, forced them into a type of self-examin- ation they had studiously avoided until they hit a wall of loss – of hair, of energy, of ambition, of interest in their spouses. They saw wasted lives funnelling ever faster towards the void of death. Now that she faced consideration of the condition, Mrs Pugh, who prided herself on never being less than fair, could quite see why so many of them fell into the arms of willing, life-affirming women younger than themselves. And the fall was made easy. Emily did not need a magazine to confirm the legion presence of single and disappointed women who patrol the cities and towns and lobbies of hotels like Finbar's waiting and watching for opportunities. If her instincts were right, hadn't that T-shirt woman in the door- way of the bar downstairs been doing just that?

Was this what had happened to her Terry? And was it her fault?

She thought back to just three months ago. They were happy, were they not? Or were they?

She was certainly not happy now. The supports under her own life, which she had thought so broad and secure, had shrunk to the dimensions of the sharpened tip of a fence post, so that now she teetered this way and that, bound to fall in the gales which assailed her, with only chance dictating in which direction.

Groggy from all this thinking and unaccustomed emotion, she stumbled into the bathroom. Perhaps a nice soak, she thought. That always relaxed her and she would be enabled to think more clearly. At least she was safe for the present. Terry did not know she was in Finbar's and if she calmed down and worked things out properly, he need never know she had made such a fool of herself.

If she had made a fool of herself . . .

She ran the bath, added Finbar's bath foam from its classy little bottle, undressed, and to avoid catching sight of her fifty-year old nakedness slipped quickly into the warm, camouflaging water.

There had been other worrying signs. If she was truly honest, Emily would admit that her relationship with her husband had over the years become a little pat, one-third communication, two-thirds sludge underneath that neither cared to disturb. She had frequently found him to be remote, even while they were sharing a meal or doing something together they both enjoyed, like planning their garden. On the occasions when she had mentioned this he had always been ready with a logical answer. Too ready and too logical.

He had problems on his mind which were nothing to do with her, pet. His job. His immediate superior, whom he detested. A planned sales campaign in which all the senior reps were being pitted against one another in competition. And she had allowed both of them to be content with these answers. Ignoring tiny prods of conscience, she had told herself that to probe further was to pry. Individuals within marriage did not cease to be individuals and were entitled to individual thoughts, even worries. If it were anything serious, if he was genuinely not happy, Terry would tell her. Of course he would.

She forced herself now to banish all this rí-rá and to empty her mind. To think of woolly clouds in a blue sky. Of marigolds. She was almost successful, the warm, soft, drifting bubbles acting so soporifically that she found herself sliding towards a pleasant doze.

Oh God! Emily slopped water and bubbles all over the floor. Her laptop! Where was her laptop? She had left her laptop back in Room 106.

She scrambled out of the bath, uncaring now about wrinkles or sags, rushed back into the bedroom, leaving dark black footprints on the pristine pile of the carpet. Then had to rush back to fetch a towel to dry herself. In her fright, with her legs damp, she couldn't get her tights on and pulled violently, severely laddering one side of them. She had no spares.

This time above all others for it to happen. Emily subsided against the rim of the bath and the tears came.

Not for long. The problem was too urgent.

Emily finished dressing, minus her tights. She telephoned Mr Pugh's room. No reply. Thank God. There was still time.

Almost giddy with relief, she searched for the key. Where was his room key? Yes, here it was, still in the pocket of her skirt, thank God again.

She eschewed the lift and walked up the flight of stairs between the first and second floors. On the first bend she faltered. Descending towards her was a slim young man with bleached hair, wearing trainers and gold-coloured trousers. He was shouting into a mobile telephone. All Mrs Pugh's instincts told her that he had to be American and wouldn't know her – or care a jot that the words 'fool' and 'stupid' were written large throughout the pink ABCs on her bare shins. As she passed him, she heard – she could not avoid hearing, he was screeching— 'We lost the order, everything, all because of her goddam father . . .'

The fire door to Mr Pugh's corridor was heavy, glassed. It swung shut behind her with a heavy thud. Assuming an insouciance she did not feel, Mrs Pugh hurried along the corridor. But before she could reach Mr Pugh's door, the lift opened and the pair of Americans she had observed previously in the lobby emerged. Looking right and left as though unsure of where they were, they seemed finally to make a decision and came towards her. Emily's stride had not broken. She nodded towards them in what she hoped was a pleasantly casual manner, inserted Mr Pugh's key, opened his door and closed it behind her. She took a deep, shuddering breath.

Then another moment close to hysteria. She had thought the laptop to be somewhere near the bed, but it took a few seconds for her to locate it. Here it was, against the wall, right beside her feet.

She snatched it up and swivelled, opening the door again. To find her husband's amazed eyes staring into hers. His key was in his hand. (There must have been a spare.) His other hand clutched a carrier bag. He was not wearing a tie.

This much Emily Pugh took in before a type of mist clouded her vision. She stumbled and might have fallen, if it hadn't been for her husband's sustaining grasp. He led her to the bed, made her lie down. It was difficult to know who was more shaken, he or she. Did she want a glass of water, would she like him to call a doctor?

No, she was fine, really she was. She was grand. She'd be grand in a minute.

Neither as yet had mentioned the big question.

Emily recovered her strength. Stared up at her husband with eyes wide as an owl's. Now that her trap was sprung, she was speechless. She left the next move to him because she was incapable of any.

'What were you doing here, Emily?' he asked, when they ran out of reasons for a pause.

Emily started to weep for the second time in less than ten minutes. She was not a weeper, her husband knew this, therefore he was alarmed beyond reason. 'Emily, pet, please . . .' At the same time he seemed more dismayed than even this bizarre occasion warranted.

Emily noticed and stopped weeping, sitting up and finding strength.

'Where were you on the Spring Tear? I rang the hotel in Cavan. You weren't there—'

She stopped because Terry Pugh, electrified, was staring at her. He was making no attempt to rebut, a fact which collapsed Emily's anger. She stared back at him, realizing that underneath all the planning and the suspicion, a small shoot of hope had flourished. It now died swiftly and left no trace.

'Tell me the truth, Terry,' Emily whispered, aghast.

Her husband actually staggered a little, as he walked to a chair in the corner and like a closing concertina, folded into it, his carrier bag falling from his fingers. He stared at her again and suddenly, Emily didn't want to hear it. She sprang off the bed and ran to him, throwing herself on her knees in front of him.

'Don't, don't tell me. Whatever it was, don't tell me, I don't want to know. Let's just go home, the two of us. Let's go home. Our house – what about the conservatory? Pet, pet, our little conservatory . . .' She clutched at his hands, covered them with kisses. 'Whatever it was, pet, don't worry. We've been together so long, we get on so well, don't we? Don't we, pet? Whatever it was, I don't care, I really don't. Please, just come home with me.'

He stared at her for what seemed to Emily Pugh like half of a week. Then, gently, very, very slowly, he put her hands aside and stroked them. 'I'm glad, actually. I'm glad it's going to come out. I hated living a lie.'

In the past Mrs Pugh had derided students for using clichés such as *her blood ran cold*. But that is exactly what happened to her now. As she sat back on her heels, horror flushed through the small veins of her cheeks and turned immediately to ice. This ice began to spread from her cheeks to other parts of her body, particularly quickly, it seemed, to the backs of her hands and her forearms. There was no way now to stop what was coming. She knew it. It was punishment for her own transgressions. She had been smug. She had been not sympathetic enough to the marital travails of her staff room colleagues. She steeled herself to accept what God ordained to be her lot henceforth. From somewhere, she dredged sound. 'Do I know her?'

In reply, Mr Pugh reached down to his carrier bag. He

took out of it a wig, false bosoms, a red dress, patent-leather waspie, high heels, suspender belt, padded bra and black stockings. Emily stared, not understanding this needless cruelty. 'They're her clothes?' she whispered. 'Why are you showing me her clothes?'

Never taking his eyes off her, Mr Pugh shook his head.

'They're mine, pet. They belong to me.'

Almost in wonder, Mrs Pugh reached out to touch the shiny red fabric of the dress. Realization. Then relief. Ice dissolved and was swept away in waves, floods, tides of relief. No other woman. No rival. No tart, fancy woman, trollop, harlot, strumpet or doxy. This was nothing. Emily Pugh was modern. She could be inclusive. Emily Pugh could happily take this on the chin. Where there had been an abyss, there was a volcano of joy. Her voice bubbled and cracked with joy. 'Is that all, pet? Is that all?' The wonder of it. He was lost and now is found. Emily wept again and through her tears, thanked God aloud and thanked Him again for His mercy and goodness. She thanked Terry for being her husband, told him over and over again that she loved him, loved him, loved him . . .

Mr Pugh, staggered less at his wife's unexpected acceptance than at her unprecedented lack of decorum, backed against the nearest wall as though confronted with a dangerous predator. But Emily followed him, threw her arms around his neck and wept even harder. So he gave in and wept too.

Mr and Mrs Pugh talked late into the night and probably for the first time in their lives. At four minutes past five in the morning, in Room 106 of Finbar's Hotel, Mr Pugh, dressed ceremonially in his red regalia and high heels, took his wife in his arms, and over the next half-hour they became finally and truly married.

The Penthouse

TARZAN'S IRISH ROSE

The minute she walked into Finbar's Nellie could tell they recognized her. It wasn't so much the way heads turned in the foyer as the gradual numbing of conversation, as if it had been sucked into a tunnel. Imagine! She had thought no one would remember. It was good to be back on the ould sod. The stiffness in her limbs melted, she flashed a smile at some stuffed monkeys perched on armchairs and strode across the floor to the desk. 'The top of the morning to ye. I believe you have a room for me.'

The young lady eyed her oddly. Probably a bit awestruck. She ought to be nice to her fans. 'A little place to lay my head, darling. Nellie O'Meara, the name is.'

The girl's gaze travelled slowly from her toes to the top of her head. Her painted nails pawed a reservations book. Was she a wee bit gormless, maybe? Either that or English. When she finally found her voice, it was a chalky scrap, mangled with modulation – gutter Dublin with a bit of London posh sprayed over the top: 'We seem to have you down for the penthouse.'

A penthouse? At Finbar's? Nellie gave a splutter of mirth. Well, she had asked for their finest accommodation, had she not? 'Oh, nothing but the best for Nellie O'Meara.' She tossed her furs and the reception manager ducked as the irritable face of a very old ferret or fox sailed through the air on its vacant bodysuit.

'Excuse me, madam.' The one sidled past her. Her heels skittered on the marble floor as she fled.

*

'A problem, Máire? What sort of a problem?' Fiona was not pleased to be disturbed. She had been just about to celebrate the end of her third month in the hotel business with a nice little score. Now she had to scatter her precious white powder, tut-tutting about the way no one bothered with dusting any more.

'Well, you know that bit of awkwardness about the penthouse this morning. We couldn't let you-know-who have it because it had been reserved. The party who booked it has just arrived.'

'And?'

'It's a crazy old lady. She doesn't look as if she has the price of a pint, never mind the penthouse. Frankly, I don't think she's the right sort for Finbar's.'

Fiona looked at her new front-of-house manager as if she was snot on her sleeve. 'Frankly, my dear, that makes two of you. Are you telling me you can't sort out some old biddy? Make yourself useful soothing our celebrity guest. Tell him the penthouse is his and I'll go and deal with the problem. As usual.'

Nellie was relieved when a different girl appeared. This one was a wild, lovely Irish girl, never mind the peroxide locks. She glanced at the reservations book and then came to Nellie all smiles.

'I'm Fiona, proprietor of Finbar's. There's been a bit of confusion. We had you down for the penthouse but that has been requested by a celebrity. We have a lovely room all ready for you. Shane here will take your bags and we'll send you up a cup of tea, with the compliments of Finbar's.'

Nellie put her head on one side. 'Oh, a celebrity? Now what class of a celebrity would that be?'

'Well, he has requested confidentiality, but I'm sure I can trust you to be discreet about our famous American guest.' She leaned across, girlish and scented, and whispered.

Nellie examined her shoes. Lovely shoes, they were. They didn't make them like that any more. You couldn't get a decent pair for love nor money since the war. 'I don't know would I let my room go to a Yank.'

'Oh, now,' Fiona coaxed. 'He's not just any American. He is an icon.'

'An icon, is it? And what sort of rubbish do you think you're dealing with here?'

Fiona's expression told her. She saw now the kind she was. Not wild and lovely at all, despite the leather catsuit, but convent-school-and-selvage-stitched-arsehole written all over her. She put a hand on the girl's arm. 'Do you know what I'm going to tell you, darling?'

Fiona tried to move away but Nellie's nails had fastened on her flesh. 'Don't fuck with me, you lard-faced little cunt. I'll have the accommodation that was booked for me. Penthouse indeed! Dosshouse, more like.' Nellie smiled regally at her now rapt audience. She took the key from the girl's frozen fingers.

On the way up in the lift she could see Shane, the porter lad, trying not to smile. Good-looking young buck, though the Edwardian get-up didn't quite go with the earring in his ear. Gay, of course, but all the good-looking ones were nowadays. She got a fit of the giggles herself. Fancy Finbar's getting notions! Mind you, it had changed. The mouldy oul' rugs and curtains were gone. Everything was shiny now, glass everywhere – no comfort or privacy. In the old days, there wasn't even a lift. She had asked for the cheapest room then, and she remembered the long trudge up rickety stairs with her suitcase, praying to the Virgin that there wouldn't be rats. When she saw the room she wanted to run home to her mother. But even if she did run home, it wouldn't be to her mother, but to Billy Shaughnessy and the pigs. She had sat on the edge of the bed and bawled her eyes out, and then, when that was out of the way, she dried her face determinedly, put on her dance dress, took her sponge bag out into the freezing corridor to look for a bathroom, and there painted on to her frightened face a set of features so bold it would give bad thoughts to a bishop.

'So, what's this penthouse like?' she asked the porter.

'Deadly,' he said.

Deadly. Well that would stand to reason. All the same, she got an awful fright when she saw it. She just stood there with her mouth hanging open, gazing all around her.

'Are you all right, madam?' the lad asked her.

She felt unsteady as she waded across the carpet and peered out of a porthole window at a view of mammoth yellow cranes munching the old parts of the city in a leisurely vegetarian fashion. 'Where's the bed?' There was a grand piano and a wooden hot tub like they had in the Wild West films, sitting right in the middle of the floor, but there didn't seem to be any place to sleep.

'Which one?' he beamed. 'Master or junior? There's two bedrooms and three bathrooms. The third one's for the Secret Service.'

'The Secret Service?' The old woman looked bewildered.

'International politicians always stay in the penthouse but they don't like sharing a john with the goons.' He showed her the kitchen and its fridge stocked with full-sized bottles of champagne. 'You can get anything you want up here,' he added. 'Not just regular room service. You can sit here thinking up weird things that you'd like, and it's our pleasure to find them for you. It's a special service that goes with the penthouse. We pride ourselves on that.'

'Like what?' she wondered. They must have knocked out all the rooms on the top floor to make the suite. There was a kitchen, an office with a computer and even a little film screen, a bathroom the size of a skating rink, real gold leaf on the tiles.

Fiona had impressed on the new porter that he must be positive. The truth was, they hadn't really had all that many interesting parties on the top deck in the few months they had been open. Rich, sure, but not newsworthy – not until that old guy from the sixties turned up today. 'Barbecue-flavour popcorn,' he decided. 'Joe Elliot of Def Leppard asked for barbecue-flavour popcorn.' That had happened in the Berkeley Court where Shane worked before, but how was she to know. 'There's a limo service too – your own private limo to take you anywhere you want. Now what can I get you, madam?'

Depressed by the thought of a deaf leopard, she sank onto a sofa covered in mushroom-coloured suede and tried to figure out something she could ask for. 'How much does this cost?'

'Fifteen hundred pounds,' he said.

'A week?'

'No, a night.'

After that she went so silent he thought she must have

died but she was only thinking. 'I'd like a pet,' she said. 'Nothing fancy, just a small kitten. Or a canary would do.'

The boy guffawed. 'If I suggested that to Fiona she'd probably have a canary for you personally. Actually there was some joker smuggled a cat into Finbar's once. In them days it probably would have met its dinner coming up through the floorboards. Things is different now – very different.'

'I'll say,' Nellie murmured. £1,500. Three thousand dollars. Jesus, how did they get away with it? How was she going to pay for it? Last time she had been to Finbar's, she had been charged fifteen shillings for her room by Finbar FitzSimons himself, and it was still robbery. For some reason the kid was hanging around, looking at her sort of expectantly. What was he waiting for? Of course. She had been too long out of the limelight. She picked up a room service menu and signed it with a flourish. 'There you are, son. My autograph.'

*

The celebrity was sulking.

'First there's no goddam penthouse, then there is a penthouse, now there's no penthouse again. What kind of a joint is this anyway?'

He didn't sound like an icon. His voice came out as a sort of low-grade whine, like a fly dying inside a window on a hot day. She still couldn't even be sure if he actually was who he claimed to be. So many things were fake, from breasts to orgasms, that nothing would surprise her. And this guy wouldn't even win a look-a-like competition.

'If you had let us know in advance, sir,' Fiona said. Sir, indeed. She hated having to toady. She longed to let him know that she had handled far bigger celebrities than him in her time – and in ways that would have stiffened the strings of his guitar.

'Hey, you know I can't do that,' he grizzled. 'Press gets wind of where I'm staying, the creeps are climbing all over the place.'

'You can be assured of your privacy at Finbar's,' she promised him. 'In fact, I think you might prefer one of our executive suites. The press is always interested in who's staying in the penthouse. Let me show you our senior executive suite. I really think you'll be impressed.'

'I don't want to be impressed.' He followed her but the whine had risen to electric-drill pitch. 'When I book a suite in a so-called high-class hotel, I want to be fuckin' astounded.'

*

Marooned in her private paradise, Nellie froze like a rabbit on a runway. She scooted as a chandelier rained down diamond light on her. In spite of her little victory, she felt lonely and scared. She couldn't think of anything else to do so she went to her own personal bar and poured herself a large drink. She needed to think. She had spent most of her money on the fare coming over. She had an urge to phone down and tell Fiona she had changed her mind, that she didn't care for the penthouse after all and would take a plain ordinary room, but she wouldn't give the little rip the satisfaction. She had taken a hell of a chance coming to Ireland with nothing in writing but what else was she to do? Spend the rest of her days in a dingy two-room apartment that wouldn't even let her have a cat?

After she had had a second drink, the panic began to

subside. When young, she had believed herself to be a creature of destiny. Why not now? Fate must have led her to the penthouse. Now no one would ever know she was poor, that she had taken to feigning illness in order to get into hospital to get fed and get warm. It was in hospital that she had met old Harold Zadblatt and he told her about the new big-budget movie being made in Dublin with Hugh Grant as W. B. Yeats and Helena Bonham-Carter as Maud Gonne. They need someone to play the old Maud. 'Someone with a bit of style.' The big C had got him by the throat and his voice was like bathwater going down a drain. 'Not one of those hard-bitten broads who has outstayed her welcome as the mother of the bride, but an actress last seen as a youthful beauty. That little prick of a nephew of mine, Ed Horseshit, is producing. Play your cards right, babe, and the part is yours.'

She would show them style. It was right that she should have the penthouse. She grabbed the phone and dialled the number of Proxy Productions. As soon as the contract was signed they would surely give her a little advance – probably insist on paying her hotel expenses. She would throw a party, have a press conference. She paced the room, phone in hand, selecting locations for her photo shoot. When she was a girl, it would have been the hot tub. Perhaps not now. The grand piano! She would be photographed by the grand piano wearing her Balenciaga, her old posters and photo-graphs ranked around her. Mercifully, they had not gone into the hock along with everything else. She crouched down to take her studio shots from her case. Nellie O'Meara, the Flower of Fermoy! Nellie O'Meara, the Wild Irish Rose! And then there fell into her hand a blurred snapshot of Nellie at nineteen – pure as a primrose and sweet as a mountain stream.

'Yes?' A bored voice came on the line.

'I'd like to speak to Ed Horscht.'

'Mr Horscht is very busy. Do you wish to leave a message?' It was one of those stonewalling young women that were around everywhere now. Pre-cast concrete. You couldn't imagine a man ever laying them. Trowelling, maybe.

'He'll be available to me, darling,' she said. 'Tell him it's Nellie O'Meara – the famous Nellie O'Meara.'

At nineteen, Nellie O'Meara was famous for only two things – her beauty and her way with animals. She had hair the colour of a red setter, skin like cream with a hint of strawberry on the cheekbones and a coltish energy that electrified all her movements. She had set her cap at Billy Shaughnessy because he was good-looking and a farmer and she thought it would be lovely spending your life raising creatures. Her own da only owned a pub. When she married him she knew nothing about men and even less about pig farms. She knew about sex all right, growing up in the country, but the poor old sheep and cattle didn't belt each other in order to get themselves excited. So within a month she found out all she ever wanted to know about men and pigs; that men were the real pigs and that their unfortunate namesakes died a horrible bloody death. There was nothing remotely pleasant in her life, except her own reflection in the mirror, so she grabbed a bag and twenty quid from Billy's trouser pocket, hitched a lift on a donkey cart and took the train to Dublin.

She booked into Finbar's because it was the nearest hotel to the train station and she couldn't afford to waste money on a taxi. Christ, what a hole! Light bulbs the colour of cow gum, and the dining room reeking of soup and must. In a way, she was sorry it was changed so much. She had a feeling the key to her old self lay in Finbar's, for that was where everything had begun.

The little bitch was back on the phone. 'I'm afraid Mr Horscht is unavailable at the moment. What did wish to speak to him about?'

'About you losing your job if you don't change your tune. Nellie O'Meara, the name is, and I am playing a very important role in Mr Horscht's new film.'

'I've got the cast list in front of me. Your name is not on it.' The girl's voice was still without expression.

She wondered if girls like that ever felt anything – the joy of being young, the pain of love, the excitement of living. At seventy-three she still felt everything, and right now it was pure panic. She ran to the master bathroom to splash her face with cold water. Four huge mirrors threw back her reflection. She looked hideously old and small. With rattling hands she shook out the contents of her washbag. Sleeping pills! She had brought enough to last a fortnight. She poured herself a glass of water and began cramming the pills into her mouth. As she grunted and gulped she caught sight of her reflection again. Behind the lines and the wispy hair, there was still the ghost of her old self – those lovely cheekbones and sleepy eyes – but what was lost was not just the beauty but the courage of her young self.

'Nellie O'Meara, you should be ashamed of yourself!' she told the mirror. She spat the pills into the sink and ran the tap. 'Ready to throw in the towel because of one small setback. Imagine the mere notion of doing away with your-self just because you can't pay a hotel bill. God would strike you down for such a thought. Young Nellie would have had better sense.'

The young Nellie had refused to let her terror show. She

put on her good dress, went back down the rickety stairs and sat in the smelly residents' lounge. There were two kinds in the lounge – a random assortment of no-hopers coming from or going to the country, girls in trouble or young ones such as herself up from the sticks with no education and no money, plus a few drunks. The other kind were all males of a different order, silent, watchful types, well dressed and cautious with the beer. They were here for one class of business only, to pick up the young girls, green as nettles, and initiate them in the ways of city life. Culchie vultures, she termed them. They assumed it was a one-way transaction, with all the advantage going to them. Nellie knew otherwise. As long as a man owned a wallet, he was worth getting to know.

Back then, it was astonishing the number of men in a city the size of Dublin who knew someone who knew someone who could get you a part. Mostly the only parts on offer were private ones. Nellie didn't care. She was never a fool and was well aware that the path to Hollywood would be interior sprung and stuffed with horsehair. Having a horrible start to your sex life was a great advantage to a girl. It meant that your expectations were low and the temptations were fewer. She knew that if she kept her nerve and avoided falling in love, then sooner or later there really would be someone with a bit of influence. In the meantime, she got a job in the Gresham as a waitress, where the pickings were rich and so were the clients. After two years she met an American who actually worked in films. He took her back to Hollywood and got her some screen tests. To her surprise, she was told to accentuate her Irish accent and throw in all the corny phrases she could find. She was never much of an actress but she was a beauty and she got parts in animal pictures because of her calming way with even the most intractable brutes. Soon she was being suggested for a new Tarzan picture. Being Irish was a help. Tarzan hadn't had a really decent mate since Maureen O'Sullivan. When Gideon Stillbrook took over from Johnny Weismuller as the new Tarzan in 1948 they even wrote a picture specially for her – *Tarzan's Irish Rose*.

It was a gorgeous story. An Irish missionary nun gets separated from her group and is kidnapped by a hostile tribe who tie her to a tree, preparatory to devouring her. The animals she has befriended chase away the savages, who head off for weapons and reinforcements. Tarzan hears her singing hymns and frees her and they flee together, Nellie hitching up her long robes to shin trees and swing across ravines on ropes. She teaches Tarzan his prayers and falls in love with him. They nearly get to grips with one another, but a priest finds the pair of them and hauls her away back to the nuns. The last scene shows Tarzan looking desolate, but finally finding consolation in prayer.

The film was a humdinger and in spite of the fact that there wasn't even a real kiss in it, it was sexy as silk knickers, for the sight of Nellie, with those long, long legs, shinning up a tree with her habit hitched up around her waist caused a lot of crossed legs in the viewing room. She still had the photograph. That was the one MGM used for promotion. Now she took it out of her case, polished it on her sleeve and placed it on top of the piano. It looked so good she was about to sit down at the piano and play a tune to it, but her attention was caught by another picture – of her co-star, Gideon Stillbrook.

Gideon Stillbrook! He had the body of Schwarzenegger and the face of Keanu Reeves. His real name was Harvey

Blumberg and his real dream in life was the manufacture of disposable tableware. Nellie thought it was the nuttiest thing she had ever heard of. 'You mean you eat your dinner and then throw the plate away? Why not have disposable dinners for people on a diet – throw the whole lot away?'

'No, seriously, Nellie.' In spite of his sexy looks, he had a sombre manner, and he was sensitive. 'Synthetic materials are getting cheaper and labour is getting dearer. Day will come when it's cheaper to buy new cups and plates than to hire someone to wash them.'

Those were the best days of her life. She loved Harvey and it was grand to be surrounded by jungle animals. There were no animatronics back then but lions and tigers held little fear for her. If things had been different they could have gone on in Tarzan pictures for the next ten years. If things had been different, she could have married her Tarzan. He was the only man she had ever really cared for. Of course things were never different. They were only the way they were.

All the same, just thinking about her early success made Nellie feel better. She decided to put in a personal appearance at the offices of Proxy and speak to Ed Horscht herself. She had given in too easily. In all probability he was making two pictures at the one time and the girl had a different cast list in front of her. She pulled from her suitcase an emerald-green Balenciaga gown. Really good garments never aged. When she put it on, it didn't quite meet at the back. Her figure was still the same. It just wasn't in the same place. Her tits fell down like schoolboy's socks. She covered the top with a swansdown coatee. Oh, she had had some high old times in that ensemble. That was fifty years ago, but the magic still hung about in the folds of the fabric. She felt good. She felt terrific. If the meeting went well, she would invite everyone back for a party. 'The fact of the matter, girl, is that the suite is yours, paid for or not, and you are going to enjoy it.'

On her way out, she heard music. She followed the sound past the dining room to Fiona's Bar. My God! It was the old residents' lounge, where she spent her miserable first night at Finbar's. She had sat at a table on her own with a lemonade in front of her, advertising her innocence. And sure enough, within ten minutes the men were sniffing around her like dogs at a dung heap.

'Are you all on your own, miss? It's a desperate city for a young girl on her own.'

'Let me buy you a decent drink on a cold night like this. Hotels are terrible expensive. Would you like to come and stay with my sister?'

And all the time Nellie kept her head on one side, that trick she learnt when she was angry but didn't want to give anything away.

'What's your name, miss? You're a very pretty girl. Has anyone ever told you that? What is it that you do for a living?'

And then Nellie spoke for the first time. 'I'm going to be an actress.'

Fiona's was empty now, except for an old American with old yellow American skin the colour of a boiling chicken. Creep, she thought automatically, dismissing him as one of the raincoated package tourists who spend their days clambering on and off buses and trying to find their luggage. He was skinny, as if he had been boiled down for stock, and that architect-designed chair must have been giving his old bones hell, but he would have been a big man once and had a kind of nobility, like some prehistoric toad that has seen other species come and go and rules over his desert rocks. He wore his check jacket like a flag of nations and communed with his cigar, toying with it, tonguing it, eyeing it, tooting on it, in a way that made it look like public sex. She could tell now that the old geezer had money.

Nellie went to the bar and ordered a highball. She did it without thinking, forgetting that no one in Ireland drank cocktails and a request for one would only earn you the barman's contempt and a long glass full of ice and umbrellas, but the young man behind the bar produced a shaker and there followed the reassuring aerobic flourish, the gravelly sloosh that never failed to cheer. She took out her cigarettes and was further heartened when the kid produced a tiny box of matches and lit her up. The matches were blue with gold tips and he left them with her on a little saucer. God, she liked this joint.

The buzz of a perfect cocktail in her mouth, the sound of piano notes being sprinkled over her, made her feel that she was coated in stardust. She could stay here drinking cocktails until her nose went numb. If things didn't work out at Proxy, she could float back up to the penthouse, swallow some Smarties and exit left for heaven. It wasn't such a bad way to go.

The old man called for another drink. Nellie thought that sounded like a fine idea. 'And the same again for me, son,' she told the barman; 'God be with you, and His holy mother.'

She looked around, smiling, as the barman made her second drink. When she caught the beady stare of the old American, she even gave him the eye. He frowned at her sharply. Well, fuck you, she thought. And your holy mother.

'Haven't we met before?' he said.

'No, and you need a new scriptwriter,' she said, but there was something about his voice.

'Blumberg's the name,' he enunciated heavily. 'Harvey Blumberg.'

'Tarzan!' She gaped at him in astonishment.

The pleats of his face folded even closer as he tried to place her.

'It's Nellie,' she prompted. 'Nellie O'Meara.'

'Good Christ! Aren't you dead? No, wait, I saw you a few years back on some dumb-assed ad on cable.'

'I'm here to make a picture.'

His croaky laugh made a dry percussion against the music of the cocktail shaker. 'Of what? Dorian Gray?'

'No, it's a biggie. About Yeats and Maud Gonne.'

'Oh, sure, I heard about that. *Gonne with the Wind*, they're calling it. What are you playing?'

'I'm playing Maud in later life.'

He stirred his drink with his finger. 'Oh, Nellie, I doubt it. It's all over the place. Martha's got that part – Martha Vernon.'

Nellie felt shock seeping into her bones. 'There must be a mistake. She's not even Irish.'

He laughed his slow, deep, death-rattle laugh. 'Neither was Maud Gonne, if I remember rightly.' Nellie began to tremble. The part was hers – well, practically hers. She had been promised the role – or at any rate that it had not yet been cast. She would sue. But she had nothing on paper. And that included cash.

'Aw, Nell.' Tarzan regarded her with compassion. 'It's a lousy, dirty business. You should have quit years ago.'

'Like you?' A tear fell down her jaw. She tried to sniff it back but it went on rolling. 'Or did you make a comeback?

Is that what you're doing here? There was a time when everyone in Ireland was writing a novel. Now everyone is making a picture.'

'I'm not making a picture, but my wife is. The Coen boys are shooting here – *Dirty O'Gill and the Little People*.'

'You're here with Martha?'

He shook his head. 'That ended a very long time ago.' He leaned back against the wooden counter of Fiona's Bar with a smug look. 'I'm on my honeymoon.'

'Oh, yeah? You and your cigar.'

'Yes, well, a woman is only a woman . . .'

'You're having me on, Harvey Blumberg.'

'I just got married for the fifth and final time.'

'So where is this wife?'

'Nikita's in our room. We only just arrived. She's having a little sulk. She wanted the penthouse because she heard Brad Pitt slept there, but some other jerk booked it.'

'I suppose she's some young bimbo. What is it with old guys, always looking for some beautiful young girl to flatter their ego?'

Harvey shook his head. 'You've got it all wrong, Nellie.'

'Hah! I suppose you're going to tell me it's true love.'

'No, Nellie. No, I'm not. I'm too old for love and men don't marry younger women to flatter their ego, they marry 'em to titillate their prick. I've lived a long time and I've done a lot of things and I can tell you something. When all's said and done, there's only one thing in life matters and that's a good fuck.'

'In your dreams, Tarzan,' she said sourly. 'At your age it would take a parachute to get it up.'

He looked gravely away and she thought she had offended him, but he was watching a girl coming through the door.

'I've got one,' he said softly. She wore a tight black leather dress and high black leather boots and neither seemed to cover anything that mattered. Her hair was big and blonde and her lips as wet as a squashed tomato. She barely glanced at Harvey as she went to the bar.

Nellie pointed. Harvey nodded. Nellie looked disbelieving. Harvey made a rubbing motion with thumb and forefinger. Cash.

When the girl and the barman had finished flirting she sat beside Harvey, looking bored.

'Had a nice rest, Nikita, honey?' he said. 'What would you like to do now?'

'I'm going out,' she said. 'I need some money.'

'Sure, sweetie.' He took out his wallet and removed a wad. 'Want me to come with you?' She gave him a look of contempt and snatched the cash. 'I'll see you back here at eight.' She got up to leave and then, as an afterthought, composed the squashed tomato and presented it. Nellie saw the girl wince very slightly as the granite fissure of Harvey Blumberg's lips attached itself. The girl put up with this as long as she could and then drew back bad-temperedly and stalked out of the room. Harvey watched her retreating bottom with reverence. When Nellie caught his eye he put a hand over his mouth and yodelled softly.

'She's making a fool of you,' Nellie said. 'Can't you see she doesn't love you?'

Harvey shrugged.

'How can you have a relationship with someone who doesn't like you?'

'That drink probably doesn't like you, but you seem to be getting along just fine with it.'

'Oh, grow up, Harvey Blumberg. At least what's in my

242

glass is the real thing. There's nothing genuine about her. I'll bet her breasts are made of styrofoam.'

'Silicone,' he corrected.

'You mean, you know that, and you don't care?'

'I don't know from nothing,' he laughed. He signalled the barman for two more drinks. 'These days a man can ask a girl to remove her dress, but it's still not decent to ask her to take off her skin off. Anyway, I kind of like the idea of silicone. It's non-biodegradable. Think of it, honey, when she's your age, her breasts will still be sticking up like Mount Vesuvius. Makes me horny just to think of it.'

There was a time when she had made Harvey horny. And vice versa. She couldn't believe that the creaky old buzzard beside was the man she had loved for more than forty years.

'So you're rich, Harvey?' She couldn't think of anything else to say.

'As Croesus.'

'Doing what?'

'Doing what I wanted before some jerk spotted me in a gym and offered to put me on the screen – making paper cups for the catering trade. Freshen up your glass, doll?' he said.

'No thanks,' she said. 'I've got business to do.' She snapped her fingers at the boy behind the bar. 'Fetch me the penthouse limo.' She enjoyed doing that. Even Harvey looked impressed.

As she waited for the car behind the glass doors in the lobby she looked out at the broad grey sweep of the city – soft sky, grey buildings, river curdling like grosgrain silk. It was a beautiful day but blue skies never suited this city. The bright sunshine seemed to hurt its eyes. It was too harsh for her eyes too, and she screwed them up, feeling suddenly old and defeated. When she opened them to a veil of sunspots, there was a woman watching her. She looked as if she knew her. Well, Nellie knew her too – knew a lot more than she would ever have guessed. She knew from the lacquered perfection of her grooming that she'd lived in America, but she wasn't American. Nellie could tell a mile off the fresh and indignant look of an Irish complexion. She gave the woman a friendly wink. 'Ah, we all come back in the end. Well, they say women always love a bastard.'

The woman stared at her in amazement. Maybe Nellie should have said bitch, in the case of a city. Dublin sure was a bitch. The woman continued to stare. In fact she nearly seemed to be in shock. At last Nellie copped. Another autograph hunter! There was she in her Balenciaga and the creature was rooted to the spot by the sight of the famous Nellie O'Meara in all her glory. Oh, lovely, lovely fame. Why had it stayed away so long when she loved it so much she could eat it with a spoon? And why, in the name of God, had she come out without a pen?

'Excuse me, darling,' she edged closer to her admirer. 'Could I possibly trouble you for a p—'

'Of course,' the creature cut in, stupefied with embarrassment, as people often are in the presence of the famous. 'I hope your luck changes,' she whispered at Nellie as she thrust something into her hand.

This time it was Nellie's turn to stare. How on earth did she know? But then the limousine pulled in outside and Nellie moved through the glass doors as the driver got out to open the door for her. Nellie turned to sign her name but the woman had remained inside the lobby. 'Hey, you forgot your pen!' Nellie called back to her. But when she looked in her hand it wasn't a pen she held at all, but a pound coin.

'Where is everyone?' she asked the chauffeur as she slid into the glossy black sarcophagus. 'There's hardly any traffic. Don't they have a rush hour in this city?'

'There's an international friendly in Landsdowne Road,' he told her. 'A testimonial. That might explain it. Maybe there's even a tiger escaped from the zoo. You know, ma'am, I just think there might be. I was talking on my own radio on the time, but I'm sure I heard something about a tiger escaping on the news. Ha, ha! Must be the Celtic tiger.'

'It's all a zoo,' Nellie murmured. She was beginning to feel sleepy after her cocktails. 'Tigers are the least of it.'

The first person Nellie walked into in Proxy was Martha Vernon. It was a shock. Finding the cast of her old life assembled like this was like going to her own funeral. The other shock was the way Martha was dressed. Apart from the dinosaur complexion, she looked like a teenager. She wore old jeans and a pale pink cashmere twinset. Her hair was bobbed like a girl's. She was a big woman but she had always had the trick of looking like a gamine. Up to the age of fifty, she had worn her hair in plaits. Nellie's confidence began to ebb. She realized she was dressed all wrong. You didn't wear designer clothes in the day any more – especially not fifty-year-old ones. Just looking at Martha one knew she was rich. And in the same way, Nellie realized at once that anyone looking at her would know she hadn't a bean.

'Martha!' After the first moment of recoil, she managed to sweep her old enemy into an embrace. 'Gorgeous to see you! Everyone I've met all day is a film star. Dear, dirty Dublin has turned into Sunset Boulevard.'

Martha received the tribute coolly. She was still cold and hard enough to sink the *Titanic*. 'Call me Maud,' she said.

'I've got to get used to that now – and a wig that I shall sell on to Joan Collins for her declining years.'

Nellie managed to conceal her alarm. 'You up for the part of Maud too?' She went to the reception desk. 'I have an appointment with Mr Horscht,' she said bravely. 'Tell him Nellie O'Meara, star of *Tarzan's Irish Rose*.'

'A Rose born to blush unseen,' Martha muttered as she nibbled girlishly on a fingernail.

'Mr Horscht is out to an early dinner,' the girl said.

Nellie swallowed her disappointment. 'Well, Martha, may the best man win.'

'She has, sweetie,' Martha said.

'Signed, sealed and delivered?' Hope leaked out of Nellie's voice.

'Signed and sealed,' Martha preened. 'I have yet to deliver.'

Nellie fought off the old, bewildered look that she knew sat on her face. 'Well,' she said. 'I suppose I'm relieved, really. At my age, I prefer to live off my memories.'

Martha gave her girlish giggle. 'Oh, darling! I do hope there's something more than that in the piggy bank.'

'You bet,' Nellie said. 'But nothing that matters more. I don't imagine any other film could quite match up to *Tarzan's Irish Rose*. Wasn't it wonderful, Martha?'

'Of course, sweetie, and wasn't it a shame?'

'Let me buy you a drink to celebrate your new picture.' Nellie tried to knock her off course.

'I would, sweetie, but I have to dash. I'm due for a photo call. Actually, I'm late already. You can't get a taxi for love or money in this squalid little city.'

'Take my limo,' Nellie said. 'My driver will take you

anywhere you want. Come and have a drink with me afterward. I'm in the penthouse at Finbar's.'

There was more than a little satisfaction in that, even if Nellie had to walk all the way back. The city had changed almost beyond recognition and she kept getting lost. No longer any Nelson's Pillar for a marker, and she wasn't helped by the tears that blurred her eyes. Damn and blast Martha Vernon. She had taken everything that mattered to Nellie. Why did she have to take her memories? *Tarzan's Irish Rose* had been a hit – at least until some American bishop protested at the notion of a nun showing her legs. In no time there were priests denouncing it from the pulpit all over the world, forbidding the faithful to see it under pain of mortal sin. Distribution got hit on the head, and although the picture had a cult following for some years it was the end of Nellie's career. MGM terminated her contract. Harvey, out of loyalty, resigned and asked Nellie to marry him. She would have married the big lump, but she was married already. In less than a year, Harvey was replaced by Lex Barker in *Tarzan's Magic Fountain*, and Nellie was replaced as Harvey's bride by an insipid blonde, name of Martha Vernon.

By the time she got back she was worn out and had taken another wrong turning. She arrived at the back of the hotel instead of the front and wouldn't you know, for all their penthouse and fancy exterior, it had stacks of garbage bags outside, just like anywhere else. There was a poor little cat pawing at the rubbish.

'Here, puss,' she said. Actually, it wasn't a little cat. It was the largest cat she had ever seen.

The cat turned and smiled at her. She was delighted by

that show of teeth. It was the first genuine smile she had seen since she arrived in Ireland. 'Good fellow.' She clapped her hands. The cat opened its jaws even wider and roared. That set her back a bit. 'Aw, cut the crap, pussy. You're not really mean – only hungry. You just come with me.'

The cat attempted another protest but Nellie had always had a way with animals. It merely shook its head to keep its dignity and padded after her. 'Now, stick with me and stay quiet,' she instructed. 'We'll go in the back way. I get the feeling they're kind of down on dumb beasts and smart old broads in this joint.'

There was a private lift for the penthouse. She had got the animal settled, except for its tail, when some drunk appeared and attempted to climb in after them.

'This lift is for the penthouse,' she said sharply. 'It is not for the use of regular clients.'

'Don't you know who I am?' The man spoke in a muted American whine. 'Do I look to you like a regular client?' He was a bit spooky, hair all over the place and chewed-looking clothes.

'Frankly, no, you don't,' she said. 'You look like a low-life. I'm surprised they let you past the door of a respectable establishment.'

'Madam, I'll have you know that the penthouse is mine by rights. I am—!' He stopped and gulped. He appeared to have forgotten his name. His eyes seemed about to pop out of his head. 'Do I see what I think I see?'

'Indeed you do!' she snapped. 'You see before you the famous Nellie O'Meara, star of *Tarzan's Irish Rose.*' She swished the tail at him, backed into the lift and shut the door in his face.

'Isn't this fun?' she said to the cat. 'I haven't had as much fun in half a century.' The cat was laughing too, showing all those marvellous teeth. Its yellow eyes, though, were small and full of murder. It raised a paw, showing a freshly sharpened set of Elm-Street-Freddie fives. 'Oh, back off, you big ape.' She swatted him with her handbag. 'There's no decent dining on an old bird like me. You'll get a proper dinner soon.'

Back in her suite she rang for room service. 'Penthouse here. I want something from the menu. I'll have the sirloin steak. Twenty pounds, please. No, I did not say ounces. Oh, and I want it raw. To drink? About three gallons of fresh milk. Yes, that's right. Just bring it in a bucket. Oh, and tell the boy not to come in. I'm having a bath. Just knock on the door and leave it outside.'

The cat was getting the feel of the place. It paced by the window and then, as cats do, ran up the curtains. Nellie chortled as the swagged drapery transformed itself to tapers. The animal did not like this loss of face. It shredded the film screen, then sharpened its claws on the mushroom-suede sofa and let out a mighty bellow.

*

'Fiona!' Shane rushed into her private office without knocking. 'There's something funny going on in the penthouse. That oul' one!'

'Not her again!' Fiona snapped.

'You'd want to hear the roars out of her. And she's after ordering up half a cow – raw.'

'Primal therapy. They're all into it in America. And the meat will be for some sort of Californian beauty treatment. As you should be aware, guests can do anything they want in the penthouse. Now make yourself scarce or I'll give you primal therapy.'

*

Nellie watched, enchanted, as the cat lapped up the milk, kicking huge scoops back down its throat with its doormat-sized tongue, its eyes half-closed with pleasure. It took the meat to the bedroom, grinding gore into the embroidered linen bedspread. When it had finished eating, it climbed off the bed and selected a thick white rug. Squatting slightly, it raised its tail and peed. Nellie laughed delightedly. She had never seen such a river. Not since the time Errol Flynn . . . oh, but that was a story she had promised never to repeat. Steam rose off the sodden mat and the penthouse filled with a strange pungent odour. The suite was losing its minimalist look. This was much better. It was getting to resemble the jungle. As if in agreement the animal climbed back onto the bloody bed, rolled on its back and purred.

Nellie could use some dinner herself. It was after eight and she hadn't eaten all day. She glanced at the room service menu but she didn't fancy anything on offer. She craved all the things she hadn't been able to afford in years – scallops, duck, asparagus. She wondered if she could rely on puss to behave if she left him alone. She was contemplating this when there was a knock at her door. Must be the porter wanting his trolley back. She closed the bedroom door care-fully before wheeling the implement to the exit. Good God! As soon as she opened the door, she had an urge to slam it again. It was Martha Vernon.

'I decided to take you up on your invitation, sweetie. I'm impressed. You really are in the penthouse.'

'Of course I am,' Nellie said. 'Didn't I say so? I was just on my way down to dinner.'

'Lucky you, not having to worry about your figure any more! But you did invite me, so you can pour me a glass of champagne.' Her bones crackled as she tiptoed around the lounge. 'Actually, I wanted to know your secret. Rooms like this are for the rich. Last I heard of you, you were short of your rent money. Hey?' She paused in her prancing. 'What happened up here? The curtains? This place looks like a wild animal's run amok. What's that noise?'

'It's the plumbing.' Nellie opened a bottle of champagne, hoping the pop would divert from the catcall. 'I just had a bath and the water makes a lot of noise draining.'

'What are you up to?' She sniffed. 'What's the smell?'

Nellie drained her glass in a single swallow. The bubbles shot through her head like a comet. 'Bath oil,' she said. 'Patchouli.'

Behind her the animal emitted a low, lonesome moan.

'You've got a scene going in there!' Martha's eyes lit up. 'How lovely, a little scandal!' Nellie tried to hold her back but Martha pushed past her and flung open the door. Her smile stayed in place but her features froze. The cat let out a mighty bellow and crouched for a pounce. Martha tried to scream but could only spring a tiny mew from the back of her throat. Very slowly, she turned her stiff head to Nellie in appeal and then fell on the floor with a thud. The cat licked its lips.

'Naughty puss! You scared her,' Nellie said. 'Now you just stay put or I'll swat you one.'

She dragged Martha into the other bedroom and heaved her on to the bed. Poor thing, she did look awful. Best just leave her to sleep. She shut the door. She didn't want the cat thinking she was dessert. She couldn't take a chance on him misbehaving further, so she ground up some sleepers and mixed them with fresh milk from the fridge. He was getting peckish again and lapped up his nightcap with relish.

By the time she got downstairs the Echo Room was full, but she spotted Harvey at a table on his own. 'Aren't you dining with young what's her name?' She sat down and grabbed a menu.

'Nikita?' He shook his head. He seemed downcast. 'Young women never eat. All they do is wash their hair and fuck.'

'Well, I guess you can't do either at the dinner table. But couldn't she toy with a stalk of celery?'

'Not while she's fucking.' Harvey was heavily engaged with a bottle of wine.

Nellie ordered asparagus and then duck. 'She can't do that without you,' she said cautiously.

'Oh, yes, she can.' He looked at her with hangdog eyes. 'Kita knows I'm always punctual so when she said she'd meet me at eight, she could be sure our room would be empty then. Well, I was here by eight, but in the bar I realized I was wearing odd socks. It happens at my age. I nipped back for a straight pair. She was in bed with the porter. Never even saw me.'

'Shane? Are you sure? I could have sworn that boy was gay.'

'He certainly looked quite sunny when I saw him – what I could see of him,' Harvey said through gritted teeth.

Poor old guy. No matter what he had said earlier, she could tell his heart was busted. It seemed rude to eat under the circumstances but she was starving and the food really was excellent. She wolfed down the delicious meal, feeding him morsels on her fork as she used to do when they were lovers. Funny thing – even thought he looked like a dehydrated toad, he still had good chemistry.

'You like some dessert?' he asked her.

'Let's have a cognac,' she said. 'Not here, though. Come upstairs to my penthouse. I have something to show you.'

'What?' He made no move.

'A surprise.' She winked at him. 'It'll take you back.'

'Aw, Nellie, not that. Not you too.'

'Better than that,' she promised. 'Better even than that with Miss Non-biodegradable-boobs.'

'I'll come with you if I can have a snooze. Can't even get into my own goddam bed.'

*

Harvey let out a yell when he went into the bedroom.

'Big cat, huh?' Nellie was busy fixing the brandies.

'Yeah, she's big. She's also dead, Nellie.'

He had wandered into the wrong bedroom. He was looking at Martha Vernon stretched on the bed.

'Oh, I forgot about her,' Nellie said. 'Don't mind her. She just fainted. There's something else you have to see.'

'I don't mind her,' Harvey said. He had a finger on Martha's neck. 'But she's definitely dead.'

'What'll we do, Harve?' She was scared now. She hooked a hand into Harvey's tweeded elbow. 'Phone the police?'

He let out his slow chuckle. 'No, doll. Phone the studio. With Martha gone, the part of Maud is definitely yours.'

A slow rumble came from behind them. 'Good Christ! What was that?'

Still clutching his arm, she led him through to the bedroom. The tranquillized cat blinked and yawned.

'Holy carnivore!' Harvey gazed in awe.

Nellie smiled proudly. 'Isn't he wonderful? Doesn't it take you back?'

Harvey approached the beast with caution. The animal tried a snarl but it turned into another yawn. 'All the way,' Harvey said gleefully. 'You know something? That jungle smell! I'd forgotten. It really gets the testosterone going. If there was a tree in the goddam room, I'd swing from it.'

'There's a chandelier,' Nellie pointed out.

'Ah, to hell with that, I've done all that. There's just one thing Tarzan never got to do in those movies.'

'I'm all yours,' she said. 'But I'm not Nikita.'

'In this light, baby,' he said, 'you look a million dollars. Anyway, I've got a confession to make. Sex with a young broad isn't all it's cracked up to be. When I go swimming I like to get my feet wet, but these babes won't go on the pill. If you don't wear a rubber, they get pregnant and you never know who the father is.'

She was glad she hadn't been able to fasten up her dress, because it fell to the floor at the touch of a single hook. She and Harvey did likewise. 'Well, you're safe with me,' she promised. 'It's Jurassic Park in there.'

*

In the dark, the driver of the limousine didn't get a good look at the three passengers climbing into his car. Then he glanced in his mirror. 'Suffering Jaysus! Get that thing out of here.'

'Drive!' Nellie said. 'If you don't drive, he'll get angry. You wouldn't like him when he's angry.'

They had to climb the gate to get into the zoo. They used the driver's tow-rope to make the tiger a lead. Leo, they had named him. Leo, after Leopold Bloom, another innocent pilgrim in a spiteful city on a summer's day. They had planned to tie him to his cage and then head back. Back where? Harvey had no desire to return to Finbar's and Nellie couldn't really stay – not after Leo had taken a little rest-stop on the bed. Besides, she had completed her business there. She left a message on the answerphone at Proxy to say that Martha Vernon had passed peacefully away, adding the number of her own agent. She had also left a note for Fiona.

'Can you still climb?' Harvey asked Nellie.

'I climbed the gate, didn't I?'

'See that tree. Looks like a real easy one. What about your good dress, though?' Nellie tied the Balenciaga around her waist and began to scale the branches. Harvey whistled. Her legs were not what they used to be, but they still went all the way up. Nellie got about a third of the way and clung to a bough. Her heart was in her mouth, but it had been in her boots too long. Harvey shinned up painfully behind her. When he got a few branches higher he put down a hand and hauled her to a lofty limb. They reached a fork and rested. The summer sky was spread above them for a canopy – indigo velvet, sprigged with sparklies. Harvey put a hand over his mouth and yodelled. He was answered at once with grunts and whirrs and howls. He felt utterly at peace. King of paper cups and lord of the earth!

'Nice joint you've got up here.' Nellie nestled into his arms. 'What's it called?'

He kissed her leathery cheek and chuckled. 'It's the penthouse, doll.'

*

It was after midnight before Fiona got around to reading Nellie's note. The last thing she needed was more grief from the belligerent old bat. She had been having a wretched day. The wake for that old porter in the Irish Bar had turned into a full-scale hooley. Drunks were reeling in from all over Temple Bar, brimming over with song and vomit. Her celebrity was still on the prowl – said he couldn't sleep without a crowd around him. He was used to having his own space. She had been relying on his goodwill to bring in more star custom. She slit open the envelope as if it was the white throat of an adversary.

Fiona, darling. She scanned the spidery scrawl. *I am returning your lovely penthouse to you, safe and sound. As you rightly guessed, it's far too grand for the likes of me and as I haven't a mortal bean I am leaving, in lieu of payment, a few reminders of my Hollywood past.*

Fiona then did something that she thought she would never, ever again in her life do. She fell on her knees and gave thanks.

She ran to find the celebrity. He wasn't in his room, nor in the Irish Bar where there had been an earlier sighting. When at last she found him stumbling out of the lift, still fixing his clothes, she had to avert her gaze and concentrate on a giant Graham Knuttel of five lewd-looking persons around a dinner table. 'Wonderful news, sir! We have succeeded in vacating the penthouse.' God Almighty! Things were wild in the eighties, but those people from the seventies! At least in her day people were taught to look respectable afterwards. She couldn't look at him. She just couldn't. Bits of him hanging out everywhere! 'Just give me an hour,' she told the painting, 'and it will be ready for occupation.'

'I don't have an hour,' grumbled the real-life icon, half

dressed, and large (surprisingly large, actually) as life. 'For God's sake, it's one in the morning. Just how much damage can an old lady do?'

'Oh, none at all, sir,' she assured him. 'In fact, she didn't even sleep in it.'

Five minutes later she rang the penthouse. She couldn't resist it. After all that grovelling, she needed her praise. 'I just wanted to make sure that your new accommodation is the sort of thing you're used to.'

There was silence. Dead silence. And then a small, hoarse whisper: 'Fuck me!'

'Well, I might if I wasn't a married woman,' Fiona jested happily. At last things were coming together. The press might call her an amateur, but try as he might to sound cool, she could safely judge that her celebrity was astounded by the penthouse she had personally designed at Finbar's Hotel.